Praise for Anna Bennett's Del...

When You Wish Upo.. ....

"Expertly tugs at the heartstrings."   —*Publishers Weekly*

"Readers who love a grumpy-to-smitten hero will swoon."
                                        —*Kirkus Reviews*

"A dashing Regency romance featuring a wounded earl and an unyielding heroine with strong convictions."
                                        —*Library Journal*

The Duke Is But a Dream

"The pace of their story is steady and the flow is smooth, with plenty of chemistry and passion . . . A deeply satisfying tale of love persevering despite social constraints."
                                        —*Publishers Weekly*

"In this story of finding yourself, it's the family the central characters create together that's the most satisfying discovery of all."   —*BookPage*

"Again she creates relatable heroines similar in force and tone to those created by her sister historical romance authors Tessa Dare and Sophie Jordan."   —*Booklist*

"A wonderful read, one that is hard to put down."
                                        —*Affaire de Coeur*

"Anna Bennett is a fantastic storyteller . . . A delight of a read with characters you will love and subplots that add to the fascinating tale of old memories, new beginnings, and a happily-ever-after that made me smile."   —*Fresh Fiction*

"A finely crafted historical romance novel and a wonderfully entertaining read from cover to cover."

—*Midwest Book Review*

First Earl I See Tonight

"A kind, funny heroine is the perfect match for a stoic, brooding hero in Bennett's delightful first Debutante Diaries Regency romance. Sexy, clever . . . will bring smiles to its readers."   —*Publishers Weekly* (starred review)

"We love a heroine who doesn't wait to be rescued, so thank you, Anna Bennett! . . . A crumbling estate, mysterious letters, and a villain hiding among friends add a dash of intrigue to this tantalizing Regency adventure."

—*Apple Books Review*
(Apple Books Best of the Month)

Praise for the Wayward Wallflowers series

The Rogue Is Back in Town

"Fans of Regency romance authors Eloisa James, Tessa Dare, and Mary Jo Putney will go wild for the final installment of Bennett's Wayward Wallflowers trilogy."

—*Booklist* (starred review)

"Bennett's gift for writing a page-turner of a plot is on full display . . . a solid Regency story of true love."
—*Kirkus Reviews*

"Entertaining . . . [offers] plenty to satisfy Regency fans."
—*Publishers Weekly*

I Dared the Duke

"Sharply drawn characters, clever dialogue, simmering sensuality, and a dash of mystery make this well-crafted Regency thoroughly delightful." —*Library Journal*

"Readers will enjoy this sassy Regency take on the classic *Beauty and the Beast* tale." —*Booklist*

"A captivating page-turner that will become a new favorite among romance enthusiasts!" —*BookPage*

"Bennett brings new life to traditional Regency stories and characters." —*Kirkus Reviews*

"Scrumptious . . . I devoured every word! A hot and wounded hero, a heroine you wish could be your friend in real life, and witty scenes that sparkle with life . . . The Wayward Wallflowers just keep getting better!"
—Laura Lee Guhrke,
New York Times bestselling author

Also by
Anna Bennett

WHEN YOU WISH UPON A ROGUE
THE DUKE IS BUT A DREAM
FIRST EARL I SEE TONIGHT
THE ROGUE IS BACK IN TOWN
I DARED THE DUKE
MY BROWN-EYED EARL

Girls Before Earls

ANNA BENNETT

St. Martin's Paperbacks

First published in the United States by St. Martin's Paperbacks, an imprint of St. Martin's Publishing Group

GIRLS BEFORE EARLS

For information, address St. Martin's Publishing Group, 120 Broadway, New York, NY 10271.

www.stmartins.com

ISBN: 978-1-250-79391-1

Our books may be purchased in bulk for promotional, educational, or business use. Please contact your local bookseller or the Macmillan Corporate and Premium Sales Department at 1-800-221-7945, ext. 5442, or by email at MacmillanSpecialMarkets@macmillan.com.

Printed in the United States of America

St. Martin's Paperbacks edition / January 2022

10 9 8 7 6 5 4 3 2 1

To teachers everywhere,
thank you.

Prologue

Nine-year-old Hazel Lively was well aware of the evils of eavesdropping.

There were times, however, when a girl simply couldn't help herself—and tonight was one of those times.

"You've roused me from my bed," said the exasperated lady in the next room, "to beg me to take in a poor waif?"

That last bit ruffled Hazel's feathers, but she sat perfectly still in the dark antechamber with an ear cocked toward the office where her elderly neighbor was pleading on her behalf. They were miles away from London and the only home Hazel had ever known.

A brass sign nailed to the brick wall outside the building had declared it MISS HAYWINKLE'S SCHOOL FOR GIRLS, and the room where she waited was almost as large as her family's entire flat had been.

"She's a clever lass," Mrs. Griswold said tenaciously. "She deserves a proper education. It's what her mum and dad wanted for her—God rest their souls."

At the mention of her parents, a goose egg lodged in Hazel's throat. A fortnight had passed since she'd lost them, and her grief was still so fresh, so keen that she constantly teetered on the edge of a sob. She clamped her lips together so she wouldn't cry. If Papa were here, he'd ruffle her hair and call her his little hazelnut. *Hard on the outside.*

"This is a highly reputable finishing school," Miss Haywinkle intoned firmly. "*Not* a foundling home."

"Please, ma'am," Mrs. Griswold begged. "She don't look like much, but she's well mannered and her needlework, well . . .'tisn't bad."

Hazel cringed at the blatant lie. Her needlework was *horrendous.*

The elderly woman continued, more impassioned. "I'd take her in meself, but the husband won't hear of it. And it would break my heart to leave her in a filthy, crowded orphanage. This is the sort of place she needs to be."

"What makes you so certain?" The headmistress didn't bother to hide her skepticism.

"Last time I visited her mother, the girl was in the kitchen peeling potatoes—and reading at the same time."

Miss Haywinkle scoffed.

"She were reading *Shakespeare*," Mrs. Griswold added, refusing to be dismissed.

That part was true. Hazel had been in the middle of a gloriously grisly scene in *Macbeth* and couldn't drag her eyes away from her book, which she'd propped against the flour jar. It was impossible to believe that only a couple of weeks ago, her greatest worry had been juggling chores and reading.

"Shakespeare?" the headmistress repeated, clearly skeptical. "Most of my pupils would sooner have a tooth extracted. Tell me about her parents."

"Her dad was a butcher and her mum a seamstress. Such a devoted couple," Mrs. Griswold said, her voice catching on the last syllable. "They lived in a tiny apartment in London and saved every shilling they could spare in hopes of one day sending their daughter to a fancy school . . . like yours."

Coins clinked, and Hazel guessed that Mrs. Griswold was

handing the headmistress a purse—the same one she'd hidden in the bosom of her jacket throughout their three-hour journey in the mail coach. Mama had once lifted a loose floorboard in the kitchen to show Hazel the precious pouch and had solemnly instructed her to grab it in the event of a fire.

The coins jingled again. "There's not enough here to cover the tuition for even one term," Miss Haywinkle said brusquely.

Fear skittered down Hazel's spine, and she gripped the edge of the wooden bench where she sat, helplessly waiting. Wondering what was to become of her.

Mr. Griswold didn't want her. Miss Haywinkle wouldn't take her. The foundling home didn't sound particularly appealing, but she had nowhere else to go. She'd never felt so frightened, so completely alone in the world.

"Just speak with her," Mrs. Griswold begged. "And if ye still want to send her away after that, I'll take her back to London . . . and do what I must."

In the prolonged silence that ensued, Hazel held her breath. She'd worn her best dress *and* brushed her hair. She'd rehearsed just what she'd say.

"I'm sorry I can't help." The headmistress's words echoed with a chilling finality. She would not be swayed by a few coins or sad stories.

"I'll have my assistant bring down a couple of blankets," Miss Haywinkle continued. "You and the girl can spend the night on the sofa in the antechamber. The mail coach will stop here again in the morning."

Hazel slumped. So that was it. She'd thought that after the devastating loss of her parents, nothing else would have the power to truly hurt her. She'd been wrong.

"Very well," Mrs. Griswold grumbled. "We'll be out of yer hair before breakfast."

A few minutes later, the weary woman emerged from the office and handed Hazel a quilt and a pillow. "A waste of our time," she said flatly. She flopped onto the large sofa, wrestled with her own blanket, and sighed. "Go to sleep, and we'll figure out what to do with you in the morning."

Hazel was fairly certain that any attempt she made at talking would result in sobs, and since Mrs. Griswold had no tolerance for that sort of thing, she quickly made a little bed on the floor. She lay there in the dark, her body's stillness completely at odds with the riot of thoughts in her head.

Eventually, Mrs. Griswold began to breathe heavily, and Hazel blinked at the ceiling. She was too agitated, too sad to sleep. She didn't want to dwell on the hole in her heart. Didn't want to think about her increasingly bleak future. What she needed was a distraction—preferably in the form of a *book*.

Silently, she threw off her quilt and tiptoed to the door of Miss Haywinkle's office, praying it wasn't locked. She turned the smooth brass knob and sighed with relief as she slipped inside. It only took a moment to find the lamp on the headmistress's desk and light it, bathing the room in a warm, soft glow.

Hazel gasped at the sight before her. Never in her life had she seen so many books in one place. The entire wall of shelves behind Miss Haywinkle's desk was positively stuffed, but that was only the beginning. Books covered the tables, chair seats, and floor: leather-bound reference books with gold-leaf lettering, novels with tantalizing titles, tomes with colorful and ornate illustrations.

She trailed her fingertips across dozens of smooth spines, imagining what it would be like to have access to the worlds within. To be able to choose from a hundred different stories, to read about a thousand different subjects. She'd considered herself extremely fortunate to have a few books at home, and she'd read each one more times than she could count.

But this . . . ? Surely this was paradise.

At least, it *would* be paradise—if it were a bit tidier.

Hazel reached into a pocket and withdrew her handkerchief, exceedingly glad she hadn't blubbered or blown her nose into it. With the utmost care, she pulled the first book from a bottom shelf, dusted the cover, and flipped through the pages. Then she set it down and reached for the next. And the next.

For three hours, while she sorted and straightened and stacked, she forgot she was unwanted. Forgot she was alone.

And when the last shelf of novels had been artfully arranged by color so that they made a delightful rainbow at the top of Miss Haywinkle's bookcase, Hazel yawned, turned down the lamp, and reluctantly left the office, closing the door on a future that would never be hers.

She dragged herself back to her makeshift bed and listened to Mrs. Griswold's snores until sunbeams peeked through the transom window above the antechamber door. When the elderly neighbor finally woke, she bid Hazel to put on her coat and collect her bag, then proceeded to bustle her outside.

"The mail coach will be here soon," Mrs. Griswold said matter-of-factly. "With any luck, we'll be back in Town by supper. I'll cook you a nice stew before we get you settled in the foundling home."

"Thank you, ma'am." Hazel fought back the wave of sadness that threatened to knock her feet out from under her. Her chin trembled, and she bit her lip so her kindly neighbor wouldn't see how close she was to breaking. Through sheer force of will, she kept her head high and strode down the pavement. *Hard on the outside. Hard on the outside.*

"Ah, there's the coach now." Mrs. Griswold hurried to the corner where the conveyance rolled to a stop. "I'll be needing a window seat," she murmured.

Hazel numbly handed her small, worn bag to the driver and was about to climb into the cab when a woman called out, "Mrs. Griswold, wait!"

Hazel turned and saw Miss Haywinkle scurrying toward them. She wore a smart gray pelisse, sensible boots, and a straw bonnet with a soft blue bow. She looked a little older than Mama, but it was hard for Hazel to be certain. Whereas Mama had been pretty, Miss Haywinkle was more aptly described as *proper*.

"Gads." Mrs. Griswold lumbered out of the coach and leaned toward Hazel's ear. "Tell me you didn't swipe anything from the posh lady."

Heat crawled up Hazel's face. "Er, no. Not exactly."

"What is it, Miss Haywinkle?" Mrs. Griswold called back, not bothering to hide her annoyance. "We're leaving, just like you asked us to."

The headmistress stopped a yard away and squinted at Hazel. "Did you do that?" she asked, gesturing over her shoulder.

"What the devil are you talking about?" Mrs. Griswold huffed.

Miss Haywinkle ignored her and focused the considerable intensity of her stare on Hazel. "Did you do that to my office?" she clarified.

"Yes, ma'am." Shame washed over Hazel. She'd had no right to trespass in the headmistress's quarters and tumbled over herself to explain. "I wasn't able to sleep. I only intended to borrow a book, but when I saw all those beautiful shelves . . . I couldn't help myself."

Miss Haywinkle said nothing but swept her shrewd, assessing gaze from the top of Hazel's tangled tresses to the toes of her scuffed shoes. At last, the headmistress folded her arms. "What is your name, young lady?"

"Hazel." She closed her eyes briefly, and Papa's rough, beloved face filled her head. Raising her chin, she met the headmistress's stony glare and mustered every ounce of pride she possessed. "My name is Hazel Lively."

"What you did back there—it must have taken you most of the night."

Hazel shrugged apologetically. "I tend to lose track of time when I'm around books." She hesitated, then added, "The third volume of the Prose and Poetry series is missing from your collection. I left a gap where it belongs, on the second shelf from the top."

The woman's expression remained impassive, but one elegant brow arched ever so slightly. "Retrieve your bag, Miss Lively, and come with me."

Hazel swallowed. "Ma'am?"

The headmistress's mouth was a thin, unreadable line, but her eyes softened at the corners. "You're officially enrolled in Miss Haywinkle's School for Girls."

Chapter 1

"There's a gentleman here to see you, ma'am, and he has a young lady with him." Hazel's dutiful assistant, Jane, stood in the office doorway, her expressive face beaming at the prospect of a new pupil.

Hope glimmered in Hazel's chest. Heaven knew that her newly opened school, a dream that had taken her nearly a decade to realize, needed students—especially the sort who could afford to pay tuition.

She blinked at the half a dozen books open on her desk. She'd been so absorbed in planning that afternoon's marine life lesson that she'd been oblivious to the arrival of visitors. "Give me a moment to clear off my desk, and then you may show them—"

Before she could finish her sentence, a dark-haired gentleman angled his broad shoulders through the doorway with a thin, sour-faced girl in tow. He looked around the room as he approached, his bold gaze lingering on Hazel's lace fichu and simple chignon. The office, which had seemed perfectly spacious and airy only moments before, shrunk to half its size as he stood there, looming over her desk.

"I'm Blade," he said brusquely, not offering his hand. "Earl of Bladenton. And this is Kitty Beckett."

Hazel stood smoothly, intent on making a professional, favorable first impression. The earl certainly didn't live in Bellehaven Bay, but perhaps he and his family intended to spend the summer at the seaside resort.

"It's a pleasure to meet you both," she said. "I'm Miss Lively, the headmistress. Welcome to the Bellehaven Academy of Deportment. How may we be of service?"

"I'd like to enroll Kitty," he said abruptly. "Immediately."

"That's wonderful." Hazel smiled at the girl, who seemed less than enthused. Indeed, Kitty's expression conveyed the distinct combination of boredom and displeasure perfected by most girls around the age of fifteen. "Please, sit," Hazel said, gesturing to the pair of chairs opposite her. "And tell me why you've selected our establishment."

The earl frowned as though the invitation to sit and converse was an imposition. "A friend in London gave me your card," he said, producing it from the pocket of his fine-tailored jacket and sliding it across her desk. Hazel looked at the dog-eared card, one of dozens that she and Jane had handed out over the last few weeks, desperately hoping to increase enrollment.

"You believe Bellehaven Academy will be a good fit for your daughter?"

Kitty grimaced, and the earl scowled, clearly exasperated. "She's my *niece*," he corrected. "And my ward."

"Forgive me," Hazel said smoothly. "You believe our school will be a good fit for your niece?"

Lord Bladenton clenched his chiseled jaw. "Perfect."

"Are you in town for the summer then?"

"God, no." He scoffed as though the very idea was absurd. "I'm returning to London this evening. But Kitty will be staying with you."

"I'm afraid most of our girls live in town with their families and attend lessons here in the afternoons."

He arched a dark, thick brow. "But you have some boarding students?"

Hazel inclined her head. "Only two." And they were special cases. Girls who had no family to speak of and nowhere else to go. Hazel had gladly taken them in and hoped to open her doors to many more girls whose families couldn't afford tuition. But first she needed to firmly establish her reputation. And make sure she had enough students from wealthy families so she could afford the necessities of running a proper school: rent, furnishings, and, of course, books.

"Then it sounds like you have plenty of room for another boarder." The earl slapped his palms on his muscular thighs as though the matter were settled. "I'll have my footman retrieve her bags from the coach."

"Not yet, Lord Bladenton," Hazel said firmly. She couldn't put her finger on it, but her headmistress instincts were screaming that something wasn't quite right. Turning to Kitty, she said, "How would you feel about living here in Bellehaven Bay?"

"It scarcely matters." The fair-haired girl plucked a piece of lint from her skirt and dropped it on the floor. "I don't expect I'll be here long, in any event. My dear uncle neglected to mention I've already been expelled from two schools in London. Two schools," she enunciated clearly, "in less than three months."

The earl dragged a hand through his hair and cursed under his breath.

Kitty smirked as she glanced at Hazel, no doubt hoping to find her rifling through her desk drawers in search of smelling salts.

Hazel *was* a little shocked at the girl's revelation, but she kept her expression neutral. "Impressive. How did you manage it?"

The girl shrugged. "Child's play, really. Let's see . . .

There was the Great Brandy Incident, the Hellion Heist, and my personal favorite, Operation Haunting the Headmis—"

"Enough." The earl's voice, deep and hollow, cut through the conversation more than a shout would have. "Kitty, go wait outside. I require a word with Miss Lively."

Hazel continued to sit at her desk, her hands folded, unflappable and unfazed by all appearances. But inside, her heart ached for the girl. She *was* that girl. The girl nobody wanted.

After several tense moments in which the air seemed to have been sucked out of the room, Kitty rose, deliberate and defiant. To Hazel, she said, "This is the part where he attempts to rid himself of me by throwing money at you."

"Kitty . . ." Lord Bladenton's tone brooked no argument.

The girl tossed a golden curl over her shoulder, shot her uncle a sugary smile, and blinked innocently. "Right. I'll be just outside then, diligently working on my needlepoint." She proceeded to saunter out of the office and close the door behind her with a bit more force than was necessary.

The earl exhaled wearily. "I apologize for my niece. She's been through a difficult time, but she's quite bright and perfectly capable of behaving like a lady. All she needs is a firm hand."

"A firm hand?" Hazel repeated.

Lord Bladenton shifted in his seat. "Not literally, of course. What I meant to say is that she needs rules—and consequences when she defies them."

"This is a school, not a prison." Hazel closed one of the books on her desk and slid it to the side. "It's clear Kitty doesn't want to be here, and while I understand a bit of reluctance when it comes to conjugating Latin verbs or memorizing important dates, I would not want to take on a student—particularly a boarding student—who is intent on sabotaging her own education."

The earl shoved himself out of his chair, planted his hands on his hips, and paced the length of the room. "I'll speak to her. Make sure she understands that any misbehavior will not be tolerated."

Hazel shook her head. "I wish I could help, but, as you may know, I've only recently opened the doors of Bellehaven Academy, and I'm determined to establish it as a reputable finishing school. Which means I can't afford a major scandal. Or even a minor one." She suppressed a shiver at the thought. "It would ruin everything I've worked so hard for," she added—more to herself than the earl.

Because she couldn't lose sight of that fact. Yes, she and Jane needed paying students. True, enrolling the niece of an earl would be a feather in their cap. And of course, she longed to help Kitty.

But the school's reputation was paramount. Without its good name, Bellehaven Academy would cease to exist. And unfortunately, Kitty was a walking scandal.

"I'm sorry to disappoint," Hazel told the earl. "Your niece is clearly a creative and clever girl. I'm certain you'll find another school that's happy to have her." She rose from her chair and rested her fingertips on the blotter covering her desktop. "I do appreciate your interest and wish you and your niece well." She extended a hand in business-like fashion, indicating the conversation was over, her decision made.

Lord Bladenton whirled back to the desk, ignoring her outstretched hand. "Miss Lively," he said, his voice as smooth as the bay breeze tickling the back of her neck. "I've traveled all the way from London to meet with you. Surely you're not dismissing me already?"

"Oh, but I am, Lord Bladenton." She ignored the rakish dimple in his cheek. Or rather, endeavored to. "I have lessons to plan. Students to teach. Besides, there's nothing left to say."

He placed his palms on her desk, leaned forward, and shot her a half smile that was somehow more potent than a full-blown grin. "I have *plenty* left to say," he said with a distinctly rakish gleam in his eyes. "We haven't even begun to negotiate."

"I've no intention of bargaining with you," Miss Lively countered blithely.

Blade couldn't detect a single crack in her composure. Her dark-brown hair had been tamed into a severe knot. Her fichu covered everything from chest to chin. Her expression was formidable. In short, she was all that a headmistress *should* be—if one discounted the fact that she smelled like honey and sweet cream.

"That's rather closed-minded." Blade leaned a little closer and let her scent fill his head. "Aren't you the least bit curious to hear what I have to offer?"

"Not at all, Lord Bladenton. You see, I've made my decision based on my *principles*." She paused, letting that sink in, then added, "One's principles should never be on the auction block. Wouldn't you agree?"

Blade nodded slowly, as though he'd had an epiphany. "You're absolutely correct, Miss Lively. In fact, that's *just* the sort of wisdom you should impart to my niece. Someone with your moral fortitude would make an immense difference in the life of an impressionable young lady. By taking on Kitty as a pupil, you would be doing a great service not only to her and to me, but, indeed, to all of society."

All he needed was one moment of weakness. One chink in her armor. Then he'd pounce—and next thing she knew, Miss Lively would be welcoming her newest student.

"I'm not susceptible to flattery," she informed him, as if she thought it only fair he should know. She proceeded to stack the half a dozen books on her desk, largest to smallest, making sure the corners were perfectly square. "But if I were, your empty compliments would not sway me in the slightest."

He opened his mouth to tell her how wounded he was, then quickly shut it. Either she was the best bluffer he'd ever met, or she had ice in her veins.

He shoved his hands in his pockets and stepped back from the desk, realizing he needed to take a different tack. He sauntered to the open window and looked out at the handful of tourists strolling down the sandy street, peeking in store windows. He couldn't see the shore, but he could smell the ocean air.

"How many students do you have here at Bellehaven Academy?" he asked, keeping his tone conversational.

Miss Lively cleared her throat. "Five at the moment. We've only recently launched the school, but once our reputation is established, I expect enrollment to rise quite rapidly."

Blade faced her and arched a brow. "Most families come here to spend time by the sea. They want to stroll along the cliffs, swim in the ocean, attend a few balls. I sincerely doubt anyone comes to Bellehaven for deportment lessons."

"Perhaps not." Miss Lively looked into his eyes like she was examining the remnants of his soul. "But proper behavior never takes a holiday."

"Never?" Blade asked, more curious than he should have been. He wondered if the headmistress wore her fichu to bed. Or if she ate strawberries with a fork. Or if she maintained proper posture in the bathtub.

All of which would have been a damned shame.

She turned slightly, and the sunlight behind her outlined the smooth plane of her brow, the straight line of her nose, and the plump curves of her lips. Interesting. Perhaps Miss Lively was younger than he'd originally thought. If she weren't wearing a gown straight out of his grandmama's armoire, she might have been . . . dare he think it?

Pretty.

"Proper behavior is essential at all times," Miss Lively said, snapping him back to attention. "Strength of character demands that one does the right thing—regardless of the circumstance or setting."

Blade felt a little poke in his conscience but quickly shook it off. Miss Lively was a headmistress and paid to say such things. She probably had a whole journal full of pretentious adages. She didn't know the choices he'd made. Couldn't know all the regrets that haunted him.

"I admire your conviction," Blade said, "even if I do not completely share it. I daresay you must have a difficult time convincing students to devote three hours to lessons every afternoon when you're competing with rowboat races, picnics on the beach, and cricket matches."

"Bellehaven *does* offer many entertainments," the headmistress said. "Making it the perfect training ground for the larger arena of London. Here, young ladies can attend their first formal dinner parties and balls without worrying that a tiny misstep will land them on the pages of *The London Hearsay.* And it's not as though our academic lessons are confined to the schoolroom." She turned to the shelf behind her and slowly, lovingly trailed a fingertip over the long row of books nestled there. "Books are an excellent source of knowledge, but so is the real world."

"The real world?" he repeated, more intrigued than he let on.

"We teach all the traditional subjects, of course. But we also strive to make lessons engaging and practical. We spend time studying rocks along the shore and the movement of the tides. We explore coves and sea life, and—" She paused, clamped her lips, and shook her head. As she did, a lone curl sprang free from its cursed confines and fell across her forehead. "All of this is beside the point, I'm afraid."

"Mmm," he murmured. But he couldn't take his eyes off that one rebellious curl. Couldn't help thinking that he'd found Miss Lively's weakness—her passion for her school. "I can see the benefits of the location. But it must be quite expensive. Are you able to pay all your bills?"

Miss Lively gave a curt nod. "We're doing just fine, Lord Bladenton."

"No offense, Miss Lively, but five students hardly seems *fine*. I'd wager that their tuition doesn't even cover the cost of your rent, much less your assistant's salary."

The glare the headmistress issued in return would have sent most men fleeing with their tails between their legs. Blade was just warming up.

He returned to the window, sat on the sill, and crossed his arms. "I assume your goal is to establish your school as a reputable yet refreshing alternative to stuffy London finishing schools?"

"Quite right," she said dryly. "The key word is *reputable*, my lord. That is why you and I are at a crossroads."

"I disagree. We can help each other, Miss Lively. If you don't enroll more students soon, you won't have a reputation at all. Because you'll cease to have a school."

The headmistress slowly sank into her chair and folded her hands in her lap. When she spoke, her voice was lower and, unless he was mistaken, more vulnerable than before. "Bellehaven Academy is much more than a business to me. I am seeking neither fame nor fortune. I simply want to educate as many deserving young ladies as I can, whether or not their families are able to afford tuition."

"You're a philanthropist," he mused, rubbing the rough stubble along his jawline.

"I believe everyone should have the chance to better themselves and improve their prospects."

"Everyone?" he probed.

"Yes," she said firmly.

Finally, they were beginning to understand each other. They sat in silence for a few moments while Blade made some mental calculations. He had one shot to make his best offer, without bruising her pride or flouting her principles. She sat across from him, expectant—and, apparently, unaware that he found the errant curl on her forehead utterly mesmerizing.

He dragged his gaze away, reminding himself of all that was at stake. He needed Kitty to be somewhere safe—and far away from London—for the entire summer. Three months without her interfering in his affairs or scaring away the woman he hoped to make his fiancée. Three months without a daily reminder of his numerous failings and soul-crushing losses.

"Well then," he began. "Please consider this. Kitty deserves a chance to better herself, too. I understand she presents somewhat of a risk, but this environment is precisely what she needs. If you're willing to take a chance on my niece, I'll pay all her expenses *and* three times the usual tuition—which means you'd be able to enroll a couple of other girls who wouldn't otherwise have the opportunity to improve their stations. A prospect that only comes from attending a school like yours."

She visibly swallowed, and he knew he'd succeeded in breaching her defenses—but he had no intention of letting up now. "That's not all. If you can manage to keep my niece here for the summer, I'll sing the praises of Bellehaven Academy to all my well-connected friends. And I guarantee you that by this time next year, your waiting room will be bursting at the seams with London's finest families, all vying for a spot at your school."

Miss Lively's face gave no indication of what she was thinking, but her index finger tapped the arm of her chair with the precision of a metronome. At last she said, "I want what is best for Kitty."

"As do I," he said, sincere.

"Then I will accept your offer . . . on one condition."

Thank God. He was prepared to do anything necessary. Pay five times the usual tuition. Hire a town crier to spread the word about Bellehaven Academy. Take out a full-page advertisement in *The London Hearsay*.

Fighting the urge to grin like a fool, he nodded soberly. If he played his hand right, he'd be on his way back to London within the hour—alone. Unencumbered by regrets, guilt, and shame.

"I'm gratified that you're willing to meet me halfway, Miss Lively," he said. "What is the condition?"

"For as long as Kitty resides here in Bellehaven Bay, you must agree to visit her at least once a fortnight."

"Visit?" he repeated, incredulous. "Once a fortnight?"

She nodded serenely, seemingly unaware that the weight of her demand loomed like the top half of a stockade, mocking him for believing he could break free of his past.

All he knew was that he had to try.

Chapter 2

Blade blinked at the buttoned-up headmistress sitting across the office from him, debating his next move. Because there was no way in hell he was dragging his arse all the way to Bellehaven Bay every other week.

"Forgive me," he said, mustering his last morsel of civility, "but you must realize such a requirement isn't practical. I have obligations in Town. An estate to run."

"Those are my terms, Lord Bladenton." Miss Lively stood and folded her slender arms across her chest. Every time she moved, her tantalizing scent filled his head. "I don't think I'm asking too much. If you wish for me to take on Kitty as a student, I must insist that you visit her for at least a few hours twice a month."

"Absolutely not," he ground out. He shoved himself off the windowsill and turned to look outside, bracing an arm on the wall. "I can't imagine why you'd make such an absurd and unreasonable demand, but I will *not* subject myself to these machinations."

"It's not my intention to make your life difficult," she countered, her voice infuriatingly calm. "But I think it's important that Kitty doesn't feel like she's being . . . abandoned."

Blade spun on his bootheels to face the headmistress. "You have no right to make that accusation."

"I didn't mean to imply that you are abandoning her," she said evenly. "But I do fear she may perceive it that way."

He barked a laugh at that. "In case it wasn't glaringly obvious from your brief interview with Kitty, the last thing she wants to do is spend time with me. In fact, she detests me. It vexes her that she must breathe the same air I do. My very existence upon this earth is an unbearable affront."

Miss Lively had the audacity to cluck her tongue. "How old is she—fifteen?"

He had to think about it for a minute. "Yes."

"Do you recall being that age?"

"I'm not yet in my dotage," he grumbled. "Of course I remember."

"Then I daresay you may remember feeling a measure of hostility toward adults in a position of authority. Fifteen-year-olds are not always the most rational of creatures. But we mustn't underestimate them or diminish their feelings."

Good God. He couldn't believe he was letting a headmistress lecture him about *feelings*. It was too much. "I won't do it," he said. "I refuse to travel from London to the coast every other week just to serve as a target for her vicious barbs and death glares."

"That is your prerogative, of course," Miss Lively said, irritatingly cool and detached. "You needn't accept my offer to enroll Kitty as a boarding student. I'm sure there are plenty of other schools willing to take your money without condition. This, however, isn't one of them."

Hot under the cravat, Blade swallowed a curse and counted to ten before speaking. "My niece's attempts to manipulate me are bad enough. I will not do your bidding, Miss Lively."

The headmistress inclined her head in a manner that was

maddeningly civil and said, "I regret that we were not able to reach a mutually acceptable agreement, Lord Bladenton. I wish you and Kitty well." A breeze riffled the curl at her temple, and she quickly tucked it behind her ear, blushing as though she'd inadvertently exposed an undergarment.

For the life of him, Blade could not imagine why the idea of such a thing intrigued him so.

All the more reason for him to get the hell out of Belle-haven, posthaste. He stuffed his hat on his head, made a cursory bow, and strode to the office door. Swinging it open, he bellowed, "Let's go, Kitty. We're leaving right n—"

He looked around the room and blinked at Miss Lively's assistant, who was hunched over a small table in the ante-chamber, industriously labeling the shells and carcasses of various sea creatures while Kitty was quite noticeably *absent*. "Where is my niece?" he asked. His voice was surprisingly controlled, given the potent mix of dread and anger that flooded his veins.

The flustered assistant looked up and adjusted her spectacles. "Hmm? Oh, Miss Kitty said she required a bit of air. She stepped outside to stretch her legs."

"And you let her go?" he asked, incredulous. She was probably at the local pub, tossing back her third pint by now.

"Lord Bladenton." Miss Lively said his name like a warning as she glided into the antechamber. "Jane is not responsible for your niece." To the assistant, she said, "Did Kitty say where she was going?"

"I'm afraid not," the assistant answered, contrite.

But Blade knew she wasn't to blame. *He* was—as usual.

He grumbled an apology as he burst out of the school's front door, then looked up and down the street.

Miss Lively followed on his heels. "Any sign of her?"

Blade shook his head and planted his hands on his hips,

beyond exasperated. "She's gone. And if I know Kitty, she's looking for trouble."

Oh dear. Hazel stepped back inside and grabbed her bonnet from its hook. "Jane, I'm going to help Lord Bladenton locate his niece. I don't expect it will take long, but if I haven't returned in time for today's lesson, will you stand in for me please? I've left a few notes on my desk."

Jane nodded eagerly. "Of course. Don't worry about a thing."

Hazel shot her assistant a grateful smile. They'd met shortly after Hazel arrived in town, at the bakery that Jane's parents owned. Apparently, Jane often became absorbed in her research while she was supposed to be tending the ovens, which regularly resulted in bread that was rather charred. One morning, as Hazel was purchasing a scone that was distinctly crispy on the edges, Jane expressed an interest in helping Hazel at the school during the day, and her parents readily agreed to the arrangement. Jane had worked at Bellehaven Academy ever since, and Hazel thanked her lucky stars that fate had brought them together.

By the time Hazel rejoined the earl on the street, he was already talking to a gentleman with white hair and a walking cane. Lord Bladenton raised his hand level with his shoulder. "She's about this tall," he was saying, "with blond hair. Did you happen to see her?"

The old man scratched his chin thoughtfully, and the earl turned to Hazel. "I don't require your assistance, Miss Lively," he said, his confident tone at odds with the worry lining his forehead. "I have the matter well in hand."

"But you're not familiar with Bellehaven. How will you know where to look?"

Lord Bladenton rolled his eyes. "I could walk from one

side of this town to the other in less than an hour. I daresay I'll find my way without a trail of bread crumbs."

The older gentleman tapped the earl's shoulder. "You know, I believe I *did* pass a couple of young ladies on my way back from the beach. What color gown is your niece wearing?"

The earl screwed up his face as though he'd been asked to calculate the precise distance to the sun. "Damned if I know. It's a *gown*. With all the usual"—he waved a hand around helplessly—"lace and ruffles and bows. White or yellow or pink . . ." With great reluctance, he turned to Hazel, his expression imploring.

Ah, well, she supposed she'd let the earl flounder long enough. "Gold," she offered. "Kitty's gown is a bright shade of gold with saffron trim. Her straw bonnet has an ivory bow."

"Let me think." The man tapped his cane on the ground several times while the earl stood by, impatient.

"No. I don't believe I saw a young lady in gold," the stranger continued. "But if I should pass your niece on my way home, I'll be sure to tell her that you're looking for her."

"Much appreciated," Lord Bladenton muttered. He strode toward the town's main street, one block over from the boardinghouse where Hazel rented space for Bellehaven Academy.

"Why are you heading that way?" Hazel asked. She had to take twice as many steps as the earl to keep up with him.

"Kitty is looking for entertainment, action . . . trouble. If there's none to be had at this hour of the afternoon, she'll settle for a shopping excursion. She's probably squandering my money as we speak."

Hazel frowned. "Do you really think so?"

The earl stopped short. "You have a different theory, Miss Lively?" he asked dryly.

"Yes, actually. If *I* were visiting from London," she said

breathlessly, "I'd want to explore the beach—one of the coves, perhaps, or the pier by the bay."

Lord Bladenton snorted. "Good to know. But I'll wager Kitty is at the local pub. What's it called—the Crusty Mermaid?"

"The *Salty* Mermaid," Hazel said.

"Right. Well, she's probably there, trying to convince a few young bucks to let her join their card game."

Hazel shrugged. "I suppose you could search for her in town, and I could look for her along the shore."

"You needn't bother, Miss Lively. You've made it clear that Kitty isn't welcome at Bellehaven."

"That's not true," she said. "I told you my conditions. You declined my offer."

"Yes, and now you're free to scribble some more lessons or alphabetize your slippers or . . . organize your fans by season."

"What?" She endeavored to keep her tone civil. "That doesn't make a bit of sense." And she didn't care for the earl's insinuation. Namely, that she valued order more than people.

He tipped his hat and made a mock bow. "Good day, Miss Lively."

"Good day, Lord Bladenton," she said, pleased that she'd managed to speak his name without revealing the depths of her exasperation.

If the earl thought he could tell her what to do, he was wrong—a two-plus-two-equals-five, unicorns-are-real, the-earth-is-flat level of wrong.

She whirled around and headed toward the beach, exhaling when she reached a narrow path through the tall green grasses of the sand dunes. The salty breeze whipped at her skirts, and the rushing surf soothed her nerves. She held out a hand, letting the soft grass tickle her palm as she made her way closer to the water.

She was replaying her conversation with Lord Bladenton in her head, wondering how on earth one would go about alphabetizing slippers, when she encountered Lady Rufflebum, one of Bellehaven's wealthiest, most influential matrons, walking up the path with her companion. Hazel smiled and prepared herself for the usual barrage of questions, gossip, and suspect advice.

"Miss Lively," Lady Rufflebum crooned. "How are things at that little school of yours?"

"What a pleasure to see you both," Hazel replied to the older ladies, folding her hands in front of her. "Bellehaven Academy is doing very well, thank you."

Lady Rufflebum let out an indelicate snort. "I tried to convince Lady Glenwood to enroll her granddaughter, but she says only a proper London finishing school will do. Of course, she also expects her granddaughter to marry a duke, which is about as likely as me finding a pirate's treasure buried on this beach. But enough about that," she said, peering from beneath the wide brim of her plumed hat. "Tell me, how many students do you have now?"

Hazel tamped down a sigh. "Still five. But there have been some inquiries and interest of late. I'm hopeful that we'll soon double our enrollment."

"You should seek quality over quantity, my dear," Lady Rufflebum sniffed. "The daughter of one esteemed member of the ton will do more to bolster your fledgling establishment than a whole schoolroom of ordinary girls."

"Forgive me for speaking plainly," Hazel said, "but I believe every girl is extraordinary and has the potential to flourish if given a chance." Hoping to change the subject, she quickly added, "Did you happen to pass a young lady in a gold-colored dress during your walk?"

Lady Rufflebum swiveled her head toward her companion, Miss Whitford, who mutely shook her head. "I do hope you haven't lost one of your students, Miss Lively. It's not as though you've any to spare." She chuckled, turning her plump cheeks pink with mirth.

"You are right about that." Hazel smiled and gave a polite bow. She needed Lady Rufflebum as an ally, which, unfortunately, meant swallowing her pride on occasion. "Enjoy your evening," Hazel called as she continued down the path toward the water.

When she emerged from the dunes onto the wide, flat beach, she held a hand to the brim of her bonnet and looked up and down the shore. To her right, a group of boys played cricket. To her left, a pair of women strolled near the lapping waves, twirling their parasols and chatting merrily. The bay was still too cold for all but the heartiest of swimmers, but a few children splashed and waded in the surf.

Kitty was nowhere to be seen.

Though it galled her to admit it, Lord Bladenton must have been right. Perhaps Kitty had ventured into one of the shops or pubs. Maybe he'd already found his niece, tucked her into his fancy coach, and ordered his driver to whisk them back to London—which was, no doubt, for the best.

But after her disconcerting meeting with the earl, Hazel needed a dose of serenity—the kind that only Peacock Cove, named for its brilliant blue-green waters, could provide. She strolled along the shoreline till she reached the towering pair of rocks at the cove's entrance, walked into the three-foot crevice between the rocks, and emerged onto a sandy white strip of beach that formed a semicircle around a huge turquoise pool.

The beach was deserted, but a small rowboat bobbed in the middle of the water, and, in the boat, a young woman in a gold gown waved her arms wildly.

Gads. It was Kitty.

Hazel walked to the water's edge and cupped her hands

around her mouth. "Kitty, it's me, Miss Lively. Can you row back? There should be a pair of oars on the floor of the boat."

"They fell into the water and floated away," Kitty shouted. "Which is what I'm about to do unless *someone* rescues me."

Hazel eyed another rickety rowboat still beached on the sand; it didn't look particularly seaworthy. "I don't suppose you know how to swim?" she called to Kitty.

The girl gripped both sides of the boat. "No."

Of course she didn't. Hazel yanked off her boots, set them on a rock, and shoved the old rowboat toward the water, pleased that it budged a few inches. "Hold on. I'm coming."

"Hurry!" Kitty called, more panicked than before. "This boat is sinking."

Chapter 3

Blade stalked along the shore, growing more incensed with each step. He was angry with Kitty for running off, livid with himself for letting her, and highly annoyed with Miss Lively for being *correct*.

Kitty hadn't been at any of Bellehaven's shops or inns or pubs, so Blade had resorted to searching for her along the two-mile stretch of beach, just as the insufferable headmistress had initially suggested. And now all he wanted was to find Kitty and tether her to him until they were safely home in London.

If he wasn't so consumed with the search, he might have enjoyed the breeze in his face and the salty spray in the air. He might have appreciated the majestic cliffs looming in the distance and the frothy waves lapping at his boots.

But he was too preoccupied with rehearsing the tongue-lashing he'd give Kitty, too busy dreaming up suitable punishments for her ill-advised escapade. Thanks to her, Blade was going to be stuck in Bellehaven for the night, and that meant missing a dinner party that he'd promised Lady Penelope—the very beautiful, very demanding, Lady Penelope—he'd attend.

The sun had begun to sink in the sky behind him, and

most of the tourists had left the beach for the day. However, a couple strolling toward him mentioned they'd seen a young woman near Peacock Cove. They pointed to twin rocks in the distance and said the passage between them led to the sheltered area of the bay. He'd be there in no time.

The rocks were farther away than they looked, however, and Blade started jogging, eager to find Kitty before sunset. He navigated his way through the opening, and soon found himself on a small, idyllic beach.

Fifty yards offshore, two rowboats bobbed in the water, about an oar's length apart. Sure enough, one of the boats was occupied by a young woman in a bright-yellow gown. Good God.

"Kitty," he shouted. "What the devil are you doing out there?"

"Uncle Beck!" she called back, using the nickname that melted his heart and pricked it at the same time. "I'm sinking!"

"No, you're not," shouted the woman on the other rowboat. Her tone was firm, unflappable, and familiar. "Keep bailing."

Bloody hell. He'd hoped never to lay eyes on the headmistress again. And yet the sight of her gave him an unexpected rush. A frisson of awareness.

"It's up to my ankles," Kitty called as she frantically scooped water into her soggy bonnet and flung it overboard.

One of Miss Lively's oars dragged in the water, and her boat listed precariously. A rope on her stern was tied to Kitty's bow, which didn't help matters. They were in trouble, damn it all.

Since there were no more rowboats on the beach, it looked as though he was going for a swim. He discarded his hat, shrugged out of his jacket, and began yanking off his boots.

"Training for a regatta, Miss Lively?" he goaded.

Instead of taking his bait, the headmistress, rather predictably, took the opportunity to edify him. "I discovered Kitty stranded in the middle of the bay and rowed out with the intention of towing her back to shore," she shouted. "But her boat is taking on water, and we've been battling the outgoing tide as well."

A potent cocktail of fear and guilt crept up his spine. "Can either of you swim?"

"I can, but Kitty can't," Miss Lively answered calmly. "I tried to persuade her to abandon her boat and hop into mine, but she refuses to leave her seat."

"I'd rather not sacrifice myself to the sea gods," Kitty said, her sarcasm laced with panic.

Blade unwound his cravat, tossed it onto the sand, and waded into the frigid water. "Don't move," he called back. "I'll come to you."

Hazel gripped the oars harder and endeavored not to stare as the earl strode into the water. His shirt hung open at the collar, revealing a swath of tanned skin. Wet buckskin trousers clung to his muscular thighs and narrow hips. When the waves slapped against his waist, he dove in and surfaced soon after, swimming through the surf with the ease of a dolphin.

She'd caught glimpses of other men swimming in the bay—some of them wearing far less clothing than Lord Bladenton. But she'd never found any of them half as fascinating.

The earl moved with a confidence and athleticism that made her want to study him—to understand him, inside and out. Impossible, of course. And imprudent. But inconveniently true.

Turning to Kitty, she said, "Keep bailing as much as you're able. I don't know what your uncle plans to do when he reaches us, but you need to stay afloat till then."

Kitty whimpered and flailed her bonnet.

Hazel squared her shoulders, dipped her oars in the water, and pulled with all her might. She'd rowed for half an hour before the earl arrived, and all she had to show for her efforts were aching shoulders and blistered palms. But at least the tide hadn't carried Kitty and her out to sea—yet.

She tracked Lord Bladenton's progress through the water, and before long he swam to the stern of Kitty's boat and gripped the edge with both hands. When he tried to hoist himself up, the rear of the boat dipped precariously—and was almost entirely submerged. Kitty screamed, and the earl let go.

He began to tread water near the boats, catching his breath after his exertions. "We need to get you off that boat," he told his niece, "before it ends up at the bottom of the bay."

Tears sprang to Kitty's eyes, and she shivered like a frightened rabbit. "Please, don't make me move. I can't."

Hazel cleared her throat. "I have a suggestion. If we move the boats close together, I think I could join Kitty in her boat without capsizing it. I'll sit in the bow, so the stern won't drag quite as much—and I can bail."

Lord Bladenton swam over to Hazel's boat and reached up, holding on to the side. "Right. I'll row this boat and tow you both to shore. Make way, Miss Lively—I'm coming aboard."

With that, he slung an arm over the stern. The arm was followed by a leg—an exceptionally long, muscular leg. The boat gyrated as he climbed in and tumbled to the floor in a dripping, gasping heap.

"Are you all right?" Hazel asked.

"Never better," he answered dryly. "Are you sure about this?"

"Yes," she answered—with considerably more confidence than she felt. She maneuvered past the earl so he could take the oars. Ignored the tingling sensation that radiated through her limbs. Sat until he'd managed to move their boat parallel to Kitty's.

Her knees wobbled as she stood, and she swayed pre-cariously—until Lord Bladenton grasped her hand. Hazel quickly regained her equilibrium, physically at least. But the contact of their palms left her uncharacteristically flustered. Though his hand was cool and wet, her whole body heated from his touch.

"I won't let you fall, " he said—and oddly, she believed him.

She lifted the hem of her gown and stepped up onto the bench seat behind her, careful to avoid sliding her stockinged feet over the weathered wood. As she inched her way closer to Kitty's boat, the earl shifted to the opposite side to keep the boat from tilting.

When she was as close as she could possibly get, she whispered a countdown. "Three, two, one—" and hopped into the other boat.

Kitty screamed. Hazel crouched on the floorboards as she waited for the boat to stop swaying.

"You're going to be fine," Hazel assured her. "Hand me your bonnet."

While she bailed, the earl rolled up his sleeves, grabbed the oars, and began rowing. The rope between the boats stretched taut. Lord Bladenton's arm muscles flexed with every stroke of the oars, and he grunted each time he pulled them through the water. His creased brow and clenched jaw showed his immense strain—and determination.

Finally, blessedly, they all started moving toward the shore.

"It's working!" Tears of relief trickled down Kitty's face. "Thank heaven!"

Hazel said a little prayer of gratitude and continued throwing water over the bow at a furious pace. She'd kept the water level inside the boat from rising. The earl had already managed to tow them halfway to shore. With a little luck, they'd be safely back on the beach before dark.

Hazel was surreptitiously observing the way the earl's muscled forearms flexed and the way his shirt appeared to be plastered to his chest when an ominous groan rang through the air.

"What was *that*?" Kitty whimpered, her voice laced with terror.

Hazel's gaze darted to the frayed rope that stretched between the boats. "The rope. It's breaking."

Kitty's chin trembled.

Hazel opened her mouth to warn the earl, but it was too late.

Snap.

The rope split and the severed ends whipped through the air, then plunked into the water. The boats immediately drifted apart.

"Bloody hell," Lord Bladenton muttered.

He began steering his rowboat back toward them, and Hazel tried to prepare Kitty for the only option left. "We're going to have to hop into your uncle's boat."

Kitty shook her head, resolute. "No."

"Yes. Your uncle and I will help you. We'll be holding on to you the entire time."

"Oh God." Kitty wiped her tears with the back of her hand. "Promise?"

"Promise. And I'll follow right behind you."

Lord Bladenton brought his boat alongside theirs and extended the handle of one oar to Hazel. "Grab that end," he said. "We'll keep the boats close while Kitty jumps aboard."

Hazel gripped the oar and held Kitty's hand. "Stand up slowly," she said encouragingly. "Take your time."

In the other boat, the earl stretched out an arm, coaxing Kitty to take the leap.

She stood on shaking legs and bravely lifted her chin. "Here I go," she said, her voice wavering.

With a yelp, she jumped toward her uncle, shoving off the boat with her back foot and pulling Hazel with her. Kitty landed securely in the earl's grasp.

But Hazel teetered, precariously off balance. To keep from falling onto Kitty, she shifted her weight and stumbled backward.

The sudden lurch was too much for the waterlogged boat. It flipped, and she tumbled overboard, plunging into the shockingly cold water.

Blast. She closed her mouth and squeezed shut her eyes as the ocean swallowed her whole.

Chapter 4

Icy darkness enveloped Hazel, drawing her into the deep. Her gown billowed around her head, tangling with her arms. Fear and shock paralyzed her for a moment, then her instincts kicked in.

She had to save herself.

It was familiar territory, in a way. She was used to being alone in the world. Quite accustomed to fighting for her survival.

Above her, Kitty's muted screams and the earl's muffled shouts carried through the water. She turned her face to their sounds, then kicked her legs, scissors-style, till she broke through the surface, sputtering and gasping for breath.

"Here, Miss Lively." The earl was leaning over the side of the boat several yards away, reaching out to her. "Grab my hand. I'll pull you in."

Hazel looked from his outstretched hand to the beach in the distance and made her decision. She wasn't going to risk capsizing the boat—not with Kitty in it.

"I'll swim to shore." She started churning her arms and legs in that direction.

"No, damn it!"

Hazel ignored the earl's vehement protests and Kitty's

panicked shrieks. All she had to do was make it to the beach. She could take care of herself, just as she always had.

After several grueling minutes, she made it halfway there. Her arms burned and her legs felt like jelly, but she pressed on. She was vaguely aware of the earl and Kitty in the boat alongside her, but she didn't dare stop, not even to catch her breath. If she ceased moving, she would sink, and she doubted the earl would be able to find her in the murky depths of the bay.

So she kept swimming, even when her limbs turned numb. She thought of her students and Jane, who needed her. She thought of Mama and heard Papa's voice in her head. *My little hazelnut.*

A wave crashed over her, and she choked on a mouthful of seawater but kept struggling, kept fighting—till a pair of strong arms lifted her.

Lord Bladenton scooped her up against the hard wall of his chest. He stood in the surf, holding her above the waves, his heart pounding as hard as hers.

"I can make it on my own," Hazel rasped.

"You *did*," he said soothingly. "But maybe you could let me help you the last few yards to shore."

She nodded, too exhausted to argue. She let the earl carry her to the beach, where he carefully laid her on the sand.

"Kitty?" Hazel asked breathlessly.

"She's in the boat, just over there. Perfectly safe." He raised an arm and pointed in the direction of the rowboat, which was grounded several yards away by the rocks. "She could climb down if she wanted to, but she's waiting for me to lift her out rather than risk turning an ankle."

Hazel smiled weakly. "You should help her."

"I will. Eventually." He grinned, and her belly did a strange sort of flip. "But first I needed to be certain you're all right."

"Why wouldn't I be?" she quipped, mentally sliding back

into her suit of armor. She may have had a moment of weakness, but Lord Bladenton was the last person on earth she'd allow to see beyond her hard shell.

"Oh, I don't know," he said. "Maybe because you've spent the last hour preventing my niece from floating into the English Channel? Or worse, becoming dinner to a hungry shark?"

"Thank heaven she's safe." Hazel swiped her palms together to brush off the sand and winced.

The earl growled. "Let me see your hands."

Drat. She reluctantly turned up a palm, and he held her wrist gently, staring at the raw blisters with something akin to horror.

"It's nothing," she assured him.

"It's not nothing." He cupped her hand in his, looked into her eyes, and tenderly blew on the abraded skin.

Her whole body heated, then tingled in response. Her belly fluttered like hummingbird's wings. She swayed as though she'd drunk too much wine.

She snatched her hand away, and he chuckled softly.

"Thank you for finding Kitty and keeping her alive," he said earnestly.

"It was a two-person job. I couldn't have done it without you." Hazel swept several wet tendrils away from her face. "But you're welcome."

A breeze off the water chilled her skin, and she shivered.

The earl jumped up, retrieved his jacket from the sand where he'd tossed it, and placed it over her shoulders. She snuggled into the fine, warm wool. No man had ever given her his jacket before, and since there was precious little chance of such a thing ever happening again, she savored the moment. Briefly imagined what it might be like to have that feeling of being protected and cared for all the time.

The earl smiled at her, and, in that moment, it seemed as

though the pinks, yellows, and oranges in the sky had never glowed so brilliant.

Until Kitty called out from her boat across the beach. "Shall I plan on spending the night out here?" she asked dramatically.

Lord Bladenton snorted. To Hazel he said, "I'm considering answering in the affirmative. Does that make me a terrible uncle?"

Before Hazel could reply, Kitty shouted, "If so, I hope someone's planning to bring me dinner. I'm famished."

Hazel gingerly pushed herself to her feet, testing her legs. "Your niece *is* rather demanding," she told the earl.

He groaned as he stood. "Do you think there's any hope for her?"

"Of course," Hazel assured him. "She just needs someone to believe in her."

The earl retrieved Hazel's boots from the rock and handed them to her. "I'm glad you think so. I want to enroll her at Bellehaven Academy. Immediately."

"You know my terms, Lord Bladenton. Take them or leave them."

"I tried leaving them. It didn't go well," he said with a wry chuckle. "So it seems I'll be visiting you here in Bellehaven, every other week, for the entire summer."

"Kitty," Hazel corrected. "You'll be visiting *Kitty* every other week."

The earl flashed a smug, knee-melting grin. "Isn't that what I said?"

Hazel quirked a brow. "One more thing."

Lord Bladenton snapped his gaze to hers, his expression wary. "What?"

"Kitty cannot know about our deal. You mustn't tell her that your visits were a condition of her enrollment, for that would defeat the purpose entirely. She must believe you *want* to spend time with her."

"She's bound to be suspicious."

Hazel braced one hand against a large rock as she stepped into her boots. "And why is that?"

"Our family situation is complicated." His voice was hollow, edged with bitterness. "I scarcely know my niece."

Hazel had a dozen questions she wanted to ask the earl but kept them to herself. Mostly because asking personal questions often prompted the other party to make the same sort of inquiries in response. And she certainly was not prepared to share personal details or thoughts with Lord Bladenton.

Indeed, her thoughts had taken a horrifyingly wanton turn. She found herself preoccupied with the transparent shirt painted on his impeccably sculpted torso and the drenched trousers clinging to his muscular thighs. If the earl had even an inkling of what she was thinking, she'd burrow into the sand like a crab and remain there for twenty years, minimum.

"Your visits will provide an opportunity for you and Kitty to become better acquainted," she said, pleased that she'd managed a matter-of-fact tone. "She is your ward, and even though she'll be boarding here in Bellehaven, it's important that she feel tethered to home. To family." The sentiment might have sounded trite to some, but it was a truth that Hazel understood deep in her bones.

For the space of several breaths, the earl said nothing. Then, one corner of his mouth curled in the hint of a smile. "Very well. I won't tell Kitty about our deal—or the unscrupulous manner in which you manipulated me into doing your bidding. It will be our little secret, Miss Lively." He gave her a wink before walking across the dusky violet, sunset-kissed beach.

Hazel couldn't help staring as he strode away. His trousers still dripped, and his perfectly molded backside flexed with each effortless, athletic step. Surely, her fascination with Lord Bladenton's anatomy stemmed from a natural scientific curiosity. Nothing more.

Because she had neither the time nor the inclination to engage in frivolous flirtation. There was no room in her life for romance or passion or courtship. Every ounce of energy she possessed was reserved for her school, and, more important, creating a home for the girls entrusted to her care.

No earl—not even a vexingly attractive one—would make her forget that.

The next morning, Hazel greeted Lord Bladenton and Kitty in her office once again. The earl wore a pristine cravat and a guarded expression; indeed, he bore little resemblance to the swashbuckling man she'd seen on the beach the night before. But the change in Kitty was even more pronounced—and unsettling.

Limp blond curls rested on her thin shoulders, and the feistiness she'd displayed yesterday had been replaced with resignation. The tension between her and the earl was so thick that Hazel would have needed a chisel to crack it.

She cast a bright smile at the pair. "I hope you had a comfortable stay at the inn last night."

"Quite," the earl said. He lifted the portmanteaus he held in each hand. Both bags were too stuffed to latch properly, nearly bursting with ribbons, lace, and various trinkets. "Kitty's looking forward to settling into her new quarters."

The girl stared listlessly out the window, looking anything but eager.

Lord Bladenton cleared his throat. "I settled my account with your assistant just now."

Hazel nodded, squashing the guilt niggling at her spine.

She intended to do a world of good with the substantial sum she'd demanded from the earl.

"She should have everything she needs," Lord Bladenton said. He set Kitty's bags on the floor and turned to face his niece, who refused to meet his gaze. "I'll be back in a fortnight to check on your progress," he said brusquely.

Kitty snorted—whether out of disbelief or disgust, it was impossible to say.

"You have a fresh start here," he said softly. "Try not to waste it." He lifted an arm as though he might give her an affectionate pat on the shoulder but apparently thought better of it and awkwardly stepped back.

To Hazel, he said, "I trust my niece is in good hands." For one interminable moment he gazed at her, and she felt an echo of their connection from the night before. But just when she thought he might say something more, he tipped his hat, bowed, and strode out of the office, leaving her alone with Kitty.

The earl was clearly anxious to escape the school—and the town of Bellehaven. Hazel wondered if they'd ever see him again, in spite of the promise he'd made. He'd been desperate enough to agree to anything, but now that he'd gotten what he wanted, there was little incentive for him to visit Kitty. Hazel wouldn't be surprised if he trotted off to London and forgot all about the niece who, apparently, was nothing but a thorn in his side.

The girl's chin trembled and puckered like a strawberry. The sight of her standing there, valiantly fighting to rein in her emotions, made Hazel's throat hurt. But no good would come from tears and platitudes.

Hazel was preparing her students for life—and that meant staying strong in the face of hardship. Remaining composed, even when one was reeling from heartbreak. She knew that better than anyone.

"Right." She picked up the bags and handed one to Kitty. "Let's take your things next door, so I can introduce you to the other boarding students. They're delightful and will no doubt make you feel right at home."

Kitty blinked slowly, her expression aghast. "Please tell me I won't be sharing a bedchamber."

"You won't," Hazel assured her briskly. "You'll be sharing a *dormitory*, which isn't nearly as fancy. Come along, then."

She swept past Kitty, trusting that the girl would follow. "Our classroom is just down the corridor, to the left. The dining room is through here." Hazel waved a hand at the doorway framing a long, utilitarian table flanked by solid benches before making her way up the central staircase. "A handful of women currently let rooms on the second floor. They're not associated with the school, and we must do our best not to disturb them."

"I wouldn't dream of causing a ruckus in the corridor," Kitty said dryly. "I'll save my jigs and bawdy tavern songs for the parlor."

Hazel smiled serenely as she paused on the landing, waiting for Kitty to drag her portmanteau up the steps. If the girl's cheekiness helped subdue her sadness, Hazel supposed she could tolerate a bit of sass. For now.

"Which room is mine?" Kitty asked, gasping.

"The dormitory is one flight up," Hazel replied.

"Surely you jest," Kitty said, incredulous. "You're relegating me to the *attic*?"

Hazel continued marching up the stairs until she stood outside the closed dormitory door. "It is, indeed, the attic." She pushed the door open and ushered Kitty inside the bright, airy room. "But it has one of the best views in all of Bellehaven."

"If you say so." Kitty let her bag drop on the hardwood planks with a thud and crossed her arms over her chest.

"Kitty, allow me to introduce two of your fellow students. This is Lucy." Hazel gestured toward the girl who hung halfway off her bed, the ends of her thick, auburn braids brushing the floor. Predictably, a book on mythology covered half of her freckled face.

Upon seeing Kitty, Lucy set down her book, extended her palms to the ground, and deftly flipped herself to standing. "It's a pleasure to meet you," she said, beaming.

Kitty heaved a tortured sigh. "Likewise."

"And this," Hazel said, "is Clara." The lanky, dark-haired girl sat on her bed, surrounded by colorful scraps of muslin that she'd carefully cut and laid out. "She's working on a new pelisse," Hazel added.

Kitty scoffed. "Rather tiny, isn't it?"

"It's for Lydia," Clara explained, proudly holding up her doll, who, thanks to Clara's talent with a needle, possessed a wardrobe fit for a princess.

"Lord help me," Kitty muttered as she flopped faceup on one of the two unclaimed beds. "I thought I'd been enrolled in a proper finishing school, but it's nothing more than a glorified nursery. A nursery full of misfits."

"Lucy and Clara are not much younger than you are," Hazel said to Kitty. "I've taught them for almost two years now."

Kitty narrowed her eyes suspiciously. "I thought you said this was a new school."

"It is. Until recently, I taught somewhere else." But then Miss Haywinkle had been unexpectedly swept off her feet by a kind, elderly gentleman. He'd proposed, and the headmistress had happily accepted. A few days later, she'd called Hazel into her office and told her she was retiring. And Hazel's world had been upended again.

"Were you kicked out, too?" Kitty asked with mock sympathy.

Ignoring the question, Hazel said, "The girls will help you become familiar with your new surroundings, our class schedule, and your daily chores."

"Dear God," Kitty said, pushing herself to sitting. "I'm to have *chores*? Was my uncle made aware that I'd be pressed into labor?"

"It's part of the school's arrangement with Mrs. Paxton, who runs the boardinghouse," Hazel replied evenly, determined that nothing in her manner would reveal her apprehension about having Kitty join the ranks of her beloved students. As headmistress, it was imperative that she remained calm. That she always appeared to be in control.

Even if she feared bringing Kitty on board was tantamount to plopping a wolf in a field of gentle lambs.

Hazel only prayed that her school—and her life's dream—would survive the test.

Chapter 5

Blade found his sparring partner, Will, on the edge of the ballroom's dance floor and handed him a glass of brandy. "Sorry about the eye."

"You're lucky you landed the punch. I was about to trounce you." Will raised his glass in a toast and grinned in spite of the shiner that made him look more like a devil-may-care pirate than the esteemed Marquess of Goulding.

"If it makes you feel any better, I think you cracked one of my ribs," Blade said congenially.

"That does bolster my spirits." Will smiled wryly. "At least your face is intact. You'll need those infernal good looks if you've any hope of landing a countess." He inclined his head meaningfully in the direction of Lady Penelope, who wore a sapphire gown with a daring neckline. She'd spent most of the evening doing her level best to ignore Blade. Each time he looked her way, she tossed her blond ringlets, refusing to meet his gaze.

"Penelope's cross with me for missing her dinner party last week."

Will arched a brow. "Have you apologized?"

"I've explained."

Will chuckled with mirth. "You've much to learn, my friend."

"You're hardly an expert." Blade took a large gulp of brandy. "Besides, I have no intention of becoming mired in the usual lovers' games. Jealousy, spats, guilt—they're the equivalent of quicksand."

"Ah, yes. The dreaded quicksand." Will raised his eyebrows and rocked back on his heels. "Ever the romantic, aren't you?"

Blade grunted. Perhaps he *should* make some effort to smooth things over with Penelope. Or at least determine if they were still of a like mind.

He threw back the rest of his drink and placed his empty glass on a passing footman's tray. To Will, he said, "I'm going to speak with her."

"Right. Into the jungle," Will quipped, giving him a bracing slap on the back. "Beware of the Venus flytrap."

Blade ignored his friend's laughter and wove his way through the crowd, intercepting Penelope as she left the dance floor. "I wondered if we might have a word."

She gazed at him with cool detachment, her blue eyes eerily indifferent. For a moment, he thought she'd refuse, but then she blinked and exhaled. "Meet me on the terrace in a quarter of an hour," she said. "And this time, Bladenton, don't keep me waiting."

He was sitting on a stone bench on the edge of the dimly lit garden when Penelope emerged from the house, gliding across the flagstone terrace like a queen.

She settled herself on the bench beside him and smoothed her skirts. "You wished to speak with me?" she said, clearly anticipating a fine bit of groveling.

"I regret that I wasn't able to attend your dinner party as promised," he began. "As I've explained—"

Penelope held up her palm. "I know. You were detained because of an incident involving your niece. Again."

"But now she's settled at a new school, on the coast. I don't anticipate any other crises will arise."

"No." Penelope adjusted the sparkling ruby bracelet dangling from her wrist. "You never do."

Blade rubbed the back of his neck. "I'd thought that we understood each other, that we wanted the same things. Forgive me if I was mistaken."

"Oh, I understand you," Penelope said coolly. "You want a woman who will play the part of your countess and help you raise your niece. Someone to run the household, attend social events, warm your bed, and perhaps bear an heir or two. No sentimental feelings. No distasteful drama."

Jesus, she made him sound like a stone-hearted monster. The hell of it was, she was right on the mark.

"I've been honest," he said. "No one's forcing your hand, and there are obvious advantages to the arrangement. Financial security, elevated social standing, complete independence . . . I thought those things were important to you."

"Of course they are," Penelope admitted. "But they're not quite enough."

Alarm bells sounded in Blade's head. "Tender feelings are overrated." An understatement if ever there was one. Love was combustible—a grenade that inevitably resulted in betrayal, pain, and loss. He'd be damned before he pulled that pin again.

Penelope scoffed. "I'm not speaking of tenderness or love."

Relief washed over him. "What, then?"

"I need to know I can depend on you. Imagine how I felt when you failed to show at my dinner party after promising you'd attend. You couldn't even be bothered to send word that you'd been detained."

"I didn't have time to sit down and pen a note. My niece was in trouble."

"I believe her headmistress is paid to deal with those sorts of matters," Penelope said with a sniff.

Blade recalled the scene in the cove—and the heart-stopping panic he'd felt when he'd first spotted Miss Lively bravely trying to rescue Kitty from being carried out to sea. "Yes, but . . ."

Penelope raised her gently sloped nose in the air. "I was humiliated, Bladenton."

"I'm sorry," he said, sincere. He'd never given a damn what others thought, but clearly, Penelope did.

"I'm not asking for poetry or romance. I don't need a love for the ages. But I won't be made a laughingstock by you or your niece. I need to know I can count on you."

Blade winced. "Fair enough."

"I'm glad we're in agreement," she said, her tone brisk and business-like. "But before we proceed with an engagement, I should like some assurance that you're capable of abiding by my terms."

"I am."

"Then prove it."

Blade scratched his head. "How?"

Penelope gracefully stood and paced the terrace in front of the bench. "Behave like a proper suitor for the next couple of months. Keep your wayward niece in check and refrain from embarrassing me in front of my family and friends. Take me to the theater on occasion and ask me to dance at balls. If you can manage that, we'll announce our engagement . . . and marry by the fall."

Blade stuck a finger between his cravat and neck, then swallowed. Reminded himself that Penelope was the solution to his problems. If he didn't marry and sire an heir, his title and estate would go to his wastrel of a cousin and his reprobate son. Blade couldn't allow that to happen—not when so many people depended on him. No, like it or not, he had to marry.

Penelope was the ideal candidate. Not only would she give him an heir, but she'd provide a role model for Kitty when she was home from school. Best of all, she wouldn't demand that he pry the lid off his sordid past. Wouldn't ask for anything that he couldn't give.

"Very well," he said sincerely. "I'll prove I'm capable of courting you without catastrophe."

"Courtship without catastrophe," she repeated with a wry smile. "Good heavens. Such a lofty goal."

Blade scoffed. She had no idea.

One week later, Blade braced himself for a distasteful scene as he walked through the door of Bellehaven Academy. He'd had no communication from Kitty. No desperate pleas to rescue her from the horrors of boarding school life: tedious lessons, snoring roommates, or fiendish teachers.

Miss Lively had been conspicuously silent also. He'd yet to receive a message from the headmistress enumerating Kitty's offenses, which, one could safely assume, had been myriad.

The absence of information, however, gave Blade a modicum of hope. Allowed him to delude himself into thinking Kitty had turned over a new leaf. Maybe she was fitting in. Making friends. Following rules.

And maybe he'd sprout wings and fly.

"Lord Bladenton," Miss Lively's assistant said. "It's a pleasure to see you again." She ushered him through the antechamber toward the headmistress's office and knocked once before opening the door.

Miss Lively was perched on the windowsill, with one leg tucked inside the frame and the other braced on the floor.

Predictably, her pert nose was stuck in a book, but she wore a secretive, dreamy smile—the sort that brought to mind slow, stolen kisses in the shade of an old oak tree. Or the sensuous caress of silk on bare skin.

She started and fumbled the book when she realized she had a visitor, then deftly caught it as she jumped to her feet.

"Good afternoon," she said, quickly regaining her usual composure. "You've come to spend time with your niece."

"Yes." He took a seat in front of her desk. "I had little choice in the matter—as you well know."

For several seconds, Miss Lively stared at him, impassive. Guilt for only-God-knew-what wriggled up his neck, and suddenly he was a lad again, sitting in the headmaster's office waiting for his punishment to be meted out.

"Jane," the headmistress said coolly, "would you please inform Kitty that her uncle has arrived for a visit?"

As the assistant scurried off, Miss Lively sank into the chair across from him, her spine as straight as an arrow, and tucked her book in the top drawer of her desk. God help him, he'd have given his left arm to know what she'd been reading—what it was that had turned her soft and wistful.

"Kitty will be glad for the diversion," the headmistress was saying. "What do you have planned?"

His only plan was to get in and out of Bellehaven relatively unscathed—and as quickly as humanly possible. He shrugged. "I suppose we'll go for a walk."

Miss Lively arched a brow at that but said nothing. She kept her plump lips sealed as though she were perfectly comfortable with the unnaturally prolonged silence that ensued.

"How has Kitty"—he shifted in his seat—"how has Kitty been faring?"

The headmistress met his gaze. "You should ask her."

"I intend to. But I'd like your perspective, too."

"Let me see." Miss Lively picked up a pencil and tapped

the blunt end on her desk blotter. "She snuck into Mrs. Paxton's kitchen late one night—presumably to make a tray of biscuits—and succeeded in starting a small fire."

Blade dragged a hand down his face. "Jesus."

"The following day, while she was confined to her room, she fashioned a knotted rope from the bedsheets and tried to convince her roommates to help her escape from an attic window."

"Bloody hell."

"Fortunately, my room is just below the dormitory, and I intervened before she—or either of the younger, more impressionable girls—managed to break their necks."

He winced, apologetic. "I assume that's just a sampling of her transgressions?"

"Oh yes," she assured him calmly. "I've barely scratched the surface. But I think you have a fairly good picture of what's been happening here."

A potent mix of frustration, anger, and despair whirled in his chest. Made his heart pound. Kitty was doing her damnedest to get kicked out of boarding school number three. And if he couldn't keep her antics in check, she was going to spoil more than his chances with Penelope. She was going to sabotage her own future as well.

"I'm planning to marry soon," he said, "so that Kitty will have a mother figure to guide her."

The lift of Miss Lively's brow was so subtle that a casual observer would not have noticed it—but Blade did.

"Nothing is set in stone as yet," he continued, wondering why in God's name he was divulging such personal information. "But the woman I have in mind possesses the necessary qualifications. Indeed, I'm basing my decision solely on objective criteria. No emotions are involved on either side."

"I see." The headmistress's whiskey-colored eyes looked

deep into his, as though she were searching the cobwebbed corners of his soul.

Disconcerting, that—and all the more reason to focus on the matter at hand. "I'll speak to Kitty," he said. "But I can't promise it will do any good. The truth is . . . I don't know what else to do with her."

The headmistress nodded, vexingly aloof, considering he'd just bared his soul and admitted his utter failure as Kitty's guardian. "There's one more thing I must tell you before Kitty arrives."

He shook his head. "Spare me the full listing of her misdeeds. I'll pay for the damages, of course. Just give me the bill."

"This is not an issue that can be solved with money. Or a scolding." Miss Lively folded her hands, leaned forward on her elbows, and looked into his eyes. "Kitty's roommates tell me that she has cried herself to sleep every night since she's arrived here."

Blade blinked. Tried to picture it. His sharp-tongued, mischief-loving niece had been crying? *Shit.*

Miss Lively cleared her throat. "Ah, here she is. Good afternoon, Kitty. Isn't this a nice surprise? Your uncle has come to visit."

Blade forced a smile as Kitty breezed into the room, but she looked past him and addressed Miss Lively.

"Would you please inform my uncle that he's arrived at a most inconvenient time? I'm positively drowning in school-work."

"If you were, in fact, doing schoolwork, that would be a first," the headmistress replied with aplomb. "However, as your uncle wishes to spend the afternoon with you, I shall excuse you from completing your assignments. Please, go and enjoy yourself."

"What of *my* wishes?" Kitty whined. "I don't *want* to spend time with Lord Bladenton." Her mouth contorted like she'd sucked a lemon wedge. "And I don't want to speak to him, either. The earl and I have absolutely nothing to say to each other. You referred to him as my uncle, and I cannot deny that he is—by blood. But that does *not* mean we're family."

Her words hit Blade like a dart between the shoulder blades. He opened his mouth to fire back but remembered what Miss Lively had said about Kitty crying herself to sleep.

So he counted to three in his head before facing his niece again. "I realize I'm not your favorite person. But I've driven my curricle all the way from London. Since I'm here, you may as well show me some of the shops in town. I could buy you some ribbons or even a new bonnet if you'd like."

Kitty crossed her arms and lifted her nose, refusing to look at him. "Miss Lively, would you please inform the earl that I cannot be bribed with gifts?"

Blade threw up his arms. "Fine. No gifts then. Why don't you tell me what *you'd* like to do?"

"Miss Lively, would you please tell the earl that I'd sooner pluck out my eyelashes one by one than spend the afternoon with him?"

"Kitty," the headmistress said evenly, "I had thought you far too mature for these sorts of antics."

"And yet you have relegated me to sharing a dormitory with a couple of silly girls who still play with dolls and wear their hair in pigtails." Kitty scoffed. "This isn't a proper finishing school so much as it is a charity home for outcasts."

Miss Lively's eyes narrowed ever so slightly, and the intensity of her stare made Kitty, who was not particularly inclined to shame, shuffle her feet.

Blade held his breath. If he was honest with himself, he

was relieved that, for once, Kitty had directed her barbs at someone other than him. It seemed she couldn't help but push people away, and this time, she might have pushed Miss Lively too far.

The headmistress rose slowly, walked to one side of the desk, and sat on the edge. "I understand that you're angry with your uncle for enrolling you here. And that you don't want to visit with him. But on occasion, we all must do things that we would rather not. It's part of being an adult."

"So I'm to have all of the burdens of being an adult without any of the perks?" Kitty pretended to examine a fingernail. "No, thank you."

Blade swallowed. "Maybe I should go," he said. "And come back another time."

The headmistress shot him a pointed look. "No." Turning to Kitty, she said, "I'll make a deal with you. If you agree to spend the afternoon with your uncle, I'll excuse you from dining room duty for the entire week."

Kitty gaped. "Truly?"

Miss Lively nodded. "Right. That's my final offer."

"You have a deal," Kitty said firmly.

"Excellent." Miss Lively exhaled. She swept her arm toward the door in a vaguely dismissive gesture. Clearly, she couldn't wait to have her office to herself again. "Enjoy your afternoon."

"I'll go with Lord Bladenton," Kitty intoned. "But you can't make me speak to him."

Blade's panic spiked again. What the devil was he supposed to do with his niece for the next three hours? "Miss Lively," he said. "Might I have a word before we go?"

The headmistress gazed longingly at the drawer where she'd stowed her book. "Of course." To Kitty, she said, "Please wait in the antechamber. Your uncle will join you shortly."

As soon as the door closed behind her, Blade stood and faced Miss Lively. Prepared to beg. "I realize this is a highly unusual request," he said, earnestly, "but you have to come with us."

Chapter 6

Hazel blinked at Lord Bladenton. Wished the dratted dimple in his cheek weren't quite so distracting. "I beg your pardon?"

He stood in front of her, his polished boots mere inches from the toes of her slippers. His dark hair was windblown and wild—as if he'd neglected to wear a hat during the entire drive from London. "I need you to come with us on our outing."

"Nonsense." She resisted the urge to retreat behind her desk. The earl's nearness affected her strangely. Despite the delightful breeze wafting through her office, telltale heat crept up her chest. At the same time, her skin tingled—as though she were walking naked through the soft grass on the dunes. Thank heaven she was something of an expert at masking her feelings, for if the earl could see inside her head she'd have to flee to Scotland and lock herself in a tower for the rest of her days.

Instead, she stood tall—which was still a head shorter than the earl—and looked into his troubled eyes. "In case it wasn't obvious, the whole point of your visit is for you and Kitty to spend time together . . . and begin to mend the rift between you. I would only be in the way."

"I respectfully disagree." Lord Bladenton shook his head, vehement. "Kitty is the most stubborn person I know. There's no chance of us mending rifts as long as she refuses to talk to me."

Goodness. He really was at loose ends. She moved a little closer and lowered her voice in case Kitty was listening through the door. "Can I tell you a secret?"

For a moment, the earl said nothing, then one corner of his mouth lifted in a wicked curl. "You can tell me anything, Miss Lively."

The raw heat in his voice vibrated through her like he'd plucked a harp string at her nape, but she rolled her eyes as though she were quite immune to idle flirtation. "Kitty wants to talk to you," she explained, "but her pride is wounded. She's hurt, so she's lashing out and pushing you away."

The earl held out his arms. "Then what am I supposed to do?"

"Keep showing up. Consider this is a test of sorts. She needs to know you won't give up on her."

The earl dragged his fingers through his hair, giving him the look of a man who'd just stumbled from his bed after a night of debauchery. "I have a confession."

"Now *I'm* all ears," Hazel quipped.

"I know next to nothing about children."

As confessions went, it was hardly revelatory. He might as well have told her the ocean was deep. Hazel waited expectantly.

"Kitty is my brother's daughter, but my brother and I were estranged. Eight months ago, when he and"—the earl closed his eyes briefly—"his wife died, Kitty showed up on my doorstep. That was the first time we met."

Hazel waited to see if he'd say more, but he pressed his lips into a thin line.

"Kitty hasn't spoken about her loss," Hazel said. "But she

must feel terribly sad and alone. It's no wonder she's been acting out."

The earl scrubbed the back of his head. "You already
know Kitty better than I do. That's why you have to accompany us—just for an hour or two. Without you, this visit is
doomed. I'll be forced to talk to myself while Kitty glares
at me and plots half a dozen diabolically creative ways to
make my life a living hell." He shot Hazel a wry half smile
that she felt in the vicinity of her belly. "I realize that an
afternoon with your most troublesome student and her inept
guardian doesn't hold quite the same appeal as your book,
but I'm begging you to come. Please."

She blew out a long breath. Five minutes ago, she'd have
had no difficulty giving Lord Bladenton a firm *no*. But then
he'd gone and shown a different, more vulnerable side of
himself and left her feeling uncharacteristically persuadable.
Almost—Lord help her—*soft*.

"A short outing," she said reluctantly. "I'll come along to
act as a buffer between you and Kitty, but it will be up to you
to earn her trust."

"Of course, I understand." His eyes shone with relief.
"Thank you."

Hazel was already kicking herself for agreeing to accompany them, but there was nothing to be done for it now.

She breezed past him, plucked her straw bonnet and
paisley shawl from a hook on the wall, and opened the office door. When she entered the antechamber, both Jane and
Kitty looked up at her, their faces questioning.

"I'll be joining Lord Bladenton and Kitty on their outing," Hazel said to her assistant. "I expect to return before
dinner."

Jane pushed her spectacles up her nose and squared her
shoulders. "No need to rush. I'll mind things here."

"Excellent." Hazel felt rather than saw the earl standing

just behind her. Though her skin prickled with awareness, she endeavored to appear impervious to the heat of his body and the light puffs of his breath on her neck.

To Kitty, she said, "Since you've no interest in browsing the shops today, I thought we could take a stroll through town. Perhaps show your uncle some of the local landmarks."

"How enthralling," the girl said flatly.

"Do you have another suggestion?" Hazel said.

"I was thinking my uncle could return to London, and I could return to my bed for a nap."

"I'm afraid that's not an option." Hazel tossed a glance at the earl. "Both of you, please follow me."

A moment later, the three of them stood outside of the school, breathing in the soothing, salty air. A humid breeze swirled around Hazel's legs, playfully puffing out her skirt. The vivid blue sky was punctuated with clouds resembling large dollops of clotted cream, but neither the earl nor his ward seemed inclined to notice the glorious scenery.

Hazel needed to think of an activity that would let them momentarily escape their troubles. Something that would let them appreciate the beauty of Bellehaven as she did.

She glanced down the street, and inspiration struck. "I have an idea."

"Kitty and I are amenable to whatever you suggest," the earl said stoically.

The girl sniffed and tossed her golden curls in silent protest.

But Hazel refused to be deterred. "Let's go for a curricle ride . . . on the beach."

Blade cocked an ear, certain he must have misunderstood. The headmistress was so regimented that she probably wore a corset to bed. So disciplined that she probably translated bloody Latin texts in her dreams.

"A curricle ride on the beach?" he repeated.

Miss Lively nodded in the affirmative. "I've seen one or two gentlemen racing across the sand. It looked rather . . . exhilarating."

Kitty's eyebrows slid halfway up her forehead, proving that the headmistress had shocked her, too—which was no small feat.

"Then a curricle ride, it is," Blade said. "My horses are in the stable, being watered and fed, but they should be rested soon. Shall we walk for a while?"

Their odd trio strolled down the pebbled streets, stopping occasionally so the headmistress could point out various shops and establishments. Kitty scowled, while Blade tried to ignore the scents of honey and sweet cream that wafted around him each time Miss Lively was near.

When they circled back to the block where the school was located, Blade ducked inside the stable, readied the curricle, and climbed onto the seat—the rather *small* seat that he was unaccustomed to sharing. It was cozy for two people and would definitely be a tight squeeze for three. On the bright side, since Kitty wasn't speaking to him, he wouldn't have to endure a barrage of complaints.

He drove the curricle to the corner where Miss Lively and Kitty waited, then hopped down to help them up. Predictably, Kitty walked past him without taking the hand he offered. As she climbed onto the vehicle, she called over her shoulder to the headmistress. "I won't sit beside him. You'll have to take the middle spot."

Miss Lively shot a dubious glance at the seat, clearly pondering how the three of them were going to fit. She hesitated, and for a heartbeat, Blade wondered if she'd object. Or if she'd take his hand.

But then, as she stepped onto the curricle, she slid her

fingers into his palm. A shimmer of desire traveled through his arm and warmed his whole body.

He wondered if Miss Lively felt it, too.

Unlikely, since the headmistress seemed immune to mortal foibles like attraction and longing and loneliness. And yet Blade detected the faintest blush glowing from her cheeks.

He climbed into the seat and wedged himself next to her, determined to banish wayward thoughts from his head. He reminded himself that the visit was supposed to be about forming a bond with Kitty. But he was only human—and all too conscious of Miss Lively's soft, shapely body pressed against his side.

She stared straight ahead as she directed him to drive one street over, toward a sandy path wide enough to permit the horses and curricle to pass across the dune and onto the deserted beach.

"The gusty winds and large waves have kept the swimmers at home today," the headmistress said conversationally. "It's as though the beach is all ours."

Blade drove toward the broad strip of shoreline just out of reach of the greedy waves. His horses trotted lightly across the compacted sand, and the curricle wheels rolled freely. With a slap of the reins, he urged the horses into a gallop—and the world began to rush past.

The roar of the surf thundered in his chest. The powerful headwind rushed at him, slicking back his hair and taking his breath away.

For a moment, he was a lad of sixteen again, unencumbered by regrets or grief. Blissfully free and full of hope.

He looked to his left, making sure neither of his passengers minded the brisk wind or breakneck pace. Miss Lively's bonnet blew halfway off her head, so she untied the ribbon at her chin, held the hat in her lap, and turned her face to the sky. Kitty extended an arm toward the ocean, reveling in the spray of the ocean against her palm and the flow of the air between her fingers.

Maybe the three of them had something in common after all.

Blade nudged Miss Lively, held up the reins, and spoke next to her ear. "Why don't you drive for a stretch?"

Surprise, then delight flitted across her face. She began to take the leather straps from him, then stopped as though she thought better of it. She shot him a pointed glance and inclined her head meaningfully toward Kitty.

Blade stared at the headmistress like an idiot. Of course, he might have been distracted by the long, thick curls that had escaped the knot at her nape. Or the pure joy that had transformed her face. Whatever the reason, he didn't have an inkling what she was trying to say to him.

"You don't want to drive?" he asked.

As she leaned in closer to respond, the curricle hit a dip in the sand. She squeezed his upper arm to brace herself, and his heart started beating triple time. "Ask Kitty," she said. "She won't be able to resist."

Right. He probably should have thought of that. But his niece hadn't said a word to him all damned afternoon. The chances of her acknowledging his existence were approximately one in a hundred.

As if privy to his thoughts, Miss Lively said, "Just try."

"Kitty," he called, "why don't you take the reins?" He offered the straps to her, fully prepared to be rebuffed.

Her gaze snapped to his, wary. "Do you mean it?" There was a mixture of awe and hopefulness in her voice.

He nodded. "Just keep us out of the ocean," he said wryly, slapping the side of the curricle. "She doesn't float."

Kitty grasped the reins and faced forward solemnly, as

though determined to keep them on a straight path. The wind whipped wildly at her blond hair, and a euphoric smile lit her face.

"This is amazing!" she shouted gleefully. "It feels like we're flying!"

Apparently, the silent treatment was over, and Blade had Miss Lively to thank.

They exchanged a look, and—unless Blade was hallucinating—the headmistress winked at him. Of course, it was entirely possible a grain of sand had flown into her eye, and she was merely blinking it out.

But hours after he'd returned Kitty and Miss Lively to Bellehaven Academy and taken a room at the Bluffs' Brew Inn, Blade was still thinking about that wink. Still remembering the feel of Miss Lively's body pressed against his side.

He reminded himself of his plan to marry Lady Penelope, but when he laid his head on his pillow and closed his eyes that night, he didn't dream of her.

It was the unexpectedly intriguing, undeniably alluring headmistress who haunted him.

They were in her office, all alone. She sat in the window, reading. But when she saw him, she smiled, set down her book, and slowly, deliberately removed her lacy fichu. Let it drop to the floor.

The tiny sleeves of her gown slipped off her shoulders, catching on her elbows. Her neckline dipped tantalizingly low across the swells of her breasts. As she glided toward him, she removed the pins from her hair, one by one, releasing a riot of rich brown curls down her back.

With an arch of her brow, she grabbed him by the lapels and led him to her desk. She perched on the edge, pulled him close, and leaned back, shoving aside books and papers and

God-knew-what. As though she were mad with desire—and as crazed with passion as he was.

Even while he dreamed, he knew that a romantic encounter with Miss Lively was about as likely as him flying to the moon.

But that didn't stop him from savoring every second of the fantasy.

Chapter 7

Hazel woke the next morning feeling more optimistic than she had in weeks. Kitty was speaking to her uncle again, and though the girl's relationship with the earl was still shaky, progress had been made. Lord Bladenton had even decided to stay in Bellehaven overnight, reasoning that as long as he was there, he might as well take his niece to luncheon before returning to London.

Hazel hummed a happy tune as she poured herself a cup of tea at her office desk. Aromatic steam tickled her nose, and the caws of seabirds floated through the open window. At last, her life was moving in the right direction.

Thanks to the considerable sum she'd received from the earl, she'd been able to pay her rent for the entire summer, buy several beautiful books for the school's library, *and* order dresses for Lucy and Clara to replace the ones they were quickly outgrowing. Hazel could scarcely wait to see the looks on their faces when she surprised them with the pretty new frocks.

In honor of her gloriously sunny outlook, Hazel had worn a pale-yellow gown embroidered with cheerful green sprigs. Her choice of gown had nothing to do with Lord Bladenton's impending visit. Or the odd stirrings she felt whenever he was near.

The thought of seeing him when he came to fetch Kitty for luncheon caused a vexing flutter in her belly, but surely that was merely a natural, if highly inconvenient, biological response to an attractive man. One she was fully capable of ignoring. After all, it wasn't as though she inspired the same sort of reaction in the earl. To him, she was simply a head-mistress, and moreover, the solution to a problem.

The sound of muffled conversation in the antecham-ber jolted Hazel from her musings, and she instinctively checked that her starched linen fichu and tidy hair twist were secure. Someone rapped on the door a moment before it swung open.

Jane stood in the doorway, her spectacles propped haphaz-ardly on top of her head. "You've a visitor, Miss Lively."

Hazel set down her teacup, hoping her cheeks weren't as pink as they felt. "Oh?"

"Mrs. Covington," her assistant announced, waving the stylishly clad woman into the office.

Gads. Mrs. Covington was Prudence's mother—one of her local students. Hazel stood and gestured toward one of the chairs in front of her desk. "Welcome, Mrs. Covington," she said. "I trust Prue is doing well?"

"Very well." The woman forced a smile as she sat.

Hazel lowered herself into her chair, perplexed. Mrs. Cov-ington hadn't paid a visit to the school since enrolling Pru-dence several weeks ago. "Would you care for some tea?"

"No, thank you." She shook her head, and the plumes on her elegant peacock-blue hat quivered. Her hands, donned in immaculate gray kid gloves, were clasped in her lap. "I shan't stay long. I simply wished to inform you of a deci-sion that Mr. Covington and I have made in regard to our daughter's future."

The hairs on the back of Hazel's arms stood on end. "A decision?"

"As you know, Prudence adores her lessons here at Belle-haven Academy. She's constantly prattling on about this novel or that outing. And she's very fond of the other girls."

"They adore her as well," Hazel said. "Prue is a wonderful student—so inquisitive and studious. She never tires of learning."

Mrs. Covington wrinkled her nose. "Precisely. My husband and I worry that she's a bit *too* studious. We fear she'll develop eccentric tendencies that are off-putting to potential suitors."

Hazel frowned. "With all respect, Mrs. Covington, I don't think you need to worry. Prudence is intelligent and kind."

"Yes, there's no denying that. But she'll need more than a pleasant disposition to compete in the marriage mart. To that end, my husband and I believe she'll be better served by having a tutor—someone to teach her to play the harp and speak French and carry herself properly. In short, someone who will transform her into a fashionable young lady."

"Prudence doesn't need to be transformed," Hazel countered. "She's lovely as she is."

Mrs. Covington's face softened. "She is. However, she's not likely to attract a gentleman if she spends every afternoon reading as she walks on the beach, heedless of her soaked hem and sand-filled slippers. What my daughter requires is a bit of polish."

Oh God. Losing Prue as a student would be a hardship for the school, but it would be even more devastating for Hazel personally. Prue was a ray of sunshine, both inside the classroom and outside of it. She adored her studies and her classmates and would be heartbroken if her parents withdrew her.

Hazel played her last card. "Once the summer is in full swing, I intend to give the older girls opportunities to attend social events where they can practice their manners and deportment."

"Oh?" Mrs. Covington's brow creased as she mulled over the new information. "I suppose some exposure to the social whirl would be useful. Anything to get Prudence's nose out of a book. Perhaps she can continue her lessons here through the summer and start with Miss Lavelle in the fall."

"Or maybe you and your husband will change your—" Hazel stopped, cocking an ear to better hear the scuffle coming from the antechamber. Oh dear.

"Miss Lively!" The elderly boardinghouse owner, Mrs. Paxton, burst through the door and marched into the office clutching her beloved tabby cat to her chest. "Your girls have gone too far this time."

Oh no. Hazel attempted a serene smile, praying her alarm didn't show. "Good morning, Mrs. Paxton. Whatever the trouble is, I wonder if we could discuss the matter a bit later?" She inclined her head meaningfully toward Mrs. Covington.

The gray-haired woman walked farther into the room, undaunted. "Look at this." Her spindly arms trembled as thrust forward her cat. Her extremely well-dressed cat.

"Is that . . ." Mrs. Covington leaned toward the creature, as though she couldn't quite believe her eyes. "Is that animal wearing a ball gown?"

Mrs. Paxton nodded as she lifted the hem and the cat's sizable belly to reveal its hind legs. "With matching slippers!" she cried, clearly appalled.

Hazel stood, glided toward Mrs. Paxton, and inspected the cat more closely, searching for a way to diffuse the woman's anger.

"You must admit, the azure silk looks lovely against the orange fur," Hazel ventured. "And I hadn't realized there was a tiara here between the ears." The cat yawned, unimpressed.

"I am not amused, Miss Lively," the older woman intoned.

"I didn't mean to make light of the situation," Hazel said sincerely. "But it does seem a rather harmless prank. Your cat shows no signs of distress."

"Harold may appear unperturbed on the surface but look into his eyes."

Hazel inched closer and obediently searched Harold's whiskered face. His eyelids drooped as though he longed for a nap.

"He's utterly humiliated," Mrs. Paxton exclaimed. "Your students have wounded his dignity."

"I'm sure that was not their intent." But the girls knew how Mrs. Paxton doted on her cat and should have guessed she wouldn't be pleased to discover him looking as though he'd pranced directly out of a duchess's boudoir. Hazel would bet her favorite poetry book that Kitty had put the younger ones up to it. "I'll speak to the girls and have them make amends somehow. Perhaps they could sew you a new apron or make Harold a proper bed—one that's fit for a prince."

Mrs. Paxton huffed, only slightly mollified. "I cannot abide this sort of mischievousness in my boardinghouse."

Mrs. Covington clucked her tongue. "Such pranks certainly don't reflect well on the school—or your students. You know, I think it best if I withdraw Prudence immediately."

Oh no. "Please," Hazel choked out, "give me a chance to sort this all out." She walked behind her desk and gripped the back of her chair in a futile attempt to keep the room from tilting.

If Prue left, other students would follow suit, and Hazel would soon have an empty classroom. Her life's dream was evaporating faster than morning clouds over the ocean.

All because Mrs. Paxton couldn't stand to see her darling Harold in puffed sleeves and a flounced skirt.

Hazel closed her eyes for several breaths, determined to compose herself. A headmistress was supposed to be confident, capable, and strong. Her toughness had brought her this far, and she couldn't falter now.

No matter what, she mustn't surrender to the flood of panic. Mustn't lose control.

And she absolutely could not, under any circumstances, *cry*.

She swallowed the ghastly lump in her throat and addressed Mrs. Covington. "I'm begging you to reconsider."

"Good morning, ladies." Lord Bladenton strode into the office wearing a snug-fitting jacket and a charming grin. His gaze flicked to Hazel's face, then meandered around the room, eventually settling on Harold. "I hope I'm not interrupting."

Mrs. Paxton arched a white brow and pursed her thin lips.

Mrs. Covington fluffed the ringlets that hung over her shoulder and beamed.

"Not at all," Hazel lied. "Lord Bladenton, this is Mrs. Paxton, owner of the boardinghouse."

"A pleasure," the earl said smoothly. He reached out and rubbed the cat under the chin. "And who might this delightful creature be?"

"Harold," Mrs. Paxton said proudly. "He's not given to wearing dresses—he's usually quite dashing."

Hazel held her breath, praying the earl wouldn't say anything to make matters worse. "Handsome fellow," Lord Bladenton drawled. "But he'll need to trade the gown and slippers for a waistcoat and cravat if he's going to impress the ladies. Maybe I should give him the name of my tailor," he added with a wink.

Mrs. Paxton's cheeks turned pink, and she tittered like she was suddenly five decades younger.

Hazel blinked and gestured toward the woman sitting across from her desk. "And this is Mrs. Covington, the mother of one of my students."

Lord Bladenton flashed his dratted dimple and made a polite bow. "Delighted to meet you. I enrolled my niece a couple of weeks ago."

Mrs. Covington fanned herself. "How wonderful. Prudence mentioned a new boarding student."

"Forgive me for barging in," he said smoothly. "I came to collect my niece but didn't realize the three of you were conducting business."

"I was about to take my leave," Mrs. Paxton said. Addressing Hazel, she added, "Inform your girls that they'll have after-dinner duty in the kitchen this week."

Hazel nodded, grateful for the relatively light sentence. She supposed she had the earl's charm to thank for that.

He inclined his head as the elderly woman walked out of the office, cradling Howard in her arms as if he were a fragile newborn baby instead of a lethargic cat weighing nearly two stone.

Mrs. Covington's appreciative gaze swept over the earl. "Tell me, are you staying here in Bellehaven, Lord Bladenton?"

"I'm afraid not. I'm returning to London tonight—although I must say this town has much to recommend it." He shot her a pointed, brooding glance. Almost as if he were . . . flirting. Hazel bristled. Not because she was jealous—the very idea was absurd—but because of the earl's sheer audacity.

"Yes, well," Mrs. Covington said breathlessly. "Perhaps we'll persuade you to join us for some of the summer's popular festivities." To Hazel, she said, "We can resume our conversation another time, Miss Lively."

"Then I'll see Prue on Monday?" she asked hopefully.

Mrs. Covington stood and, unless Hazel was mistaken,

surreptitiously examined the earl's backside. "Yes, of course," she answered—more than a little distracted. "Good day, Lord Bladenton."

His mouth curled into a semi-smoldering smile. "Until next time."

The dark-haired beauty swept past him as she left the office, and he closed the door behind her.

Leaving the earl and Hazel alone.

She sagged against the edge of her desk and gaped at him. "What. Was. *That?*"

He stared at her as if the simple question had left him dumbfounded. "*That* was me, saving your skin."

Hazel snorted. "Truly? Because it looked as though you were shamelessly flirting with one of my clients—who happens to be married. Are you mad?"

"Undoubtedly." The earl chuckled smugly, raising her ire from a simmer to a boil.

"I'm glad you find the situation humorous, my lord." She shoved herself off her desk and stood directly in front of him. "Let us hope that *Mr.* Covington is similarly amused—and that he doesn't own a set of dueling pistols."

Lord Bladenton scoffed and crossed his arms, causing the fabric of his jacket to hug his biceps in a most vexing manner. "The only thing I'm guilty of is a bit of harmless banter, intended to improve Mrs. Covington's mood. I overheard her threatening to pull her daughter out of your school. And I happen to know you can't afford to lose any students."

"I can't," she grudgingly admitted. "But I certainly don't need you unleashing your formidable charm on their unsuspecting mothers."

He grinned, and the force of it hit her in the belly. "You think my charm is formidable?"

For the second time that morning, a shiver stole over her skin. But this one warned of a different type of danger. She quickly pondered her options and decided to answer him as objectively as possible.

"You seem to have enchanted Mrs. Covington and, to a lesser extent, Mrs. Paxton, which is no small feat. So, yes. Empirically speaking, I must conclude that you do, in fact, possess a modicum of charm."

He moved a fraction of an inch closer and quirked a brow. "Empirically speaking?"

"Yes." She kept her voice steady despite his nearness and her racing pulse. "You've capably demonstrated your dubious powers."

He rubbed his chin, thoughtful. "So, the results are conclusive."

"I suppose you could say that." She gave a noncommittal shrug.

"But . . . ?"

"Two women hardly constitute a wide sampling." The moment the words left her mouth she wished she could stuff them back in. But she saw the gleam in his eyes. Knew it was too late.

"If only there were another test subject available," he said, his suggestive tone making his meaning perfectly clear.

"I'm not a suitable candidate," she said crisply.

"And why is that?"

"As I've told you, I'm not susceptible to flattery or amused by innuendo." She planted her hands on her hips. "And I'm definitely not moved by brooding glances."

"I know. I learned the hard way." His gaze swept over her face, neck, and body, caressing her like a feather. "But you're different today."

She narrowed her eyes. "How so?"

"Less rigid. More like the rest of us mortals," he mused. "Perhaps you're not as immune to my charms as you claim to be."

"You overestimate your rakish talents." She resisted the urge to look away or tidy the items on her desk, because doing so would only prove his point. "And, moreover, your appeal to the opposite sex."

His eyes crinkled in amusement, but his gaze remained fixed on her—and turned hot. Almost feral. "Then why don't we conduct an experiment?"

Blast. She'd naively backed herself into a corner. She blamed the earl's dimple for that.

"I'm afraid I limit experiments to the classroom," she said dryly. "But then, maybe you'd like to enroll? I have a few openings."

"I know what you charge," he quipped. "I can't afford your prices."

As he studied her, the room grew warmer and smaller. More intimate. He rubbed his jaw thoughtfully, and Hazel's own fingers itched to feel the light stubble there. To trace the fullness of his lower lip. She swallowed and prayed the earl couldn't see the desire that burned deep in her belly. It was growing harder and harder to keep her wits about her when he was near. Hiding her attraction to him was both mentally and physically taxing. Like trying to calmly recite multiplication tables while hanging from a window ledge by her fingertips.

"Surely you don't believe scientific inquiry should be confined to the schoolroom?" The deep timbre of his voice purred in her chest. "Not when the world is ripe with opportunities for learning . . . and exploring."

Heavens. He was shamelessly attempting to provoke and manipulate her. To seduce her with his words.

God help her, it was working.

Her shell, the one that had served her so well, seemed to have developed a hairline fracture. Against her better judgment, she took the earl's bait. "What sort of experiment do you propose?"

"A simple one." He took another step closer, leaving a scant inch between her chest and his torso. "I propose . . . that we kiss."

Chapter 8

Hazel laughed. "Surely, you are joking."

The earl stared at her mouth. "I would never joke about kissing. Especially not with you."

The air between them was thick with untapped energy, like a moody sky moments before it unleashes its first, fat raindrops.

Running for shelter would be the sensible thing to do. But she wasn't feeling prudent in the slightest. She wanted to let the tempest swirl around her. She wanted to revel in it.

"What are you trying to prove?" she asked.

"Ostensibly, the hypothesis that I'm irresistible to women." He flashed a lopsided smile.

"Why ostensibly?"

His expression turned sober. "Because that's not really the question that keeps me awake in my bed at night."

She swallowed. "Dare I ask, what does?"

With a feather-light touch, he brushed a strand of hair from her forehead; her whole body tingled in response.

"This curl," he murmured. "This wayward curl that refuses to do your bidding. It haunts me if you must know. It makes me wonder what else you're hiding behind your books and your rules and your fichus. And whether you ever long to do something rebellious. It makes me wonder if you feel even a hint of the spark I feel when I'm near you."

His words intoxicated her, loosened her tongue like one too many glasses of wine. "Perhaps a hint," she whispered.

His heavy-lidded gaze caressed her cheeks. Lingered on her lips. "Then let me kiss you—just this once. If nothing else, we'll satisfy our curiosity."

"We'll rid ourselves of these perplexing symptoms," she murmured.

"Right." His eyes beckoned like dark, bottomless wells, brimming with mystery and desire. "What do you say?"

"Yes."

She'd scarcely spoken the word before he slanted his mouth across hers.

He cupped her head in his large, warm hands. Pulled her body closer. Teased her lips apart with his tongue. Every move he made enticed and enthralled her, expertly coaxing her to loosen her grip on control—till it slipped through her palms like a silken rope.

Her eyes fluttered shut and her arms circled his neck. Her breasts brushed against the hard wall of his chest, and beneath her chemise, her nipples puckered.

She'd always considered a kiss to be a relatively straightforward matter—the simple act of two people's lips coming in contact. But this kiss . . . was infinitely more complex.

It was the hot melding of their mouths and the desperate tangling of their tongues. It was a low growl, deep in his throat, vibrating through her limbs. It was falling and floating and flying—all at the same time.

She didn't want it to end. And it seemed the earl didn't, either.

He skimmed the pads of his thumbs over her cheeks. Trailed scorching kisses along the column of her neck. Growled when he reached the blockade of her fichu.

"Of all women's fashion accessories, I find this to be the most vexing by far." With a lightly callused fingertip, he traced a path along the top of the lace garment, lingering near the sensitive hollow of her throat. Her whole body tingled in response.

"You could remove it," she said, her voice unexpectedly raspy.

His fingertip froze and his eyes flared with a heat that could easily consume her if she let it. For the space of several heartbeats, he said nothing. "I am tempted. More than you could possibly know."

She held her breath, waiting for his next move. With one effortless tug, he could free the scrap of lace from her bodice and toss it to the floor, catapulting their kiss into an altogether different realm. An exhilarating prospect—but also a dangerous one.

He gazed deep into her eyes and shot her a half smile that launched a meadow's worth of butterflies in her chest.

When at last he spoke, his voice was low and gruff. "In in the not-so-distant future, this fichu *will* come off. But I won't be the one to remove it. You will."

Hazel hoped he couldn't hear the drumbeat of her heart. Prayed he couldn't guess the dizzying effect of his words. "That is a bold prediction, my lord," she managed. "And highly unlikely. Your fortune-telling abilities are sadly lacking, I'm afraid."

"You think so?"

She resisted the urge to run her palms over his chest. Barely. "I know so."

"We'll see about that." There was an earnestness to his voice that echoed in her chest as he lowered his head and captured her mouth in a knee-melting encore of their kiss. Every sensuous stroke of his tongue and tantalizing brush of his lips echoed with the promise of pleasure . . . and perhaps something more.

At that moment he was completely attuned to her—a far cry from the privileged, haughty earl who'd sauntered into her office a couple of weeks ago, throwing his money around. No, this was the man who'd carried her out of the frigid surf and slipped his jacket around her shoulders. The man who'd let his niece drive his curricle on the beach and who'd stepped in to save Hazel from losing a favorite student.

She let herself sink into him, imagining what it might feel like to count on someone besides herself. To have a partner who would always stand by her. Someone who'd never leave.

Tenderly, he speared his fingers through her hair. Moaned into her mouth.

His touch thrilled her. So much so, that she contemplated eating her words and removing her fichu—along with his cravat, jacket, and a wide assortment of other articles of clothing.

His fingertips massaged her scalp, loosening the tight knot at her nape and draining the tension from her body. A few tendrils escaped their confines, drifting around her shoulders and down her back.

And then, in the midst of their passionate encounter, a hairpin hit the floor. The subtle clink of silver on wood jolted Hazel to her senses as though she'd plunged her head into a bucket of ice water.

What on earth was she doing? She was a headmistress at a school that taught girls *deportment*, of all things.

And there she was, kissing a man who had paid her to look after his niece, in her *office*, of all places.

It was beyond improper—it was reckless.

She broke off the kiss, took a step back, and touched a fingertip to her lips.

The earl blinked at her, clearly dazed, then shook his head

as if to clear it. "Forgive me for becoming carried away. I hope I didn't hurt you."

She let her hand drop to her side. "You didn't," she assured him. "And you don't need to apologize. I agreed to the experiment, after all."

His forehead creased. "Experiment?"

"Experiment. Test. Whatever you'd like to call it." She quickly gathered the curls dangling around her face and attempted to tuck them into the remnants of her bun.

"Right," he said. "I'd forgotten."

She searched his face to see if he was mocking her, but he appeared quite sincere—which only made her feel worse. "I believe I'm the one who should apologize," she said.

"You?" he said, incredulous. "For what?"

"For being swept away in the moment." Heat crept up her neck. "And succumbing to a grave lapse in judgment."

He blinked at that, then fired a sultry smile that hit her squarely in the knees. "I've been called many things, Miss Lively, but 'a grave lapse in judgment' is quite possibly my favorite." He tugged at the sleeves of his jacket and raised his chin, inordinately pleased with himself. "I'm honored."

"I'm not surprised." she quipped, relieved to be back on familiar ground. It felt much safer when he played the part of a devil-may-care earl and she assumed the role of a prim headmistress.

He rubbed his chin thoughtfully. "The question is, what are we going to do about it?"

The back of her neck prickled. "What do you mean?"

"We conducted our test, and I think it's fair to say the results were conclusive."

She rolled her eyes. Pretended to be impervious to the attraction that still crackled between them. "I disagree. What happened here was nothing more than an aberration—an accident. We should proceed as though it never happened."

He raised his brows in mock disbelief. "Those who ignore scientific evidence do so at their own peril. As a scholar, I'm certain you'd agree."

"As the headmistress of a finishing school, I am cognizant of myriad forms of peril," she countered. "Including silver-tongued rogues."

He grinned at the barb, like it was another feather to stick in his proverbial rake's cap. "Your point is well taken," he said smoothly, "but some of the most significant discoveries were accidental. Archimedes in his bathtub. Newton under his apple tree. Even the discovery of the Rosetta stone required a bit of serendipity."

"Perhaps," she said soberly. "But there is a fine line between serendipity and stupidity. For my sake, and the sake of Bellehaven Academy, I'm asking you to forget that this kiss ever happened."

His smile faded, and his eyes glowed with a sincerity that made her chest ache. "You can't erase this like it's chalk on a slate. Asking me to forget that kiss is like asking me to forget the colors of a sunset or the taste of ice cream. It's like asking me to forget the melody of a song or the smell of wildflowers. Even if I wanted to, I couldn't."

Sweet heaven. She curled her fingers into her palms so she wouldn't do something foolish like kiss him again, or worse, tell him she felt the same way.

Instead, she swallowed and shook her head. Remembered the motto that had brought her this far, the mantra that had always served her well. *Hard on the outside.*

She glided behind her desk and pretended to straighten a stack of papers that was already perfectly tidy. "Those things are entirely different, as you well know. Regardless, you must find a way to forget . . . if you want Kitty to remain here."

He winced as though she'd slapped him. "I hadn't realized you'd go to such lengths."

"I'm simply being practical—I'd encourage you to do the same. Your visits to Bellehaven Bay are an important part of Kitty's healing, which means it will be impossible for you and I to avoid each other entirely. No one can know about our indiscretion, and we certainly can't risk another."

He paced slowly in front of her, as though he was pondering what she'd said. At last, he halted in front of her desk and leaned across it, his broad shoulders testing the seams of his jacket. "I can't promise to forget the taste of your lips or the touch of your fingers on my skin. But I do understand our dilemma, and so, I will promise you this: I won't speak of our kiss again. Not to you and certainly not to anyone else. Just know that the memory is not going away. Ever."

She exhaled slowly, feeling an odd mix of relief and melancholy. "Thank you."

He stood and raked a hand through his hair. "May I ask a favor in return?"

"Of course," she said, bracing herself. A traitorous part of her hoped he'd ask for one more kiss so that the foolish part of her could answer in the affirmative.

"Will you tell me your given name?"

She rotated a stack of books five degrees to the left to avoid meeting his gaze. "Whatever for?"

"So that I can use it," he said, quickly adding, "only when we're in private."

"I don't anticipate that happening in the future," she said—an obvious yet futile attempt to convince herself.

"Stranger things have happened," he said smoothly. "Why not indulge me?"

Why indeed? "Everyone in Bellehaven knows me as Miss Lively," she said with a casual shrug.

"Yes, Miss Lively—the capable, calm, and confident headmistress."

"Is there something wrong with that?"

"Not at all. But I've seen another side of you—a part you shouldn't keep locked away."

Drat. Why couldn't he have asked her something, anything, less personal than her name? She would have happily volunteered her age, weight, and financial status instead. Anything but the childhood name that was inextricably tangled with poignant memories of love and loss.

"Is it something awful?" he teased. "If it is, I promise not to laugh. On the contrary, I'll feel even more honored that you shared it with me."

She raised her chin, aware he was trying to coax her out of her shell and quite cognizant of the danger that posed. And yet, she wanted to trust him. "My name isn't embarrassing, but very few people use it. I suppose it reminds me of a painful time."

His expression turned sober. "I have a name like that too. It's Beck—short for Beckett, my surname. Only two people besides Kitty ever called me Beck. And they're gone now."

"I'm sorry," she said.

He waved a dismissive hand, as if it were an old wound that scarcely troubled him anymore, but there was a rawness to his voice, a flash of pain in his eyes, that suggested otherwise. "I wanted you to know I understand," he said. "And I won't press you further. You can call me anything you like, by the way. Blade, Devil. Even Beck."

She nodded, warmed by the sentiment, but it was time for them to put this entire wonderful, unfortunate incident behind them. "Kitty is probably waiting for you."

"Yes, I should go." He hesitated then said, "I'll see you in two weeks, Miss Lively."

He turned toward the door and was halfway across the room when she heard herself say, "Wait."

He faced her, and she slowly walked toward him, stopping

when she was close enough to see the warm, golden flecks in his eyes.

"My name is Hazel." She felt exposed, like she'd been caught removing her gloves or letting down her hair, and yet the feeling was not entirely unpleasant. "You may call me Hazel."

Chapter 9

Several days later, on a glorious summer afternoon, Hazel decided to set aside the history lesson she'd planned in favor of an outing. Armed with a few oil lamps and some rudimentary hand tools, she and Jane herded their six students to the foot of the cliffs overlooking the sea where they could explore the caves, study the rock formations, and search for fossils.

When they'd reached a suitable spot, Hazel lifted a glowing lantern in front of the cave wall, pointing out the distinct horizontal stripes on the damp surface.

Prue raised her hand. "Sedimentary rock?" she asked.

Hazel nodded. "Each layer contains clues about a different time in the earth's past. There's a story hidden in each one."

"May we start digging?" Beatrice asked, impatiently waving a chisel in the air. She'd already announced her intention to unearth an ancient fossil—preferably a dinosaur bone—before it was time to return for dinner.

"You may," Hazel said with a chuckle. "But please stay close. A few hours from now, when the tide comes in, the water will be waist-deep, cutting off our path to the beach. I wouldn't want anyone to be stranded here."

Winnie shuddered and rubbed her hands over her bare arms. "Do you suppose there are creatures lurking back there, in the dark?"

"Perhaps a few crabs and insects," Hazel said. "Nothing to be frightened of."

Winnie moaned. "Nevertheless, I think I shall stay close to Miss Jane."

Kitty cleared her throat. "May I ask a question, Miss Lively?"

"Of course," Hazel said, pleased that her most reluctant student was taking an interest. In fact, she'd been brooding since breakfast when she'd learned it was her turn to take dish duty in the kitchen.

"Do you find my uncle attractive?"

Sweet Jesus. A chorus of gasps echoed off the walls, and every pair of eyes in the cave blinked at Hazel, expectant.

She took a moment to compose herself, then said, "Your question is neither appropriate nor relevant, Kitty. Please remember the purpose of our outing."

"Forgive me if my natural curiosity seemed rude," Kitty said in a parody of sweetness and innocence. "What I *meant* to ask was, have you set your cap for my uncle?"

Hazel ignored her and rummaged through the basket near her feet in a blatant attempt to avoid the current line of questioning. "Does anyone require a shovel? Trowel? Hand pick, perhaps?"

Kitty crossed her arms and paced like a prosecution lawyer in the Old Bailey. "I only ask because I happened to notice that the two of you were quite cozy during our curricle ride when he last visited."

"Carry on, girls," Hazel said casually, even as her belly tied itself in knots. "You'll want to make the most of your time."

"Even *I* must admit that you made a striking pair," Kitty

prattled. "But alas, as you well know, my uncle will neces-
sarily wed a woman from a respected family. Someone who
was born and bred to be a countess. Someone like Lady Penelope."

Hazel's skin prickled as though she were covered in burrs,
but she attempted a serene smile as she pulled an apron over
her head and cinched it at the waist. Kitty was obviously trying to ruffle her feathers—and she'd succeeded, blast it all.
Who the devil was Lady Penelope, and why on earth did
Hazel care?

The girls seemed to have forgotten all about fossils. Even
Jane appeared to hang on Kitty's every word. "Who's Lady
Penelope?" Lucy asked, echoing the question in Hazel's head.

She picked up a chisel and hammer and attacked one wall
of the cave. But as she chipped away at the rock, she couldn't
help hearing the conversation behind her.

"Lady Penelope is the most beautiful woman in London," Kitty announced. "Widowed, worldly, and wealthy.
She dresses in the most gorgeous gowns and always looks as
though she walked straight off a fashion plate."

"Oh," Clara said, wistful. "I wish I could meet her."

"Unlikely," Kitty replied with a sniff. "She only mingles
with society's most elite. Why would she spare a moment for
a nobody like you?"

Hazel turned around. "That's enough, Kitty," she said, her
voice forceful but even. "You owe Clara an apology."

Kitty shrugged and faced the dark-haired girl. "Forgive me
for speaking plainly," she said dryly. "I should have known
it would be difficult to hear the truth." With that, she strode
to a large rock near the entrance of the cave, sat, and stared
sullenly at the ocean.

Clara sifted through her satchel, glided toward Kitty, and
handed her a sketchbook. "If you don't feel like digging, could
you draw me a castle? Like the one you made for Lucy?"

Kitty said nothing but took the sketchbook and flipped past Lucy's gown patterns to a clean page.

Jane clapped her hands briskly. "Back to our lesson, girls. We haven't a moment to waste if we're to become renowned paleontologists."

Kitty snorted as she began making sure, graceful strokes with her pencil. "You'll be lucky if you find a snail."

A couple of hours later, Hazel and Jane shepherded the girls out of the cave and back onto the sunny beach. They had dust in their hair and sand in their slippers, but Hazel considered it a successful lesson—even if Kitty's prediction had been correct. The most exciting find of the day had been a mussel, which Lucy wanted to pry open and Prudence wanted to leave in peace. Hazel suggested that the girls take a vote, and, in the end, the mussel was spared from an untimely death.

The group marched along the shore, chatting and laughing, but Hazel was still thinking about the things Kitty said. She'd thought her attraction to the earl—er, Blade— was invisible to everyone else, but she was wrong. And that was a dangerous thing.

Worse, she found herself wondering about Lady Penelope and whether she was someone special to him—or the woman he intended to marry. Not that it mattered to Hazel. After all, she'd begged him to forget their kiss. She should be glad that he was interested in another woman. Someone who came from the same world he did.

Lady Penelope probably didn't wear fichus or spend her afternoons digging up mollusks. She probably didn't have to worry whether a minor indiscretion with a dashing earl would destroy her life's dream.

"Miss Lively!" Clara skipped alongside her, snapping Hazel from her thoughts. "Look at the castle Kitty drew for me." She handed Hazel her sketchbook, beaming.

In the center of the page, a fantastic fortress sat high on a cliff, with enormous ocean waves licking at its rugged stone walls. Every battlement, footbridge, and turret was drawn so skillfully and with such detail that the castle seemed to move and breathe.

"Isn't it magnificent?" Clara said with a sigh. "I want to live there."

"So do I," Hazel murmured, stunned. Kitty had been in Bellehaven almost four weeks now, and she'd never mentioned her talent for drawing. Never shared any of her work with Hazel. "Thank you for showing it to me."

"Oh, Miss Lively!"

Hazel glanced up to see Lady Rufflebum waving a lacy handkerchief in the air as she and her companion toddled down the beach toward them. "How fortuitous that I found you," she called.

Hazel sent up a silent prayer that her students would be on their best behavior in front of the countess. "Good afternoon, Lady Rufflebum," she said, gesturing toward her students. "We were just returning from an outing."

The countess wrinkled her nose at the girls' sandy dresses and windblown hair. "Your students certainly do not suffer from a lack of fresh air," she said in a valiant attempt at diplomacy. "Now then. I wanted to personally extend you an invitation to a dinner party I'm hosting Saturday evening."

Hazel heard several of the girls giggle behind her. "That's exceedingly kind of you," she said smoothly, "however I generally spend Saturday evenings working on my lesson plans for the upcoming week."

"Come now, Miss Lively," Lady Rufflebum cajoled, "surely you can set aside your books and leave your office for an evening. Besides, it will be an excellent opportunity for you to meet some of the most respected members of our fair town. You might even gain a student or two," she said pointedly.

Jane gave her a not-so-subtle jab in the side. "You should go," she whispered.

"It will be a rather small affair," the countess reassured. "Nothing too formal."

Hazel couldn't think of a polite way to refuse. "Very well," she said. "I'd be delighted to attend."

The girls erupted in cheers, and Lady Rufflebum recoiled as if the sound hurt her ears. "Excellent." Casting a critical eye at Hazel's dusty apron, she added, "I look forward to seeing you in a gown that's not quite so . . . schoolmarmish."

The countess's comment caused more titters, but Hazel smiled. "I fear you may be disappointed. I am a headmistress, after all, and as I'm fond of telling my students, proper behavior never . . ."

". . . takes a holiday," the girls chimed in, punctuating the motto with a groan.

"Perhaps not," Lady Rufflebum replied. "But there's nothing improper about accentuating one's natural assets." She wagged a finger at Clara's sketchbook and added, "You might want to write that down, girls."

Clara and Prue dutifully began scribbling, while Jane and the rest of the girls stared at the countess, their mouths agape.

Lady Rufflebum clasped her hands, pleased. "This teaching business is rather simple, isn't it? But don't worry, Miss Lively, I've no intention of competing with your fledgling school. I'm too busy trying to bring a measure of culture and sophistication to Bellehaven. Enjoy your evening, everyone," she said magnanimously. As she and her reticent companion continued down the beach, the countess turned and called over her shoulder, "Oh, and Miss Lively? I shall send my carriage round for you at eight."

*   *   *

Three days later, Blade was back in Bellehaven, sitting across from Kitty in a rowboat. He'd shed his jacket and rolled up his shirtsleeves before picking up the oars, but the afternoon sun was hot enough to make him envious of the swimmers splashing in the bay.

The brim of Kitty's bonnet shaded most of her face, making her expression unreadable. She'd said little since Blade picked her up from school, despite his awkward attempts to make conversation, but she wasn't displaying any hostility toward him, so he considered that a victory.

"The innkeeper mentioned that this inlet is the starting point for regatta next month," Blade said. "The boats race around Devil's Point and along the shoreline, finishing at the piers across from Main Street."

Kitty perked up. "Are you going to compete?"

"Absolutely not," he scoffed. "I don't even know if I'll be in town that weekend."

"The prize is a silver cup," Kitty said. "It might help you impress the ladies."

"I don't need a trophy to impr—" He stopped, cursing himself for taking the bait. "I'm not racing," he said firmly.

"Suit yourself." Kitty gave an indifferent shrug. "I'm simply saying that it couldn't hurt."

"Noted." He continued pulling the oars through the water, grateful for the breeze on his neck. "How are your classes progressing?"

"I'm not exactly poised to take first honors," she said dryly. "But I haven't managed to get myself kicked out yet."

Fair enough. "Have you made any friends in Bellehaven?"

Kitty shook her head. "Not like my friends at home."

"Do you mean in London?"

"No. I mean at *home*. In Somerset."

Blade swallowed. He and Kitty didn't discuss Somerset or her parents—or his estrangement from them. "I'm sorry. You must miss them."

"I miss many things," she said stoically, but her lip trembled. She looked so much like his brother: fair hair, light eyes, and wide mouth. But her expressions—the ones that sliced open your chest and grabbed you by the heart—those were solely from her mother.

"I know," he said truthfully. Grief still had a grip on him too. "Maybe we can arrange a visit with your friends when you return to London. You can go shopping on Bond Street and eat ice cream at Gunter's."

"What's the point? It's not as though I can return to my old life. Things will never be the same."

"No," he said regretfully.

For several moments, they floated along in silence. Then Kitty said, "My parents talked about you all the time. 'No one can jump a hedge like your uncle Beck. No one can shoot an arrow like your uncle Beck. No one can make the ladies blush like your uncle Beck.' You were always in the forefront of their minds. Yet you never talk about them. It's as though you want to pretend that they didn't exist."

Blade tightened his grip on the oars and willed his pulse to slow. "That's not true."

"Then why won't you speak their names?"

"It's complicated," he said. If he weren't on a boat in the middle of the bay, he'd walk away from this conversation, from this pain, and pour himself a good, stiff drink. "I only know two things: They loved you very much, and they named me your guardian. We both have to respect their wishes in this . . . and find a way to make it work."

"And you think they would have wanted you to send me away to a boarding school?"

He let the oars rest in the water and looked at Kitty, earnest. "I don't know. Probably not. But I've never been responsible for another person. Despite what you may think, I'm trying to do what's best for you."

For several heartbeats she said nothing, then she nodded bravely. "I trust you."

"Thank you," he said, oddly touched. It was hard to fathom she was the same girl he'd brought to Bellehaven Academy four weeks ago. Or maybe it was hard to believe he was the same man. Either way, he supposed he had Hazel to thank.

"Which is not to say I agree with you," she added quickly.

He chuckled and picked up the oars again. "How is Miss Lively?" She'd been conspicuously absent when he'd picked up Kitty.

"As dedicated as ever. Dreadfully so," she said, as if she were describing a dire medical condition. "Why do you ask?"

"Hmm?" He couldn't very well admit that he'd thought of Hazel constantly since kissing her two weeks ago, so he made a dismissive face and shrugged. "No reason."

Kitty removed her bonnet, leaned back on her palms, and gazed at the marshmallow clouds dotting the sky. "Miss Lively takes her duties quite seriously," she said. "But I suppose that even headmistresses are entitled to attend the occasional social engagement."

Blade blinked. "Why do you say that?"

"Hmm?" Kitty shot him a serene smile. "No reason."

Chapter 10

Hazel peered through the window of the coach as it rolled to a stop in front of Lady Rufflebum's grand manor house. Majestic marble steps rose to meet a massive front door flanked by towering columns. White stone walls blushed beneath the pinkish hues of the sunset, and lush, colorful blossoms overflowed from urns lining the porch.

When a footman opened the door of the carriage, she alighted and smoothed the skirt of her gown. The burgundy muslin had seemed perfectly adequate when she'd stood before the mirror in her bedroom. Pretty, even. Now she wasn't so sure.

But there was nothing to be done for it. She patted the simple twist at the back of her head and glided up the front steps, determined to make the most of the evening. She'd enjoy dinner, a glass of wine, and some adult conversation. With any luck, she might even gain a new student.

A young, barrel-chested butler greeted her at the door and escorted her through the grand foyer, up a gleaming staircase to the drawing room.

Hazel stood on the threshold and quickly scanned the room for any familiar faces. Lady Rufflebum, of course. Her sour-faced nephew, Mr. Bradshaw, and his long-suffering wife. Dr. Gladwell, whom Lady Rufflebum called upon almost daily to treat a variety of maladies, some real and some imagined. A striking young woman whom Hazel had never met. A dashing light-haired gentleman who was also unfamiliar.

And, Lord help her, a broad-shouldered rogue who was all *too* familiar.

The butler stepped just inside the doorway, cleared his throat, and intoned, "May I present Miss Lively."

Hazel held her head high as every pair of eyes turned in her direction. Felt her cheeks flush as Blade's gaze locked with hers.

He stood beside the fireplace looking impossibly handsome in his dark-blue jacket, buckskin trousers, and polished boots, but the shadow of stubble on his jaw and his longish hair saved him from appearing *too* respectable. Indeed, it was his slightly dangerous air that Hazel found difficult to resist. Which was precisely why she'd avoided him when he'd come to the school to pick up Kitty earlier in the afternoon.

And now she would have to endure an entire evening with him.

Lady Rufflebum, who was holding court on a royal-blue settee in the center of the room, quickly waved Hazel over. "Come sit beside me, Miss Lively, and I shall introduce you to everyone."

Hazel painted on a smile and joined the countess's small circle. "Good evening."

"Here she is, headmistress of Bellehaven's very own girls' school," Lady Rufflebum announced. "Miss Lively, I believe you know my esteemed nephew, Mr. Bradshaw, and his wife, Mrs. Bradshaw, who are staying with me for the summer."

"It's a pleasure to see you both," Hazel said to the couple.

Mr. Bradshaw grunted in response, but his wife offered a warm smile. "Likewise."

The countess gestured toward an auburn-haired woman wearing a stylish gown in lemon silk. "This is Mrs. Bradshaw's friend, Miss Lavelle. She's also visiting from London—but I'm hoping to convince her to move to Bellehaven permanently. We need accomplished young ladies here if we're going to attract eligible bachelors to our fair town," Lady Rufflebum added in a stage whisper.

"It's lovely to meet you," Hazel said, trying to recall where she'd heard Miss Lavelle's name.

"And speaking of eligible bachelors," the countess continued, "we have *three* in our midst. Gentlemen," she called over her shoulder, "cease your talk of horses and politics so that I may introduce you to Miss Lively."

The men dutifully sauntered across the room, brandy glasses in hand. All of them were handsome, but the truth was that Blade was in a class unto himself—a Gainsborough among amateur scribblings.

"I'm certain you've heard of Dr. Gladwell, my personal physician," Lady Rufflebum said. "He also tends to Bellehaven's residents and all the tourists who flock here seeking the restorative effects of the seashore."

Hazel inclined her head. "A pleasure."

The brown-haired doctor had serious eyes and a winsome smile. "The pleasure is mine, Miss Lively."

"And here is the Viscount Dunmire. He's having a house built down the road. He claims to be in town checking on the builders' progress, but I suspect he's training for next month's regatta," Lady Rufflebum teased.

The viscount smoothed the front of his peacock-colored waistcoat and scoffed. "No need to practice. I won by two boat lengths last year," he said, flashing a devilish grin. "Charmed, Miss Lively."

"Last, but certainly not least, we have Lord Bladenton," the countess said, beaming. "I understand he has enrolled his niece in your school, Miss Lively."

She nodded and said, "Good evening, Lord Bladenton," aiming for a tone that was cordial but professional. A tone that indicated she was in no way smitten by a broad pair of shoulders and roguish dimple.

Blade made a polite bow, then gave her a look that melted her insides. "This is an unexpected surprise. It's always nice to see you, Miss Lively."

She gave a curt nod, willing Blade to remember his promise to act as though their kiss had never happened. "Likewise, my lord."

"Well then," the countess said. "That's everyone—except for Maude."

Lady Rufflebum's faithful companion sat beside her, faithfully fanning her with enough force to launch a small sailboat. "Good evening, Miss Whitford," Hazel said.

She congratulated herself on surviving the introductions. No one at the dinner party seemed to suspect that her heart was beating out of her chest. Or that she and the earl had once quite seriously discussed removing her fichu. No one seemed to know that she'd had disturbingly arousing dreams of him every night for the last two weeks.

The other guests were blessedly oblivious to her discomfort, and the conversation flowed freely. When Miss Lavelle asked Lord Dunmire about last year's regatta, he was all too happy to regale her with the details of his victory. Hazel did her level best to focus on the viscount's story—mostly so she wouldn't be tempted to look at Blade.

"We were behind at the halfway mark," the viscount said,

"but the gentleman in the lead boat had consumed a few too many drinks at the Salty Mermaid the night before . . ."

As Lord Dunmire continued his tale, a delicious tingling stole over Hazel's skin, telling her Blade was nearby.

"Would you care for a glass of claret, Miss Lively?" His voice, deep and warm, wrapped around her like a towel that had been hanging in the sun.

She turned to find him standing next to her and took the glass he offered. "Thank you."

"I trust you've been well?" he asked softly.

"Quite." She smiled and continued to give her attention— at least ostensibly—to the viscount and his regatta.

"I've heard this story before," Blade whispered in her ear. "You're not missing anything."

Hazel blinked. "I shouldn't want to appear rude," she whispered back.

"Dunmire's the one monopolizing the conversation," Blade said. "Rambling on about some provincial rowboat race."

"That sounds like sour grapes, my lord." Hazel managed to speak out of the side of her mouth while giving the appearance that she was listening to the viscount. In truth, she was far too distracted to follow the conversation.

Blade scoffed. "Sour grapes? Over the Bellehaven Bay regatta? I think not."

"I understand it's an event not to be missed," Hazel said, unable to resist ribbing him. "You shouldn't dismiss it out of hand. In addition to the prize money, the winner is awarded a silver cup and an endless supply of ale at the local pub."

He grunted. "So I've heard."

". . . and when we glided across the finish line, the cheers were deafening," Lord Dunmire concluded.

Miss Lavelle clasped her hands. "How exhilarating! I look forward to watching this summer's race."

"It's an all-day celebration," Lady Rufflebum said proudly.

Her shrewd gaze flicked from the viscount to Miss Lavelle, and back again. "I'm sure Dunmire would appreciate having a lovely young lady cheer him on."

The viscount pressed a hand to his chest dramatically. "Always."

"Good grief," Blade muttered.

"Miss Lavelle is a talented harpist and singer." Lady Rufflebum dabbed her forehead with her handkerchief and motioned for her companion to fan her more vigorously. "In fact, one of Bellehaven's prominent families has asked her to tutor their daughter in the social graces."

Hazel sipped her wine, thoughtful. *That's* where she'd heard the name. Miss Lavelle was going to be Prue's tutor—unless Hazel could convince her mother to let her stay at Bellehaven Academy.

"What's wrong?" Blade whispered.

"Nothing," she said discreetly. "Why do you ask?"

"You looked worried all of the sudden."

Hazel opened her mouth to respond, but was saved by the butler, who enthusiastically announced, "Ladies and gentlemen, dinner is served."

"I'm going to escort Lady Rufflebum to her seat," Blade said smoothly. "Then I'll return for you."

"No need. I can see myself through to the dining room."

Blade chuckled. "I hope we're seated next to each other."

"Not likely." He'd be near the head of the table; she'd be at the opposite end.

"Then I hope we have a chance to speak after dinner," he said earnestly.

Before Hazel could inform him that was a horrid idea, he was striding toward the countess and offering her his arm.

Hazel had been correct about the seating arrangements. She sat next to Dr. Gladwell, who was amiable, and across from Mr. Bradshaw, who was not. While the countess's nephew grumbled about being relegated to the foot of the table, the charismatic doctor drew Hazel into conversation, inquiring about her school and her teaching philosophy. She asked about his practice and his decision to establish himself in Bellehaven, and it became clear they had much in common. He even agreed to come to the school one day and give the girls a lesson on how to best treat common maladies.

Blade sat several places away, but she could feel his gaze on her, and she was aware of him, too. Especially when he spoke to Miss Lavelle. Each time she broke out in melodious laughter or tossed her gleaming curls, Hazel's grip on the stem of her glass tightened.

As a pair of footmen dressed in bright shades of green and gold served the first course, Lady Rufflebum raised her glass. The spots of rouge on her cheeks were darker than usual, and her upper lip glistened with perspiration. "To Bellehaven Bay," she began, "and all its wonderful residents."

"Hear, hear," everyone chorused, before eagerly diving into their turtle soup.

But Hazel couldn't help noticing that the countess was swaying in her chair, and when her eyes began to roll back in her head, she sprang out of her seat. "Dr. Gladwell," she called, already halfway to the head of the table.

The countess had slumped against one armrest, so Hazel gently propped her up, picked up a napkin, and began fanning her. Within seconds, the doctor was there, too, snapping his fingers in front of Lady Rufflebum's face.

"I'll grab the smelling salts!" Miss Whitford cried, scurrying from the room, and the table erupted in exclamations ranging from mild concern to complete panic.

"Lady Rufflebum." The doctor lifted her limp hand and patted the back. "Can you hear me?"

After several anxious moments, her head lolled from side

to side, and her eyes blinked open. "Yes, I must have suffered a spell."

Dr. Gladwell frowned and pressed the back of his hand to the countess's cheek. "You're feverish. We must take you to your bedchamber," he said firmly.

"Very well," Lady Rufflebum said. "But let the party proceed. You and Miss Lively may assist me."

The doctor shot Hazel a questioning look, and she nodded. "We'd be happy to."

Carefully, they helped her to her feet, and she was able to walk with a little support under each elbow. When the countess's companion, who'd finally located the smelling salts, met them on the staircase, she wrung her hands. "What shall I do?"

"Perhaps you could prepare a cool cloth and a pot of willow bark tea," the doctor said calmly.

Clearly relieved to have a task, Miss Whitford nodded. "Straight away."

Hazel spent the next hour tending to Lady Rufflebum. She and Miss Whitford helped her don her nightgown, then tucked her into her bed. Dr. Gladwell examined her, prescribed tea and rest, and promised to call on her tomorrow.

While Miss Whitford tended to the countess, Hazel picked up the book of poetry on the bedside table and read softly. It took approximately twenty pages, but Lady Rufflebum's feverish moans finally gave way to peaceful snores.

The countess's companion thanked Hazel profusely and urged her to rejoin the dinner party, so she quickly washed up and made her way to the dining room—only to find it dark and empty.

"Everyone left." The voice, deep and familiar, made her heart flutter, and she turned to see Blade leaning against the doorjamb.

"Not everyone," she said pointedly.

He grinned at that. "It didn't feel right to continue the party without our hostess. How is she?"

"Resting comfortably. The doctor says it's probably nothing more than a head cold."

"Her nephew is bound to be disappointed."

Hazel stared at him, aghast. "Why would you say such a thing?"

Blade shrugged innocently. "It's no secret that he and his wife are impatiently waiting to come into their inheritance."

"I thought they were staying here. Where have they gone?"

"Minutes after the countess fell ill, they retired to their room and asked plates to be sent up. Miss Lavelle announced she was much too upset to eat and excused herself as well."

"What about Lord Dunmire?"

"He headed back to town to drink a few pints and play some cards. Tried to persuade me to join him."

"And why didn't you?" she asked.

He shot her a lopsided grin that made her wish she had some of Miss Whitford's smelling salts. "I was waiting for you."

Chapter 11

"You shouldn't have waited for me," Hazel said.

Blade shot her an amused smile. "Why not?"

She swallowed. "You could give people the wrong impression."

He craned his neck around, scanning the obviously vacant dining room. "Which people?"

It was a fair point, blast it all. "It's not only about appearances," Hazel said slowly. "You promised."

His eyebrows rose halfway up his forehead. "Promised what?"

She poked a finger at his chest—his ridiculously hard, perfectly sculpted chest. "You're pretending you don't remember in order to make me recount what happened, and it's not going to work."

"I thought you wanted me to forget," he drawled. "But don't worry. I haven't."

Her face heated. "I'm not worried. At least not about that. But it has been a long evening."

"My coach is outside," he said. "Let's go."

"You want me to leave with you?" she asked, incredulous.

He shrugged. "You could ask the butler to rouse a footman to send for the driver to bring Lady Rufflebum's carriage around, but all that seems rather unnecessary when I'm headed to town myself. Besides, you must be hungry. I'll take you to dinner on the way home."

She shook her head firmly. "I cannot go to dinner with you."

"Fine," he said. "I'll take you directly home."

Oh, he was smooth. But he did have a point. And the sad truth of the matter was that even if someone *were* to discover that she rode home with him, they'd never suspect that a dashing earl had designs on a headmistress. They'd assume he was merely doing a kindness—and perhaps he was.

"I did want to ask you something about Kitty," she said. "I suppose we could discuss school business during the drive."

"An excellent plan." Blade reached for her hand like it was the most natural thing in the world, leading her through the drawing room, down the grand staircase, and out the front door. All the while, she stared at his large hand wrapped around hers, wondering how a simple touch could make her insides melt like chocolate. How it could make every nerve ending in her body light up like the stars on a cloudless night.

When they stepped out the front door, he waved the coach around. Blade helped her inside, then spoke briefly to the driver before returning and settling himself on the plush velvet seat beside her.

A gentleman would have sat opposite her.

But then her heart wouldn't be fluttering like it was about to take flight.

He angled his body toward hers, till a scant inch separated his thigh and her skirts. "What's this about Kitty? More trouble?"

She shook her head. "Nothing that I can't handle. On the contrary, I wondered whether you'd seen any of her drawings."

"No," he said, his expression wary. "What sorts of drawings?"

"Of buildings, mostly. Her sketchbook is full of castles, palaces, cathedrals, and cottages that she's imagined. The pictures are extremely detailed and beautifully executed. When I asked where she learned to draw like that, she said she hadn't had any formal training. But apparently, her mother was an artist."

Even in the dark interior of the coach, Hazel sensed that Blade flinched. "She was," he said curtly—as though he had no wish to dwell on the matter.

"Kitty has a gift," Hazel continued, undaunted. "And while I can't quite explain it, I feel like her drawings may be the key to helping her work through her grief."

Blade rubbed the back of his neck. "I had no idea. Do you think she'd be willing to show the pictures to me?"

"It can't hurt to ask."

"I'm going to take her to tea before heading back to London tomorrow. I'll broach the subject then." He let out a long sigh. "Besides that, how has she been?"

Hazel thought about Kitty's diatribe in the cave: the pointed questions about Blade and her; the glowing description of Lady Penelope; the hurtful, but true, reminder that a handsome earl would never seriously pursue a buttoned-up headmistress. No good could come of recounting the tale. Besides, she didn't think her pride could survive it.

"There are good days and challenging days," Hazel said. "But Kitty's making progress. The younger girls follow her around like puppies, worshipping the ground she walks on."

He nodded thoughtfully. "When I took her out in the rowboat earlier today, she seemed different. Not happy, exactly, but not hollow on the inside. This place has been good for her, and I have you to thank."

His words warmed her, but it was the intensity of his gaze

that made her feel a bit light-headed. Her belly leapt like she was soaring on a rope swing, hovering weightless just before swooping toward the ground. "Bellehaven is a special place," she said softly.

"And you, Hazel Lively, are a special sort of person."

The sound of her name on his lips touched a spot deep in her soul. The heat in his eyes made her body tingle, and beneath the muslin of her dress, her nipples tightened to hard buds.

"I've missed you," he said simply.

She wanted to slip her hands inside his jacket, over his shoulders, and down his back. Worse, she was tempted to straddle him, grab his face, and kiss him like she had before—only longer, hotter, and deeper. A wicked voice inside her said they were all alone, that no one would know.

But then she remembered what Kitty had said about Lady Penelope.

"I'm glad we had a chance to talk this evening." She congratulated herself on sounding rather composed—and only slightly breathless.

"I don't want to say good night." His fingers traced a path down her neck and drew small circles at her nape. "Come to dinner with me."

"At the Bluffs' Brew?" She shook her head. "I'd feel like we were on public display."

"But you have to eat." He frowned for a heartbeat, then a gleam lit his eyes. "What would you say to a private dinner? Just the two of us, sitting on a cliff, overlooking the ocean."

She knew what she *should* say—that she wasn't hungry and would prefer to go home. But neither one of those things was true.

"That sounds lovely. Even better than a four-course dinner party. But unless you have some food stowed under the seat, it's not going to be much of a picnic."

Blade held up a hand, his expression smug. "Have a little faith. Leave everything to me."

He banged a fist on the ceiling of the cab, and the coach quickly rolled to a stop. "I'll be right back," he said with a wink. He hopped out of the cab, spoke to the driver, and returned a moment later, sliding onto the seat beside her. "I know the perfect dining spot," he said with a grin, "and we'll be there shortly."

Five minutes later, the carriage stopped along the side of the road that ran parallel to the shoreline. Hazel's heart beat wildly as Blade helped her from the coach. She was not averse to taking risks. Risks like moving to a new town and starting a school and enrolling a troublemaking student. But this was entirely different from a carefully calculated business decision.

This was a whim. An impulse. An extravagance.

She hadn't felt so daring since the night, many years ago, when she'd snuck out of the dormitory window at Miss Haywinkle's School for Girls. She'd climbed onto the roof and stared at the inky sky for hours, hoping to catch a glimpse of a comet that never made an appearance. But it had been a glorious night—a rare indulgence.

And so was this night with Blade.

The driver handed him a rolled blanket and glowing lantern, then tipped his hat as he turned the coach around and headed back toward town. Leaving her and Blade alone.

"Thomas is going to fetch our dinner. In the meantime, we can relax and enjoy the view." Blade held the lantern in front of them and helped Hazel hop over a low stone wall separating the road from a grassy spot overlooking the moonlit ocean. When they were a few yards from the cliff's edge, he set down the lantern and spread the large quilt over the soft, verdant ground.

Blade wasn't sure what he was doing, flirting with Hazel. He only knew that he felt good when he was with her. Her passion and ambition intrigued him. Reminded him of a time, long ago, when he hadn't been so cynical. When he'd believed in family and happiness and hope.

She sat on the thick blanket, stretched out her legs, and leaned back on her palms, gazing at the ocean. The warm light of the lantern gave her skin a golden glow, and a gust of wind tossed the tendrils framing her face. She shut her eyes and lifted her chin, savoring the breeze. He wished he could capture her blissful expression in a portrait and stare at it every day. All day.

"Do you want to know the reason I chose Bellehaven Bay as the location for my school?" she asked.

Blade took a seat on the blanket beside her and pondered the question. "I have an inkling."

"I'll bet you don't."

"What would you like to wager?" he ventured.

She hesitated, then said, "A question. The winner can ask any question, and the other party must answer."

Damn. His mind had wandered in a different direction, but he supposed a question could be useful, too. "Very well. I'll take that bet." He laced his fingers and stretched his arms, like he was cracking his knuckles. "The reason you chose Bellehaven as the location for your school is because"—he paused for dramatic effect—"proper behavior never takes a holiday."

She laughed, and the sound seeped into his chest. Flooded the darkest corner of his heart. "A valiant attempt," she said. "But that's not the real reason."

"No? Then I confess I'm at a loss."

"I chose Bellehaven because of the sound of the ocean. If I leave the window of my bedroom open at night, I can hear it faintly. And that constant, low, roar reminds me of how small we are."

"That's comforting to you?" he asked. "Feeling small?"

"Absolutely." She shot him an amused smile. "No matter how big my problems or how monumental my mistakes, the waves keep rolling. The tides keep changing. The sun keeps shining." She cocked an ear toward the ocean. "Sometimes when I listen to it, I imagine the surf is washing over me, pulling all my worries out to sea."

For a few moments, they sat in silence—except for the sound of the waves breaking on the rocks far below them.

"I'll have to try that sometime," he said. "I suppose I owe you a question."

"You owe me an answer," she teased.

"What would you like to know," he asked. "My middle name? My favorite flavor of ice cream?"

"I confess I'm curious about both." She propped herself on one side, mirroring his pose. "But I want to ask you something more personal—if you're willing to share."

Blade swallowed. Wondered if he'd gotten himself in too deep. "You can try me."

She gazed into his eyes. "You told me that only two people besides Kitty had ever called you Beck. Who are they?"

He rolled onto his back, tucked his hands beneath his head, and let out a long sigh.

Damn. Hazel was asking him to pry the boards off of his shuttered past. To pull out all the rusted nails and expose the ugliness he'd hidden away.

His heart pounded like he'd run a mile, so he decided to try Hazel's trick. He listened to the ocean. And he stared at the stars as he answered her.

"There was a girl named Eliza. Her family lived next to mine, and we grew up together. Running through wide-open fields, hanging from the branches of an old oak tree, keeping each other's secrets. She was my best friend—and my first love. She called me Beck."

His words hung in the air, suffocating as a cloud of smoke. Then Hazel whispered, "What happened to her?"

"She fell in love with someone else." He swallowed the infernal knot in his throat and added, "After that, she moved away. It was a long time ago."

Hazel stared at him, her eyes shining with compassion. "But you still think of her."

"Not often," he lied.

She nodded, thoughtful. "Sometimes the oldest scars are where the deepest pain lingers."

He scoffed at that, mostly because he didn't want Hazel thinking of him as some broken, jaded shell of a person— even if he was. But he also heard a rawness in her voice, and it told him she had a few wounds of her own. "What's your oldest scar, Hazel?"

"Both my parents died when I was nine," she said simply.

Jesus. "I'm sorry."

"One minute I was secure, happy, and loved, and the next . . . I was alone. Fortunately, I was taken in by the kindly headmistress of a girls' school. I owe everything to Miss Haywinkle."

"But?" he probed.

"I never felt as though we were family. I desperately miss that feeling, that sense of belonging." There was no bitterness, no self-pity in her confession. Just candor—and a hint of wistfulness. "But I've no room to complain. If it hadn't been for the generosity of Miss Haywinkle, I would have ended up in the foundling home," she said, as if picking herself up and brushing off the melancholy.

"I'll bet you were a star pupil," he said. "The sort who never caused a lick of trouble."

"That's true," she said, matter-of-fact. "Sometimes I wish I had."

He rolled onto his side to face her, intrigued. "Miss Lively, I'm shocked. What sort of trouble are we talking about here? Smoking cigars? Skinny-dipping in the lake?"

"I don't know," she said with a chuckle. "But it would be nice to have had an adventure or two. Some form of youthful mischief that I could look back on with fondness."

"It's never too late for a little mischief," he mused, pleased to see her cheeks pinken.

"You said two people called you Beck," she said softly. "Who was the other?"

Ah yes. He still owed her half an answer. "My brother, Simon. He was two years younger. Witty and charming. My parents' favorite. Everyone's favorite."

"Kitty's father?" Hazel asked.

Blade nodded. "He died in a carriage accident last year."

"How awful. You must miss him terribly."

He couldn't find the words to explain that he'd lost his brother years before the accident. That Simon's betrayal had left a gaping hole in his heart—a hole Blade had filled with anger, hurt, and guilt. But if anyone could understand the loss he felt, he suspected Hazel could. "Neither one of us has much of a family anymore," he said.

"I don't know," Hazel said. "You have Kitty. I have my students. There's hope for us both, but being part of a family takes some work."

Blade grunted. "I'm not looking for another family." He'd have to be deranged to subject himself to that sort of abuse again. "I just want an uncomplicated, carefree existence and the freedom to do what I like, when I like."

Hazel arched a brow. "What about Kitty?"

"I'm not a monster," he said, protesting a bit too much. "I'll do right by her. But she's eventually going to find her way in the world. She'll decide on her path, maybe have her own family."

"Well, I want my students—especially the ones who are orphaned—to feel like they belong. Like they have a place to call home." She spoke softly, but an unmistakable fire burned in her eyes. It said that her school, her girls, were everything to her. She wasn't simply trying to turn them into proper young ladies. She was trying to turn them into a family.

"That's admirable," he said, and he meant it. Her passion made his own plans for a loveless marriage to Lady Penelope seem rather empty. But he didn't want to think about Penelope now. Not when Hazel was lying beside him, revealing her secrets, talking about mischief, and reminding him how it felt to connect with someone. To feel accepted and understood.

"May I ask you something?" he said. "Even though I didn't win the wager?"

"I suppose." She brushed a tendril away from her face and tucked it behind her ear.

"Do you ever wish for something more?"

She shrugged. "I have my books and my school and my work. The girls challenge me and make me smile. What more could I want?"

He reached for her hand and laced his fingers through hers. "Something just for you. Do you ever wish you were free to do exactly as you pleased?"

She inhaled deeply and her chest rose, straining against the confines of her bodice. Her gaze dropped to his mouth, and her lips parted as though she was thinking of kissing him.

The way he was thinking of kissing her.

"I'm not immune to temptation," she said breathlessly.

He leaned closer and touched his forehead to hers. Swept a thumb over her satin cheek. "Well," he murmured, "should you ever decide to give into that temptation . . . or surrender to desire . . . you know where to find me."

Chapter 12

Hazel felt as though she and Blade were in one of Kitty's drawings—sitting high atop a castle wall with a diamond-studded sky as their backdrop, the turbulent ocean at their feet. His fingertips caressed her face; his words touched her soul.

And all she wanted to do was surrender. To the irresistible, palpable desire that simmered between them.

Her eyelids fluttered shut of their own accord, and she leaned into him—just as the clop of horses' hooves sounded behind them.

Blade muttered a curse at his driver's timing. "I believe our dinner has arrived," he said dryly. "I'll see what Thomas was able to round up for us. Are you able to stay out here for another hour?"

"As long as I'm home by midnight." If the dinner party hadn't ended prematurely, she would have likely stayed at Lady Rufflebum's till that hour.

"Good." He shot her a wink and effortlessly jumped the stone wall. "I'll be right back."

He returned carrying a large basket covered with a rustic cloth and placed it on the blanket between them. "I've asked Thomas to return in an hour. Until then, the night is ours."

Inside the basket, they found fruit, sandwiches, cheeses, and bread, along with a bottle of wine. Blade quickly uncorked and poured while she laid out the food on a platter, making a sumptuous spread.

He handed her a glass, and she raised it in the air. "To dinner parties gone awry," she said solemnly, "and to dinner partners who know that a sandwich on the beach tastes better than salmon on fine china."

Blade chuckled, and his rich laughter warmed her blood as much as the wine. "To dinner parties gone awry," he echoed. "And to dinner partners who look breathtaking in pale moonlight."

Her belly flipped, and she tucked the compliment away for safekeeping. He gazed at her over the rim of his glass as they each took a ceremonial sip, and she knew, deep in her bones, that they'd crossed a line that night. Not physically, perhaps—though she *had* considered it. Instead, they'd wandered into the dangerously seductive territory of intimacy. Now that she'd left the safety of her shell, it wasn't as though she could easily crawl back in. Indeed, she wasn't at all certain she would fit.

She nibbled on her sliced chicken sandwich; he devoured his. He carved a slice of pear for her then tossed another slice into the air, deftly catching it in his mouth. They chatted as they feasted, and Hazel found herself wishing that time could stand still. That she and Blade could stay on the bluff all night. Perhaps even longer.

When they'd eaten all they could, they packed up the basket and lay on the blanket beside each other, staring at the sky and listening to the sea.

"There's something different about you today," she said. "And I think I know what it is."

"Enlighten me."

"In the course of the entire evening, you haven't once

mentioned my fichu. There have been no disparaging remarks, no disapproving glares, not even a hint of frustration. I scarcely know you," she teased.

"Oh, I've noticed it," he said, disarmingly sincere. "I notice everything about you. The way the claret color of your gown turns your eyes a richer shade of brown. The wispy tendrils that flutter around the graceful column of your neck. And yes, I've noticed your ivory fichu, nestled against the delicate skin of your throat."

"And yet, you harbor no animosity toward it?" she asked, feigning surprise.

"On the contrary. Odd as it may seem, I've become inexplicably fond of that rascally scrap of lace."

"Truly?"

"Mmm." He rolled toward her and nodded. "Maybe because it seems like such a part of you."

"Oh." His simple declaration was a downy feather traveling the length of her bare spine, awakening and arousing her senses. She was suddenly all too aware that their time was running out. "Blade," she ventured. "Do you remember earlier, when you said that I should let you know if I wanted to indulge in a bit of mischief?"

His gaze snapped to hers and his eyes grew darker. "I remember."

"I want to." She reached out and traced the sharp line of his jaw. Brushed a fingertip across his full lower lip.

She ached to touch and kiss him. To give in to the desire swirling inside her.

And when it was impossible to resist him for one second longer, she leaned in—and covered his mouth with hers.

Blade remained very still as Hazel initiated a kiss—for two reasons.

First, he was clinging to control by the thinnest of threads.

He wanted to plunder her mouth, haul her against him, and explore every inch of her body.

Second, he heard the damned carriage approaching again. "Hazel," he murmured against her mouth.

"Hmm?"

"It's almost time for us to go." He could have asked his driver to come back in an hour, but he'd promised to have her home by midnight. And for reasons he couldn't quite pinpoint, it seemed vitally important that Hazel trust him.

"Oh," she sighed, and the disappointment in her voice mirrored his own.

"I'm sorry," he said gently. "I wish we could stay."

"I do, too," she said, reluctantly sitting up. "But I knew this night couldn't last forever."

Of course it couldn't. Nothing pure and good ever did.

He pressed a slow, lingering kiss to the corner of her mouth, then helped her to her feet. She walked toward the edge of the cliff, staring at the glistening sea and the star-soaked sky as if committing it all to memory. Personally, he didn't give a damn about the ocean view. He only saw her: beautiful, fearless, and free.

When she turned around, he handed her the lantern, gathered up the blanket and basket, and led her back to his carriage. Neither of them spoke as they climbed inside, but her leg pressed against his. She reached for his hand and brushed a thumb across his palm. The air between them crackled with awareness, attraction, and desire.

As the coach started rumbling down the road, she turned toward him, grabbed the lapels of his jacket, and pulled him against the soft, sensuous curves of her body.

Every noble intention, every thought of maintaining control, flew out the carriage window and floated out to sea. Her tongue tangled with his. Her arms circled his neck. His hands slid up her sides. And he was lost.

She tasted of wine and ocean air; she felt warm and ripe as a freshly picked peach. He craved every part of her—her satin skin, soft sighs, and quiet strength—and it seemed as though she craved him, too.

Which meant there was no time to waste.

He speared his fingers through the knot at her nape and lightly cupped one of her breasts, teasing a taut nipple with his palm. He kissed her long and hard and deep, savoring the eager thrusts of her tongue and the hungry moans in her throat.

"You wanted to indulge in mischief," he murmured.

"Mmm," she said, greedily running her hands over his waistcoat.

"How much, precisely?"

She went still and shot him a sultry smile that made him even harder.

"I'm not certain how to quantify mischief," she said. "Shall I tell you when I'm approaching my limit?"

"Perfect."

They clung to each other as the carriage rolled along. He slid a hand beneath the hem of her dress. Traced a path up the back of her calf. Caressed the soft flesh of her inner thigh.

He moved slowly at first, listening to the hitch of her breathing and feeling the tension in her muscles. Each little sound, every subtle shift was a road map, telling him what she liked. What she wanted. Soon she was clutching his shoulders and lifting her hips to meet his touch.

God, she felt good—warm, wet, and tight. He kissed the column of her neck, sucking and nibbling all the way down to her fichu. He wanted her to cry out in pleasure. Wanted to hear his name on her lips as she came undone—and she was close.

Her soft whimpers filled his head, and her body coiled tightly, poised to unfurl.

"Blade," she rasped.

"Mmm?"

"I'm . . . I'm afraid we've arrived at the school. I should go."

Shit. Reluctantly, he pulled down her skirt and covered her lithe legs. He gave her one last sensuous kiss, a shameless attempt to imprint himself on her body and soul.

"Can I see you tomorrow?" he said. "I'm taking Kitty shopping in the morning, but I could come to your office afterward."

"I don't think that's a good idea," she said regretfully. "But thank you for giving me an evening to remember. It was . . . just the right amount of mischief."

The hell it was. "Hazel, we need to talk about what happened tonight."

She reached behind her head and twisted a few long curls into her bun, hastily pinning them in place. "There's really nothing to discuss," she said. "Tonight was an aberration, and we both know it. Nothing can come of it. Nothing *will* come of it."

He opened his mouth to refute what she was saying but stopped himself. Maybe she was right. She was dedicated to her school and students. Her life was here in Bellehaven.

He wasn't dedicated to anything or anyone but himself. He wanted no part of a family—at least not a real one. His future involved a loveless marriage to Lady Penelope. In London.

And yet he couldn't go back to thinking of her just as Kitty's headmistress. He couldn't let Hazel walk away and pretend that she hadn't changed him.

"Please," he said. "I know our situation is complicated, but we can't go back to the way we were before."

She glanced out the window at the dark boardinghouse, straightened her bodice, and let out a long breath. "Actually, we can."

Just like that, her armor was back in place. He felt her retreating into her shell, leaving him outside in the cold.

"What if I don't want to go back to the way we were before?" he pressed.

"Given time, I think you'll agree it's for the best," she said. "We'll remain civil, of course."

"Civil?" he repeated, incredulous. "After what we just shared?"

"I know it seems abrupt. Maybe even unfeeling," she admitted. "But the truth is—how can I say this delicately?"

"Please, don't mince words."

"Very well. The truth is we're not thinking clearly right now."

He scoffed. "What are you talking about?"

"I fear we're under the influence of desire."

Holy hell. "Is that so terrible?" He leaned forward, forced her to look into his eyes. "Why must you analyze everything so logically and rationally? Why are you so measured and detached?"

She winced as though he'd landed a verbal blow.

"Hazel," he said, "I didn't mean that."

"No, it's all right. I *am* guarded—perhaps to a fault."

"No," he backtracked, dragging his hands through his hair. "I shouldn't have implied—All I'm saying is that I'd like to see you again."

She avoided his gaze. "We're bound to see each other, on occasion, when you visit. Bellehaven isn't so big a place."

"That's not what I'm talking about, and you know it." He reached for her hand and brushed his thumb across the back. "This thing between us—I don't know exactly what it is. And I definitely don't know what we should do about it, but we can't pretend it doesn't exist."

At last she looked at him, her heart-shaped face pensive. "Perhaps not. However, I don't think now is the time to make any important decisions. It's been a long evening . . . and I find it difficult to think clearly when you're holding my hand."

Reluctantly, he let go.

"I have a suggestion," she said.

Hope sprouted in his chest. "Go on."

"I propose that over the next two weeks, we give our feelings a chance to settle. That we each return to our normal lives and do our best to forget about tonight."

"And what if we cannot?" he said.

"Then," she replied, slowly, "when you return to Belle-haven, we can discuss how to proceed."

He exhaled and shot her a conspiratorial smile. "I suppose I can live with those terms."

She raised a finger, indicating she wasn't done. "But in the meantime, we must try to think practically—and not allow ourselves to be carried away by fanciful notions."

He rubbed his jaw, wondering if she intended the warning more for him or herself. "Right," he said. "Level heads. Feet rooted firmly in the ground."

She nodded her head in approval and reached for the carriage's door handle. "Enjoy your outing with Kitty tomorrow."

"I'll see you in two weeks," he said. "Do you think you can stay out of any more mischief till then?"

She gave him a wan smile. "I like my odds better than yours, my lord."

Chapter 13

"Miss Jane said you wanted to see me." Kitty strolled into Hazel's office a few days later wearing a sprigged green gown and a surly expression. "What am I in trouble for this time?"

"Nothing." Hazel arched a brow. "Unless you have something you'd like to confess?"

"No, no." Kitty slouched into one of the chairs in front of the desk. "Let's just have this conversation done with so I may move on to more important things, like organizing my ribbon drawer or watching tourists shake the sand out of their shoes."

Hazel sat across from Kitty and folded her hands on her blotter. "I wanted to speak with you about your drawings."

"Again? Why is everyone so obsessed with my sketchbook? Surely you and Uncle Beck have something better to do than fuss over my silly scribbles."

The offhand mention of Blade made Hazel's belly flutter, but she remained focused on the task at hand. "They're not silly at all, as you well know. You have a gift, and it's my duty to help you nurture it."

"Let me guess." Kitty rolled her eyes. "You'd like me to take up watercolors, or perhaps oil painting."

"What?"

"You'd prefer me to 'channel my energies into a more dignified and refined art form,'" she replied in an exaggerated impression of a teacher's voice.

Hazel blinked. "Not at all. That is, there's nothing wrong with those media if you'd like to explore them."

"My uncle already offered to purchase any supplies I wanted. But all I really want is my sketchbook and pencils." Kitty heaved a sigh. "Am I free to go now?"

"Not quite." Hazel steepled her fingers beneath her chin. "I wondered if you might be interested in having a mentor."

"You?" Kitty asked, clearly skeptical.

Hazel laughed. "Not me. Since most of your drawings are of structures, I was thinking of someone who specializes in building design—or architecture."

Kitty narrowed her eyes, skeptical. "Who might that be?"

"There's a good-natured, elderly gentleman in town named Mr. Sandford. He drew up the plans for Mrs. Paxton's boardinghouse along with several other buildings here in Bellehaven. I haven't asked him yet, but I imagine he'd be happy to show you around his shop . . . if you're interested."

"I might be," Kitty said, noncommittal. "As long as he doesn't expect me to sweep his floors, fetch his pipe, or pour his tea."

"Noted," Hazel said. "I'll stop by his office this week to speak to him."

Kitty tilted her head. "Do you think he'll balk at the idea of mentoring a girl?"

"Honestly, I don't know. But I suspect that when he sees your drawings, he'll realize you're a talented young woman with incredible potential."

For several heartbeats, Kitty stared at her hands in her lap. "Thank you," she said softly—and Hazel knew the words couldn't have come easily.

Her chest squeezed. "You're welcome."

Kitty quickly composed herself and was halfway out of her chair when someone knocked on the partly open office door.

"Come in," Hazel called, pleased to see her young protégée, Poppy, breeze into the room carrying a large basket of books on one arm.

"Good morning, Miss Lively. I've finished all these." Poppy's hair hung down her back in a riot of strawberry curls, and her freckled cheeks glowed with excitement. "You were right about the gothic novel," she started, then drew up short when she spied Kitty. "Forgive me for intruding. I didn't realize you were busy."

"It's all right," Hazel said. "Poppy Summers, this is my newest boarding student, Kitty Beckett."

"Nice to meet you," Poppy said, but her expression turned wary as she set down her basket. "I'll just leave these with you and come back another time."

"No," Hazel urged, "please stay. I've set aside several more books I think you'll like."

Kitty sat up in her chair, clearly intrigued by the unexpected visitor. "Are you one of Miss Lively's former students?"

"No." Poppy raised her chin. "Deportment lessons would have been wasted on me."

"I feel the same way." Kitty beamed, apparently delighted to have found a kindred spirit.

The truth was that Hazel *had* offered private lessons to Poppy on several occasions, but the fiery-haired young woman was several years older than most of Hazel's students and too proud to join their ranks. Besides, it was difficult for Poppy to spare an afternoon learning a bit of conversational French when she could be working—casting her fishing nets from a small boat, taking the day's catch to market, and keeping her family's business afloat.

All Poppy really wanted to do in her precious spare time was to read, and Hazel was more than happy to share books with her. In turn, Poppy insisted on bringing fresh fish to Mrs. Paxton for dinner every Sunday.

Kitty's assessing gaze flicked over Poppy's untamed tresses and her plain cotton dress. "Do you live here in Belle-haven?"

Poppy nodded. "My family has a cottage by the sea."

"You must be a good swimmer," Kitty mused.

"I suppose so," Poppy said with a shrug.

"I almost drowned during my first night in Bellehaven," Kitty said conversationally. "I'm from London and Somerset before that." She paused for a moment, then asked, "Have you ever been to London?"

"Only once, before my mother . . ." She hesitated and cleared the emotion from her throat before continuing. "It was a long time ago."

"I lost my mother and father last year," Kitty said, thoughtful. "It's strange how time divides itself into before and after."

"Yes." Poppy stared at the wooden floorboards for a moment, then met Kitty's gaze. "I'm sorry about your parents."

Hazel stood back as the girls took each other's measure. Their upbringings couldn't have been more different, but they'd both known great loss. Moreover, both were smart, determined, and feisty.

Which made Hazel wonder if they might be able to help each other.

"I can't stay," Poppy said brusquely. "Thank you for the books, Miss Lively. We can discuss them another time."

"There's the new batch." Hazel gestured toward the shelf where she'd set aside a dozen books. "Please take them."

As Poppy reverently placed them in her basket, Hazel reached into a desk drawer, withdrew a wrapped bundle, and handed it to her.

"What's this?"

The package contained one of Hazel's lightly worn calico gowns. "Just something I thought might come in handy. I no longer have any use for it." She didn't want to risk bruising Poppy's pride, especially in front of Kitty.

Poppy handed it back. "You're too generous as it is. I can't accept a gift."

"It's not a gift," Hazel said, adamant. She tucked it into the basket alongside the books, hoping that would be the end of it.

Meanwhile, Kitty looked on, fascinated by the exchange.

"Fine," Poppy said, resigned at last. "But I will find a way to repay you."

"You don't even know what it is," Kitty exclaimed. "What if it's something awful that nobody would want, like an embroidery hoop or a powdered wig or a pair of old slippers?"

Poppy chuckled. "I know Miss Lively too well and am certain it's none of those things. I suspect I'll be bringing her fish for the next decade at least."

Kitty screwed up her face. "Fish?"

Oh dear. The last thing Hazel wanted or needed was more fish, unless—

She clasped her hands together. "I have an idea. There *is* a favor you could do for me if you have the time."

"I'll make time," Poppy said, resolute. "What is it?"

"Teach Kitty to swim."

"*What?*" said the girls in perfect unison.

Hazel crossed her arms, pleased as punch. "Kitty, what's the point in living at a beautiful seaside resort if you can't enjoy the water?"

"I can enjoy it from the safety of the beach, thank you very much."

"Poppy, you spend so much time in and around the water, you must have gills," Hazel teased.

"That doesn't mean I'm qualified to give swimming lessons."

"I have faith in both of you," Hazel said firmly. "Do you want to know why?"

The girls stared at her, dumbfounded, so she continued.

"You two have something in common."

Kitty's doubtful gaze swept over Poppy's plain dress and sensible boots. "What might that be?"

"The ability to do whatever you set your mind to." Hazel brushed her palms together, signaling the matter was settled. "Poppy, under your tutelage, Kitty will be a veritable mermaid by the end of the summer."

"Very well." Poppy sighed as she hoisted her basket. To Kitty, she said, "Meet me at the foot of Brigand's Bluff tomorrow at noon."

"I shall be there," Kitty said soberly. "Now, if you'll excuse me, I must go write my last will and testament in case this all ends the way I suspect it will. Miss Lively, it will be up to you to deliver the tragic news to my uncle. I wonder what he'll say when he learns that his only niece was sacrificed to Poseidon."

Poppy shook her head and followed Kitty out of the office, leaving Hazel alone with her thoughts—which mostly revolved around Blade.

Despite her valiant attempts to forget their magical evening, she couldn't stop thinking about the way he'd made her feel. Desired. Understood. Almost . . . loved.

She knew better than to think that the earl was truly in love with her. But there was something so achingly real about their connection that she couldn't deny it. No matter how hard she tried.

She and Blade were clearly on different paths. He needed a countess—someone to attend London balls and host lavish dinner parties. Someone to warm his bed and give him an heir. None of which would have been terribly problematic if it weren't for one thing. One detail that he'd made crystal clear.

He didn't want to be part of a real family. Certainly not a large, messy family comprised of destitute schoolgirls and their on-the-shelf headmistress.

It's why she'd been opposed to seeing him again. To avoid subjecting herself to temptation and the torture of longing for what could never be. But when he'd pleaded with her, she'd been unable to resist the raw vulnerability in his eyes.

So she'd left the door open, ever so slightly, even as she'd encouraged him to forget about her and move on. Made him promise he'd try.

Already she was kicking herself for not breaking things off cleanly, once and for all, because deep in her soul, she knew that she and Blade had no future.

And yet she couldn't help hoping that he'd prove her wrong.

"There's something different about you tonight." Penelope managed to convey her irritation despite her perfect, pasted-on smile.

Blade glanced down at his dance partner and feigned ignorance. "What do you mean?"

She shrugged her slender shoulders as they twirled around the dance floor, waltzing beneath a pair of sparkling chandeliers. "You're distracted," she said. "Here, but not here."

Penelope was perceptive. Physically, he was in one of London's most opulent ballrooms, with her. Mentally, he was on one of Bellehaven's most picturesque cliffs, with Hazel.

"I'm not overly fond of balls," he said. "Not even mildly fond of them, actually."

"Yes, what a hardship," she said dryly, "to have to endure an evening of dancing, champagne, and merriment."

"Your point is taken," he acknowledged. "I have no right

to complain. In fact, I'm probably the envy of every man here." It was true enough. Any one of the ton's eligible bachelors would love to have Penelope on his arm.

She looked at him from beneath a thick fringe of lashes, clearly pleased by his admission. "Then we are still proceeding according to plan?"

Damn it. He'd planned to speak to Penelope tonight—but not on the dance floor while dozens of pairs of eyes looked on. "Could we talk later?" he asked.

Her blue eyes narrowed. "We'll go to the terrace now," she said pointedly. "If anyone asks, I am in need of some air."

He nodded and swiftly escorted her toward the French doors at the rear of the room, eager to have the matter off his chest. Penelope was bound to be displeased, but it wasn't as though feelings were involved on either side. Perhaps she'd even be relieved.

They stepped into the cool evening air, crossed the flagstone terrace, and stood beside an iron balustrade overlooking the garden. She folded her arms, then looked at him, expectant.

"I've been thinking about our courtship," he began.

"Who is she?" Penelope said, matter-of-factly.

Blade blinked. "I beg your pardon?"

"The woman who's turned your head."

He opened his mouth to deny the charge, then stopped. He owed Penelope the truth. "Someone I met in Bellehaven."

"And you intend to court her?" There was no censure or bitterness in her voice—only curiosity.

He shook his head. "She doesn't want to see me."

Penelope arched an elegant brow. "I confess I'm surprised. You're wealthy, attractive, titled," she said, ticking off the traits on her fingers. "And she wants more?"

He could still see Hazel's beautiful face glowing in the moonlight. Could hear the passion in her voice as she talked about her school, her dreams, her desire to belong to a family.

"She wants more," he repeated flatly.

Penelope nodded, thoughtful. "Then there's no reason our courtship shouldn't proceed."

He scrubbed the back of his neck. "That wouldn't be fair to you."

She rolled her eyes. "I'm not the sentimental sort, Bladenton, and neither are you. It's what makes us perfect for each other."

Blade frowned. "You could do better than me, Penelope."

"Perhaps," she mused. "But I have decided upon you."

"Why?" He wasn't fishing for compliments, but rather, the truth.

"I would rather not divulge the particulars. Let us just say that you are the safe choice for me. Just as I am for you."

He stared at the lush garden, pondering what Penelope had said. In the distance, leaves rustled, frogs croaked, and insects buzzed. He wished he could snap his fingers and trade the sounds for the roar of the ocean.

"You need a wife," Penelope continued, "whether you want one or not. This woman in Bellehaven—does she expect you to wait for her? Pine for her endlessly?"

"No." That was the hell of it. "She wants me to forget about her. Move on."

"Then you should take her at her word. Respect her wishes."

Blade had come to the same depressing conclusion as he'd lain awake in bed. He and Hazel could only end in heartbreak. And the last thing in the world he wanted was for her to feel the hurt and misery that he had. He *would* spare her that—no matter the cost.

He dragged a hand down his face. "You might be right."

"Of course I am," Penelope said, utterly confident. "This

is precisely why you need me, Bladenton. I can steer you in the right direction. I can tolerate your demons. And most important, I will never ask you for more than you can give."

"I need a little time," he said.

"There are still a few weeks left in the summer." Penelope smoothed the icy-blue skirt of her dress and placed her hands on her hips. "I'm certain all will end as it should—with you and I betrothed."

With that, she turned on her heel and headed for the ballroom doors, leaving him alone on the terrace, her words echoing in his head.

Chapter 14

"There's a huge cricket match on the beach this afternoon. Locals versus out-of-towners." Kitty sat across from Blade in the tea shop, looking through the picture window behind him and keeping an eye on Main Street—almost as though she were waiting for a particular person to walk by. "Everyone in Bellehaven will be there," she continued. "I suppose we should go."

"Fine with me," he said. With any luck, he'd see Hazel. She hadn't been in her office when he'd picked up Kitty earlier, and disappointment had hit him like a punch to the gut.

For the last two weeks, it had taken every ounce of restraint he possessed not to hop onto his curricle, drive to Bellehaven, and show up on her doorstep. But she'd asked for time and distance, and the least he could do was give her that.

Meanwhile, their time apart had given him clarity. He knew what he wanted. Knew what he could offer. What happened next was left to Hazel to decide.

"How do you like working with Mr. Sandford?" Blade asked, helping himself to a smoked salmon sandwich.

Kitty glanced around the mostly empty shop and leaned over the table. "He's rather odd," she said. "But sweet. He's teaching me to use a scale and triangle, and he likes my drawings. He says I'm as talented as his grandson."

"Impressive," Blade said, pleased to hear the enthusiasm in Kitty's voice. "And the swimming lessons?"

Kitty sipped her tea and shrugged. "I want to be able to dive into the waves like Poppy. For now, she wants me to stick to floating."

"Sounds like a good start," Blade said. "And you've managed to stay out of trouble for the last two weeks?"

Kitty shrugged. "More or less. I fear I've become a terrible bore."

"That's not a bad thing, you know," he said.

"Perhaps not for *you*," she griped. "Will you join in the cricket match?"

"Would you like me to?"

"The tourists' team could use some help," Kitty said. "I have a feeling you'd give them a fighting chance."

Blade chuckled. "Will you cheer for me?"

Kitty set down her cup and smirked. "I'm a local now, and as such, my loyalty lies firmly with Team Bellehaven."

"Betrayed by my own niece," he said with mock dismay.

"Never fear, Uncle. I suspect you'll have legions of admirers in the crowd. Especially of the female variety."

Blade didn't need legions of admirers. He only wanted one.

"You'll be sorry you didn't back the winning side," he quipped, finishing the last bite of his scone. "Let's go for a walk and you can show me Mr. Sandford's shop."

"A quick walk," Kitty agreed. She adjusted her bonnet as she headed for the door of the tea shop. "I wouldn't want the townspeople to think I'm consorting with the enemy."

Blade scratched his head. "You locals certainly take this cricket match seriously."

Kitty nodded solemnly. "You've no idea."

*   *   *

A few hours later, Hazel, Jane, and the girls emerged from Bellehaven Academy and joined the steady stream of people strolling toward the dunes. Mrs. Paxton had packed picnic lunches for everyone in the boardinghouse, and the girls were determined to secure a spot on the sand with a prime view of the cricket match.

But when they arrived on the beach, they discovered that all of Bellehaven must have had the same idea—and the festive sight took Hazel's breath away.

Enormous tents extended from the dune grasses halfway to the ocean's edge. Beneath them, protected from the intense afternoon sun, exquisitely dressed ladies and gentlemen dined and mingled around tables laden with fruits, cheeses, meats, and sweets.

Around the tents, fashionable women twirled their parasols while children chased one another. Young and old, rich and working class, all had turned out for the event.

Hazel had never seen so many people gathered on the beach, and the excitement was contagious. But her own excitement had little to do with the cricket match and everything to do with one vexingly handsome earl.

In spite of the crowd, she spotted him almost immediately. He stood near the water in a circle of young, strapping men. But he was the only one she really saw.

He'd shed his jacket, and a tan waistcoat hugged his torso. The sleeves of his fine white shirt were rolled to his elbows, exposing sinewy forearms that made her mouth go dry. The slight sheen of his sun-browned skin turned her knees to butter.

"Miss Lively," Kitty called, making her jump guiltily. "I see a spot by the rocks. If we climb on top, we'll have the best view of anyone."

"I suppose that would be all right," Hazel said. "As long

as you're careful. Miss Jane and I can spread our blankets nearby."

"You don't mind if we run ahead?" Lucy bounced as though her excitement was too much to contain.

"Go on," Hazel said. "Enjoy yourselves—but remember that you're representing Bellehaven Academy," she called after them.

The girls raced off in a blur of braids, ribbons, and laughter and were halfway to the rocks before she called after them, "Beware of the sun!"

She turned to Jane and shot her a wry smile. "Is there any chance their bonnets will stay on their heads?"

"Not the slightest," Jane said, matter-of-factly.

"Well, I can't say I blame them. I may shed mine before the end of the day, too." Hazel lifted her face toward the brisk ocean breeze and stole another glance at Blade. He stood near the surf, talking to his teammates, alternately tossing a ball toward the sky and deftly catching it in his palm—completely at ease and in command. If he'd had a single sleepless night since his last visit to Bellehaven, it certainly wasn't evident in his handsome face or god-like physique.

"Oh, Miss Lively!"

Blade looked up, and Hazel's face heated as she spun in the direction of the voice, which came from beneath one of the tents.

"Do come and join me!" Lady Rufflebum sat in an upholstered chair and beckoned Hazel with an imperious wave.

"I'll look after the girls," Jane offered kindly. "If the countess invites you to watch the match with her, you should. You might even be able to recruit some more students," she added in a conspiratorial whisper.

"I don't know about that." Hazel reached out and gave

Jane's arm a grateful squeeze. "But thank you. I'll find you later."

As she made her way toward Lady Rufflebum, Hazel endeavored not to stare at Blade, but she felt his presence with every breath she took. A frisson of awareness stretched between them, exhilarating as a chilly ocean spray on the back of her neck.

This would never do. She shook off her fanciful notions and resolved to keep her wits about her. To think more about their conflicting opinions and disparate long-term goals. To think less about broad shoulders and snug trousers.

"Good afternoon, Lady Rufflebum," Hazel said. "I'm glad to see you looking so well. I trust you're feeling improved from the last time I saw you."

"I am, indeed. I've been remiss in sending a note to thank you for your assistance on the night of my dinner party."

"Your good health is all the thanks I need," Hazel replied sincerely.

"Dr. Gladwell says that I am fully recovered, however, one can never be too careful." The countess patted her shawl like a talisman, then took a fortifying sip of claret. "Speaking of the good doctor, you should know that he has asked after you—more than once. I believe you made quite an impression that night."

Hazel glanced around, hoping no one had overheard the countess's comment. "I can't imagine why. Where is Miss Whitford today?" she asked, in a shameless attempt to change the subject.

"Visiting her sister in London," Lady Rufflebum said bravely, as if this outrageous state of affairs surely qualified her for martyrdom. "Please. You must pull up a seat and watch the match with me."

Hazel dutifully fetched a tufted footstool, placed it next to the countess's chair, and made a valiant attempt to engage in polite conversation while brawny men stretched and strategized on the beach in front of her.

"Will you be throwing your support behind the upstanding men of Bellehaven or the out-of-town folk?" Lady Rufflebum asked, leaving no doubt as to where her allegiances laid.

"I don't know the rules of cricket," Hazel said vaguely. "I'm just happy to watch the festivities."

Lady Rufflebum snorted indelicately. "There's no sport in remaining neutral." She cast a sideways glance at Hazel, then looked out at the strapping young men taking up their positions in the sand. "Unless . . . you wish to keep your options open?"

Good heavens. "I assure you, I've not given the matter much thought."

"Mmm," the countess replied, clearly skeptical. "Oh, look. Dr. Gladwell is the bowler for Bellehaven. Intelligent, attractive, *and* athletic."

Hazel hadn't noticed. She'd been understandably distracted by Blade. The sure grip of his hands on the bat. The subtle flexing of his biceps. The tiny creases around his eyes as he squinted at the crowd of spectators . . . and then focused squarely on her.

She looked away first, reluctantly forcing her attention back to Lady Rufflebum, who seemed oblivious to the brief exchange, thank goodness. "Would you like me to refill your glass?" Hazel said to the countess. "I could bring you a plate, if you wish."

"No, dash it all," Lady Rufflebum replied. "I want you to watch the match. Lord Bladenton is up to bat. Let's see how he fares against your doctor, shall we?"

"*My* doctor?" Hazel shook her head, emphatic. "He's not—"

"Of course not, dear," the countess said. She rubbed her

palms together as though she were in a Roman amphitheater, preparing to watch the gladiator games.

The next thing Hazel knew, Dr. Gladwell hurled the ball toward Blade, who smacked it down the beach, sending men running in all directions.

The crowd erupted in cheers and groans, while Lady Rufflebum clucked her tongue, thoughtful. "The earl is a formidable opponent. He must play for Bellehaven next year."

"But he's not a local."

The countess arched a mysterious brow and tapped a finger on the arm of her chair. "Not yet," she said, with a glimmer in her eye that sent a shiver down Hazel's spine.

They turned their attention back to the match and quickly became engrossed in the action. When Lady Rufflebum wasn't busy critiquing the speed, agility, and strength of each player, she patiently explained the finer points of the game to Hazel.

The teams seemed evenly matched, and before long she found herself on the edge of her stool, clutching the closed parasol in her lap as she waited to see if Bellehaven would rally to recover from a five-run deficit.

"Excellent." The countess steepled her fingertips as if she were a seasoned army general and all was going according to plan. "Nathan Gutridge is up to bat. No one on Bellehaven hits the ball harder. One swing, the match will be over, and we can finally pour the champagne."

Hazel nodded in agreement. Nathan worked at the Salty Mermaid, where he broke up pub brawls and wrestled with intoxicated patrons nightly. Hitting a ball with a bat would be child's play for the burly barkeep.

Then again, he faced a formidable opponent in his bowler—Blade.

The two men glared at each other across the length of the pitch.

At one end Blade stood like Adonis, his bronze skin glistening in the sun, his dark hair ruffling in the ocean breeze. The mere sight of him rubbing the ball between his palms did something odd to Hazel's insides.

At the other end of the pitch, Nathan crouched over the wicket and growled like a bear who'd missed dinner.

Unperturbed, Blade wiped the sweat from his brow, wound up, and launched a rocket.

Nathan grunted as he swung the bat and smacked the ball with a resounding *crack*.

It shot through the air like a bullet, and, to the horror of all, headed toward the tents.

More precisely, straight for Lady Rufflebum's head.

The countess let out a bloodcurdling scream.

Hazel's heart pounded like twenty-foot waves on the rocks.

With no time to think, she lunged in front of the countess.

The ball hit her shoulder like a snowball made of lead and she fell backward, landing on the countess's lap. For one interminable moment, the chair teetered on its two back legs.

Then it toppled over, sending Lady Rufflebum and Hazel sprawling in a tangle of arms, legs, gowns, and fichus.

"Help!" cried the countess, who had rolled off the chair and was lying on her back in the sand.

Hazel sat up, extended a hand to Lady Rufflebum, then winced. Her shoulder burned like she'd been prodded with a hot poker.

"Don't move."

Hazel blinked and looked up at Blade's chiseled face. He dropped to his knees beside her, his forehead creased in concern. In fact, he looked a little green. "Are you all right?"

She opened her mouth to answer, but the words wouldn't come. It had been so long since she'd felt as though someone cared. Genuinely, truly cared.

"Do I *look* like I'm all right?" Lady Rufflebum screamed behind him. She rocked futilely, like a turtle turned upside down on its shell.

"I'll be right there," Blade said to the countess, but his gaze didn't waver. "Hazel," he whispered, "where are you hurt?"

"I'm fine," she said, tenderly brushing off her palms. His nearness made her forget everything—her pain, her embarrassment, *and* her best-laid plans. "You should help the countess."

Reluctantly, he turned and, with the help of another nearby gentleman, hoisted Lady Rufflebum off the sand. While they assisted her into her chair and tried to assess her injuries, Dr. Gladwell sprinted toward Hazel and crouched next to her.

"Don't try to stand yet," he ordered. "I want to make sure you haven't broken anything."

Hazel rubbed the front of her left shoulder. "I'm sure it's nothing more than a bruise."

The doctor frowned, skeptical. "Still, I'd like to have a look."

"Dr. Gladwell!" Lady Rufflebum slumped in her chair while a worried young woman fanned her vigorously. "I require your attention. I don't believe I can move my neck."

Blade stood behind the doctor. "I'll stay with Miss Lively," he said firmly.

The doctor looked at Blade, hesitated, and turned back to Hazel. "I want you and the countess to return to her residence so I can determine the extent of your injuries."

"Are you sure that's necessary?" Hazel said.

"Yes," Dr. Gladwell said, his tone brooking no argument. With that, he gave Blade a curt nod and strode toward the countess.

Blade scooped the footstool off the ground, placed it near

her, and eased her onto it. "That was a courageous thing you did, Hazel," he whispered, his voice so deep it vibrated in her belly. "Foolhardy, perhaps, but brave."

Hazel's cheeks flushed, and she tried to compose herself as curious people gathered around. The girls wove their way to the front of the onlookers, breathless with excitement.

"Miss Lively, you were amazing," Lucy cried.

"Does it hurt very much?" Clara asked.

"*That's* sure to leave a mark," Kitty commented.

"I'm fine," Hazel assured them. "I just took a little tumble."

"Thank heaven." Jane exhaled. "You gave us such a fright."

"I hate to impose again," Hazel said, "but would you mind staying with the girls for the rest of the afternoon? Dr. Gladwell wants me to return to the countess's house so he can examine my shoulder."

"It's no imposition at all." Jane pushed her spectacles up the slope of her nose and lifted her chin. "We're very proud of you, Miss Lively."

"Not only did you save Lady Rufflebum," Lucy exclaimed, "but you helped Bellehaven win the match."

"What?" Hazel shook her head. "How?"

Lucy clasped her hands. "Mr. Gutridge's hit left the playing field—er, before it hit you. We scored six runs!"

"There will be ballads written about you before the night is over," Blade teased.

"Come, Miss Lively," Lady Rufflebum called, hobbling toward the dunes with the help of Dr. Gladwell. "Bladenton, would you be so kind as to escort her to my carriage?"

"It would be my pleasure," Blade said smoothly. He offered Hazel his arm, and she felt every pair of eyes on the beach watching her as she placed her hand in the crook of his elbow.

"At last, we'll have a moment to talk," he murmured.

"There are too many people around," she whispered back.

"I don't mean now. Later, at Lady Rufflebum's."

"Has she extended an invitation to you?"

"Not yet." He flashed a cocky smile. "But she will."

Chapter 15

Lady Rufflebum's kindly housekeeper, Mrs. Wallen, ushered Hazel to a sumptuous guest chamber, gave her a pretty nightgown, and tucked her into a large four-poster bed. "Dr. Gladwell will be here to check on you as soon as he finishes up with the countess." The housekeeper smiled sheepishly. "He may be detained for some time, I'm afraid. Shall I send up a tea tray while you're waiting?"

"No, thank you," Hazel said. "I'm quite content." After the chaos of the last couple of hours, she welcomed solitude—and the chance to sort through her thoughts.

Mrs. Wallen took one last tour about the room, making sure nothing was out of order. Apparently satisfied, she headed for the door and pointed out the bell pull. "Ring if you require anything at all."

Hazel had never felt so pampered, had never enjoyed such luxury. The bedchamber boasted a pair of large windows, gleaming mahogany furniture, and elegant wallpaper with leaf-green medallions on a moonlight-silver background. All of it was a far cry from her small, simple room at Mrs. Paxton's boardinghouse, and an even further cry from the cubby-like area where she'd slept in her family's flat.

Sadly, memories of her childhood home had faded, and

she could no longer recall the exact color of the walls or the position of the furniture. But she remembered the feeling of Papa ruffling her hair and Mama kissing her cheek. She remembered how it felt to belong—to love and be loved.

She wanted that again. Needed it.

If Blade didn't, she had no choice but to say goodbye, even if it broke her heart.

She loosened the tie at the neck of her nightgown and took a peek at her shoulder. It was a little red and swollen—nothing to justify the fuss that Lady Rufflebum, Dr. Gladwell, and Blade had made over her.

And yet she had to admit that even though the fuss was entirely unnecessary, it was . . . nice.

A soft knock at the door jolted her from her thoughts. She started to secure her nightgown tie, then shrugged. Dr. Gladwell would want to examine her shoulder himself.

She sat up against a silk-upholstered headboard. "Come in."

The door swung open, and Blade slipped in like a bandit in the night—or, rather, the late afternoon.

"What are you doing?" she asked, incredulous.

He silently closed the door behind him, sauntered over to the bed, and sat on the edge of the mattress. "Visiting you. How are you feeling?"

Dear Jesus. "You shouldn't be here. Dr. Gladwell could arrive at any moment."

"He's with the countess now, and she has a very long list of maladies that he'll need to address." Blade grinned at her. "In the meantime, I thought you might like some company."

Hazel gaped at him.

His smile faltered slightly. "Unless you'd like me to go?"

"No," she said quickly. "I'm glad you're here, but I'm certain I don't need to tell you how dire the consequences would be if you were discovered."

"I won't be discovered," he said confidently.

She arched a brow. "I see. I assume you have a vast amount of experience at this sort of thing?"

"What sort of thing?"

"Sneaking into women's bedchambers."

"Definitely not." He rubbed his jaw thoughtfully. "Maybe a little. But only when invited."

She rolled her eyes but couldn't hold back a smile. "Thank you for being concerned about me. But I truly am fine."

His gaze flicked to the loosened neckline of her nightgown. "May I see?"

Heat crept up her chest, but she nodded. "Yes."

He shifted closer, and her body tingled with anticipation. He swept a loose tendril behind her ear, and her blood thrummed in her veins. He gently pushed the fabric off her shoulder, and beneath her soft nightgown, her nipples tightened to hard buds.

His warm fingers caressed her skin, circling the pink mark. "Does this hurt?" he asked.

"No," she said, her voice raspy to her own ears.

He bent his head and brushed his lips over the tender spot. "How about this?"

"No."

He kissed a meandering path up the side of her neck. Trailed a wicked fingertip from her collarbone, to the hollow of her throat, to the valley between her breasts.

All the longing of the last two weeks welled up inside her. She fisted her hands in the sheets. Sighed as he nibbled on her earlobe. Moaned encouragingly as he slid a hand inside her nightgown and cupped her breast, teasing the taut tip with his palm.

"God, I've missed you," he murmured. "If you thought two weeks away would change this, you're mad."

"I've been thinking ab—"

A brisk knock on the door made her swallow her words. "Miss Lively," called the male voice from the corridor. "It's Dr. Gladwell. May I come in?"

Good heavens. "Just a moment," she choked out.

Blade planted one more kiss on her lips, straightened her nightgown, and silently hopped off the bed.

"What are we going to do?" she whispered urgently.

"You're going to tell Gladwell to come in," he said, impossibly calm.

"What about you?"

He flashed her a grin. "I'll be under the bed."

"Are you all right in there?" Dr. Gladwell called.

"Of course." Hazel yanked the sheets up to her chest, looked at Blade, and waved a hand, shooing him under the bed. "Er, you may come in."

Blade dove to the floor and rolled out of sight—just as the door opened.

The doctor strode across the room and placed his bag on a chair beside the bed. "I'm sorry it took me so long to check on you," he said.

"There's no need to apologize," Hazel said, aiming for a breezy tone. "Er, how's Lady Rufflebum?"

"I expect she'll make a full recovery," the doctor said with a chuckle. "The question is, how are *you*?"

"Perfectly fine," she said with a dismissive wave of the hand. "Never better."

"Glad to hear it." Dr. Gladwell shot her a sincere smile. "But I wouldn't be surprised if you're stiff and sore tomorrow. Let's have a look at your shoulder."

Hazel nodded and tried not to squirm as he perfunctorily examined the bruise. Tried not to look guilty as he lifted her arm and pressed his fingers to the inside of her wrist.

"Your pulse is unusually rapid," Gladwell said with a frown.

"How odd," she said, though she suspected it was perfectly normal, circumstances being what they were—namely, that she was hiding a man under her bed.

"Your cheeks are flushed as well. Do you have any chills? Fever?"

"No," Hazel said vaguely. "Perhaps I was in the sun a bit too long."

"Did you hurt yourself when you fell earlier? Or bump your head?"

"Not at all," she assured him. "The sand was quite forgiving."

"Mmm. I'm going to ask Mrs. Wallen to make a poultice for your shoulder, and I want you to stay here overnight."

"I couldn't possibly." Hazel leaned forward, aghast—and, in the process, knocked a small decorative pillow off the bed. Onto the floor.

Sweet Jesus. The doctor bent to pick it up.

"Please, leave it," she blurted.

He froze halfway down. "I beg your pardon?"

"Leave the pillow," she said. "I'll, ah, only manage to kick it off the bed again."

"Very well." The doctor stood slowly, clearly confounded. "As I was saying, I'd like you to apply the poultice and rest here until tomorrow afternoon."

"But I can't."

The doctor arched a brow. "Why is that?"

"I have a school to run. Lessons to prepare."

"Tomorrow is Sunday. Between your assistant and Mrs. Paxton, your students are in good hands. Your only job for the next twenty-four hours is to rest and take care of yourself." He snapped his bag shut, took one step toward the door, then turned back toward her. His expression softened, and he hesitated, suddenly reticent. "Send for me if you need anything, Miss Lively—anything at all."

She nodded mutely, held her breath as he walked out the door, and didn't exhale till it shut behind him.

Two seconds later, Blade emerged from beneath the bed, frowning as he brushed the dust off his waistcoat. "What in the devil's name was *that*?"

Hazel blinked. "What was what?"

"Gladwell was flirting with you," he muttered. "Never mind. We can talk about it later tonight."

"Perhaps you were unable to properly eavesdrop from your hiding spot," she said wryly. "But I'm confined to this bed until tomorrow."

Blade flashed his wicked dimple. "I heard. But there's no reason I can't come to you."

"Are you planning to scale the wall outside and climb through the window?"

"I could," he said smugly, "but that won't be necessary. Lady Rufflebum insisted that I stay as her guest while I'm in Bellehaven. She claims I'll be much more comfortable here than at the Bluffs' Brew—and she's probably correct. The mattresses at the inn are as lumpy as a sack of potatoes. I think she's plotting to have me play for Bellehaven's cricket team next summer."

"She's definitely plotting," Hazel agreed.

"But it works to our advantage. I could come back tonight after everyone is sleeping," he ventured, his dark eyes hopeful.

Hazel could have resisted him if she wanted to. Discipline was easy for her; daring was difficult. But she didn't want to resist him. And if ever a moment called for daring, this one did.

"Come back after midnight," she said. "But be careful."

Blade paced the length of his guest chamber, willing the hands of the clock to turn faster.

He needed to see Hazel. Needed to talk to her.

Because something had shifted today.

One minute, he'd been standing on the beach playing cricket. The next, he'd watched in horror as Hazel threw herself in front of a ball hurtling through the air with the velocity of a cannonball.

And his world had narrowed to a pinpoint. He couldn't bear the thought of her being hurt, or worse. True, he would have felt badly for anyone who was in pain, but this was more than empathy. This was bone-chilling dread. A nausea-inducing punch to the gut.

Even more telling was the utter relief he'd felt when he'd realized she wasn't seriously injured. He'd wanted to kiss her, scoop her up in his arms, spin her around until they were both dizzy.

It was a dangerous thing, the sense of being so connected, so attuned to someone else. Bonds like that could be severed without warning—and often were. He knew that better than anyone.

He couldn't risk that kind of agony again, but maybe he and Hazel could meet in the middle. Maybe there was a way he could at least keep her safe. Maybe there was a way they could be together.

As soon as both clock hands pointed north, Blade snuck out of his bedchamber and skulked down the long, dark, corridor to Hazel's room. He tapped lightly on the door, and almost immediately, she opened it.

Her flowing white nightgown grazed the tops of her bare feet, and rich brown curls tumbled around her shoulders. Nary a fichu nor hairpin was in sight.

She wasn't Miss Lively, the rule-bound headmistress that the rest of the world saw. This was Hazel, the woman who picnicked under the stars and stole kisses in his coach. Who courageously saved orphans and countesses alike.

And he was finding it increasingly difficult for him to picture his life without her in it.

Wordlessly, she reached for his wrist, pulled him into her room, and shut the door behind him.

"Impressive," he teased. "You're certain you haven't done this before?"

She arched a brow in his direction. "I lived most of my life in a dormitory with dozens of girls. I learned a few tricks over the years."

"Duly noted." He gestured toward the pair of armchairs flanking the dormant fireplace. "Shall we sit?"

She nodded and led the way, settling herself into one of the chairs and tucking her feet under her body. He sat opposite her and leaned forward, elbows on his knees, as he looked into her dazzling topaz eyes.

"I've been thinking about our conversation in the coach," he began.

"So have I."

"I did as you asked. I tried to forget what happened between us. I couldn't. I thought about you every day and every night."

"I tried to forget it, too," she said earnestly, "and fared no better than you. What are we going to do?"

"I think you should come to London," he said slowly. "I think you should . . . marry me."

Her eyes grew big as saucers. "Marry you?" she repeated, incredulous.

"You wouldn't have to teach anymore." He'd said it to sweeten the pot, but when her face fell, he deduced he'd made a tactical error. "Then again," he added quickly, "if you're intent on running a school for less fortunate girls, you could move your enterprise to Town and hire a staff to deal with the day-to-day details."

She shook her head as though his words made no sense. "Bellehaven Academy is more than an enterprise."

"I know," he said soberly. "But there's no reason you can't do both. Oversee your school . . . and marry me." It would be for the best, actually, if she had a project of her own. Something to pour her heart into—so she wouldn't pour it into him.

A tiny vertical crease appeared between her brows. "I thought . . . I thought you didn't want a family."

Shit. This was the difficult part—the biggest hurdle for them to overcome. But he couldn't promise something he couldn't deliver. "I don't want a family. Not in the way that you do. But I'd take care of you and any children that we might have. We'd have a good life. You wouldn't want for anything, Hazel. What do you say?"

Chapter 16

Hazel stared at Blade, trying to make sense of his proposal. His *marriage* proposal.

He'd said he'd take care of her and give her a good life. He'd made mention of London, her school, and potential children as if he were ticking off items on a list. But, somehow, he'd managed to make an offer of marriage without mentioning the most important thing of all.

Love.

She didn't delude herself into thinking that the omission had been an oversight.

Blade didn't love her. Worse, apparently, he *couldn't* love her.

She swallowed and soaked in the sight of him sitting across from her, so close she could see the light stubble along his jaw and the subtle flex of his fingers as he awaited her answer.

He'd probably never know how much she longed to say yes. But a marriage where only one of them was in love—namely, her—would be like waking up day after day and having her heart smashed to a million little pieces.

She'd have to be mad to agree to such a thing.

"I won't move Bellehaven Academy to London." She lifted

her chin and willed her voice to remain steady. "My school belongs here. My girls and I belong here."

"Fine." He nodded, unfazed. "We'll travel back and forth. I'll buy a home in Bellehaven—something spacious and elegant, where we can entertain friends from London."

Her chest ached—and it was the type of pain that no poultice could fix. "I can't marry you."

"Hazel," he said soberly, "I know you want to belong to a real family, and you deserve that more than anyone. But think about what I *can* give you. My name. Security. Maybe even a measure of happiness."

Her eyes welled. "That's the problem. I would never be content with half measures. I want the kind of bliss that makes my heart soar. The sort of joy that makes my soul sing. I want a true partnership—a deep, abiding love."

"I can't." He shook his head and closed his eyes briefly. Almost as though he were in physical pain. "It's not that I don't want to . . . but I can't give you that kind of love."

The words sliced open her chest. Like a glutton for punishment, she asked, "Why not?"

He sprang out of his seat and paced behind his chair. "Because it doesn't last. You talk about all-consuming love like it's a good thing. But what happens when it consumes you? Or me? Inevitably, someone is left with their heart torn and trampled. I won't risk hurting you that way."

"So you'd rather keep your distance from everyone." Her voice cracked on the last syllable. "You'd rather keep me at arm's length."

He faced her and braced his arms on the back of the chair. "I'd rather protect you."

"I don't want to be protected," she said, adamant. But she couldn't quite bring herself to utter the next part—that she wanted him to love her. The way that she loved him.

Maybe she *should* have told him—if only to prove she

was capable of cracking open her hard shell and exposing the most vulnerable part of herself.

Maybe she *would* have told him—if she thought it could make a difference. But Blade wasn't going to change his mind. She could bare her soul and reveal every weakness for him to see, but he was never going to fall hopelessly in love with her . . . the way she was with him.

He rubbed the back of his neck, his face a mix of confusion and torment as he came to terms with her answer. Knowing that he hurt as much as she did only made her feel worse.

She gripped the arms of her chair so she wouldn't leap out of her seat, throw herself at him, and implore him to whisk her away to Gretna Green.

"I'm sorry," he said softly. "I respect your decision, but if you should change your mind . . ."

"I won't." No matter how tempted she was to accept his proposal, she wouldn't forget the commitment she'd made to her students. To herself. She and the girls had formed their own motley little family—and anyone who wanted to be a part of Hazel's life had to love her enough to accept the lot of them.

"I guess that's settled then," he said, his voice raw with emotion. "I'll go and let you rest."

"Blade." She rose from her chair and slowly shook her head. "You don't have to leave."

He exhaled, and his anguished expression gutted her. "I think it would be best."

Perhaps it would. But she wasn't ready to say goodbye. Not like this, and certainly not now, when they were both raw and hurting.

It seemed that neither of them could give the other what they needed, but they *could* offer each other a measure of comfort—and more.

They could give each other one night. One night to burn as brightly as they dared, so that years from now they'd have a memory to pull from the distant corners of their minds. A rare, fragile memento that they could dust off and hold up to the light in order to glimpse a fraction of its former brilliance.

She wanted that, for Blade and for herself.

Silently, she glided toward him, stood a mere inch away, and cupped his cheek in her palm. He went very still, but she could hear the subtle hitch of his breath. See his pupils turn dark with desire. Feel the blood thrumming in his veins.

"Stay with me," she whispered.

He swallowed and closed his eyes briefly, as if she was testing the very limits of his self-control. "You want me to stay here, all night?"

"Yes." She let her hand slide down his neck and over the hard planes of his chest. Beneath his waistcoat, his heart thumped as hard as hers. "I want to lie with you—to be as close as two people can be."

His whole body tensed, and for several seconds he was silent. At last he said, "Jesus, Hazel. Are you sure about this?"

She wriggled her hands inside his jacket and eased it off his shoulders. Boldly loosened the knot of his cravat. "I've never been surer."

The words had barely left her lips before he captured her mouth in a kiss. Cradled her head in his hands.

Their bodies collided, and all her nerve endings came alive. Her breasts pressed against his rock-like torso. His hips rocked against her belly, seducing her with every wicked nudge.

She and Blade may not have been on the same page when it came to their futures, but physically at least, they couldn't have been better matched. Being with him was more exhilarating than cracking open the cover of a new book. More thrilling than any plot twist or turn. More satisfying than the happiest of endings.

"Tonight is ours," he said with a growl. "You and I. All. Night. Long."

He strode to the bed, laid her on the sumptuous mattress, and stretched out beside her. The warm glow of the lamp on the night table illuminated his chiseled nose, cheeks, and jaw; the night breeze from the open window danced in his rich brown hair. His cravat loosely circled his neck, and the thought of stripping it off him—along with the rest of his garments—made her tingle with anticipation.

"I don't want anything between us tonight," she murmured. "No worries, no fears . . . not a stitch of clothing." She tugged his cravat free, held it over the side of the bed, and let it drop to the floor.

He pressed a scorching kiss to the side of her neck and chuckled. "I like the way you think, Miss Lively."

She wrested free the buttons of his waistcoat. He hauled his shirt over his head, and the sight of his bare torso made her mouth go dry. She licked her lips and trailed her fingertips over his broad shoulders, across his collarbone, and over the hard muscles of his chest. Traced a path around a flat nipple, then let her fingers wander lower, over the ridges of his abdomen and the soft fuzz above his waistband.

He tensed, but if his heavy-lidded gaze was any indication, he didn't mind her curiosity. So she slid a hand around his back, down his spine, and lower, over a perfectly sculpted buttock. Charted a path around his hip and across the front of his trousers, testing the long, hard, length of his arousal.

"I think you mean to torture me," he rasped.

"On the contrary." She brushed a kiss across his lips. "I aim to please you." To demonstrate, she stroked him harder and faster—just as her trusty manual had instructed.

"Hazel," he choked out.

She froze again, praying she hadn't forgotten a vital step. "Yes?"

He arched a dark brow. "Turnabout is fair play."

In the blink of an eye, he'd grabbed her wrists and pinned them over her head with one hand.

His heavy-lidded gaze raked over her, lingering on her lips, her breasts, and her legs. "I have dreamed of this."

"You have?"

"Mmm." He undid the tie at the collar of her nightgown and pulled the neckline down—way down—exposing one of her breasts. "You're more beautiful than I dreamed."

"No one has ever called me beautiful," she said, flushing.

"Maybe no one's ever seen you the way I do." He skimmed the pad of a finger around the taut peak, spiraling round and round—stopping just shy of touching it. An insistent pulsing started in her core, and she twisted from side to side in a futile attempt to quell it.

"I think you mean to torture me," she said, flinging his words back at him.

"I do, indeed." A wicked gleam lit his eyes as he bent his head and blew lightly on her puckered nipple.

"Oh." She arched her back and whimpered.

"Maybe this will help." He drew the bud into his mouth and soothed it with his warm tongue. As he alternately sucked and teased the sensitive tip, he reached beneath the hem of her nightgown and slid a hand up her calf. Sure, steady fingers caressed the inside of her thigh, kneading the tender flesh before cruising higher—and touching the soft, slick folds at her entrance.

Her instruction manual, a French book of *poses érotiques*, depicted something similar. Hazel had flushed when she examined the lovely engraving of Aeneas reaching between Dido's parted legs—while a curious cherub holding a torch looked on.

Every night since her encounter with Blade in his coach, she'd thought about the drawing—and snuck a peek at it a time or two. Now she understood why Dido clutched Aeneas's shoulder. Why she could barely hold her head erect as she sat in his lap.

Hazel felt that intoxicating pleasure, too.

"Do you like this?" he murmured, teasing the most sensitive spot.

"Yes." But she felt slightly feverish, so she hiked her nightgown over her hips.

Blade growled his approval and slid a finger inside her. "And this?"

"Yes." Her inner muscles squeezed, then gradually relaxed. But the pulsing was still there, spiraling inside her, and Blade knew just how to stoke it. Hungry kisses. Wicked words. Sure hands, worshipping her body.

He tilted his forehead to hers and gazed into her eyes as he continued to stroke her. Their breath mingled in the space between them, and in the perfect, raw intimacy of that moment, everything else faded away. All of their worries were shoved behind the curtain of desire and diminished by the power of their connection.

"If you were mine," Blade murmured, "I'd make you feel like this every night. Every morning. Anytime you wished."

"I'd scarcely have time to teach," she rasped.

He shot her a sultry smile. "You'd never leave my bed. In fact, I might tie you to it, so I could kiss you wherever I wanted. Here"—he nibbled her ear lobe to demonstrate—"here"—he licked a circle around her navel—"and here." With that, he lowered his head between her legs and caressed her with his tongue.

Oh my. She couldn't recall an engraving like this in her manual. But she might as well toss it in the waste bin. Nothing in the book had even come close to describing this glorious feeling. No words could describe the spell she was under; no illustration could convey the magic.

Blade alternately sucked and licked, coaxing her to the very edge of a precipice. Pleasure shimmered through her limbs. Blood thrummed in her veins, so loud that it filled her ears. She fisted her hands in the sheets, arched her back . . . and moaned as she came apart.

He grasped her hips as the rush overtook her, carrying her along like foam on the crest of a wave. She soaked in the beauty and wonder of it, surrendered fully to it. And when the last ripples subsided, she nestled into the harbor of his arms, utterly spent. Thoroughly satisfied.

He stroked her hair as she curled up next to him, savoring the sight of his tanned, broad shoulders against the white bed linens. When she'd recovered sufficiently to speak, she lifted her head. "That was better than I dreamed it would be."

He gave a smug grunt.

"Actually, that's not true," she said.

A faint crease marred his forehead. "It's not?"

"I never dared to dream of anything so wicked . . . or so wonderful."

He dropped a kiss on the tip of her nose. "Then my work here is done."

"I hardly think so."

Blade blinked. "I beg your pardon?"

"You are still half dressed," she said with a frown. "And there is plenty more to be done."

"Is that so?" he teased. "What do you propose we do?"

Hazel sat up, tapped a finger to her lips, and pondered the question. Maybe she'd been hasty in dismissing the usefulness of her manual. She was thinking of a particular engraving featuring Venus and Mars. Perhaps the book would prove valuable after all.

"Well," she ventured, "I think we should begin by removing your trousers and boots."

"Hazel," he said soberly, "are you sure about this?"

She lifted her nightgown over her head, tossed it to the floor, and stretched out beside him. "I'm sure."

He almost fell off the bed in his hurry to disrobe. He yanked off his boots first, then attacked the buttons at the front of his trousers, while she watched with anticipation.

As he hooked his thumbs inside the waistband, a wicked grin lit his face. He pushed the buckskins off his hips, kicked them aside, and stood before her proudly.

He was magnificently masculine, from the sprinkling of hair on his chest to his muscular thighs to the large shaft that jutted toward her. Her palms itched to touch him, to feel his skin against hers.

"Come closer," she said.

He climbed onto the mattress, stretched out beside her, and reached for her hand, lacing their fingers together. "You always surprise me, Hazel."

She dragged her gaze away from his gorgeous body and looked into his eyes. "How so?"

"Your motto is 'proper behavior never takes a holiday,' and yet here we are in what is arguably a very improper situation." He lifted their joined hands and pressed a kiss to the back of hers. "I don't want you to regret anything."

"I won't," she said earnestly. "It's true that proper behavior never takes a holiday. We must always strive to be the best version of ourselves. But the truth is, I feel like I *am* my best self . . . when I'm with you."

His heavy-lidded gaze dropped to her lips. "I feel obliged to tell you that my thoughts are decidedly improper, wanton, and wicked—take your pick."

"Let's go with wicked." She reached for him, curling her fingers around the base of his shaft. Slowly, she stroked him, all the way to the top and down again, till a slick sheen covered the entire length. His face took on a drunk, dazed expression, and he moaned softly.

"Hazel," he murmured. "That feels . . . too good."

This morning she wouldn't have understood what he meant—but now she did. Being with someone you cared about could be so sweet, so intense, that it physically hurt. And she could ease that pain. She wanted to.

"Lie back." She placed her palm on the hard wall of his chest and pushed him flat on the mattress, then climbed above him, on all fours. Her arms were braced above his shoulders and her knees straddled his hips.

"What are you doing?" He gripped the bedcovers as though he didn't trust his hands to obey his brain.

"I should think it would be obvious." She bent her head to kiss his neck, letting her long hair tickle his chest. "I may be a novice, but I do my best to educate myself in all things—including this."

Blade blinked, clearly incredulous. "You've studied sex?"

"Perhaps it's more accurate to say I've read about it." She let her gaze wander down his torso. "Enough to become familiar with the conventions."

"There is nothing conventional about you, Hazel Lively." He reached up and cupped her breast, taking the weight in his palm.

She felt herself melting into him—physically, yes, but emotionally too. All her defenses, all her armor was stripped away. She'd thought that baring her soul would amount to surrender, but the reverse was true. In giving up a part of herself, she'd found her strength. She'd climbed out of the depths of loss and grief and emerged, ready to feel again. Maybe even ready to love.

She threaded her fingers through his thick hair. Kissed him with reckless abandon. Lowered her body and rocked her hips against his. And *that* seemed to be the nail in the coffin of his self-control.

His hands were everywhere—caressing her breasts, cruising down her back, squeezing her bottom. He grasped her hips and showed her how to move against him, so that his shaft teased and aroused her, setting her blood on fire once again.

"I want you, Hazel," he murmured hotly. "But only if you're certain you want this, too."

"Do you doubt it?" She reached between them, positioned him at her entrance, and slowly lowered herself, taking him inside. Marveling at the way her body stretched to accommodate him. Reveling in the pleasure they gave each other.

His forehead glistened with perspiration. His eyes glazed over with desire. His muscles quivered with restraint.

"Don't hold back, Blade," she urged, sinking a bit lower. "I want all of you."

He moaned as he began to thrust, slowly at first, then faster and faster. She leaned forward, letting the tips of her breasts brush against the wall of his chest. Her pulse began to pound in her ears, and a warm glow spread through her limbs.

He was so handsome, so masculine, so enigmatic. But for tonight, at least, he was hers.

His breathing turned ragged, and a low growl escaped his throat. "You feel so good, damn it."

She lightly raked her fingernails down his chest. Angled her body, increasing the friction between them. Whispered close to his ear, "I want to please you as you pleased me. I want you to come apart. Now."

"Come with me." He speared his fingers through her hair and captured her mouth in a kiss that transported her to a majestic cliff towering above the ocean. To a midnight sky dripping with stars.

They clung to each other—floating, flying, reaching.

And at last, they hurtled together through the mist.

Blade groaned as he pulsed inside her; her body clenched around him. Pleasure, pure and potent, shimmered through her veins like the morning sun dancing on the waves.

And the look of awe on Blade's face said he felt it, too.

He kissed her tenderly as they spiraled down to earth, landing gently as a feather on the grass. Deftly, he rolled her onto her side, faced her, and covered them both with a quilt.

"Rest," he said, lightly massaging her scalp. "We will talk later."

She opened her mouth to tell him the truth—that no matter how lovely the evening had been, it hadn't changed anything.

Well, that wasn't entirely true. She now knew, without a doubt, that she loved Blade beyond reason.

What *hadn't* changed was the impossibility of a future together.

He would, no doubt, be better off with someone like Lady Penelope.

But tonight didn't seem like the ideal time to mention it. Besides, her eyelids were terribly heavy, so she nestled against his chest and let herself drift off, content in the knowledge that for one magical night, she'd remembered how it felt to belong.

Chapter 17

Blade woke in the wee hours of the morning to find his legs still tangled with Hazel's. She slept soundly next to him, a serene smile on her beautiful face. But the beam of pale light streaming between the curtain panels warned their time together was quickly running out.

"Hazel." He nudged her arm gently, careful to avoid her bruised shoulder. "Are you awake?"

"No," she murmured grumpily.

He chuckled and slipped out of the bed. "I need to return to my room before Lady Rufflebum's staff begin their day. But I didn't want to leave without talking to you."

She rubbed her eyes and reluctantly sat up, tucking the bedsheet beneath her arms. "Last night was lovely."

He stuffed his arms in the sleeves and winked at her. "That was only a sampling."

"Blade." The regret in her voice turned his blood to ice, and he already knew what she was going to say.

"I haven't forgotten that you rejected my offer," he said slowly. "But that was before we made love. Surely that changes things."

She shook her head regretfully. "I haven't changed my mind about marrying you."

Damn it. He found his trousers draped over a chest at the end of the bed and stepped into them. He'd hoped, foolishly, that she'd feel differently this morning. That physical intimacy would make her realize how good they were together—and how content they could be.

If only she could compromise a little. If only she didn't demand his whole heart.

He jammed his shirttails into his trousers. "There could be a babe."

She swallowed and rubbed the tops of her arms. "My courses just ended, so it's unlikely."

"But not impossible," he countered. "You'll let me know?"

"I will inform you if I'm with child," she said soberly. "But I don't think there's cause to worry."

"I'm not worried, damn it." He pulled on his boots, strode to the bed, and sat on the edge of the mattress, wondering how in the hell a perfect night had turned into such an awkward morning. "I want to take care of you—and I don't understand why you won't let me."

"I don't need someone to take care of me." She raised her chin. "The truth is that I'd rather be on my own than marry someone who . . . doesn't want the same things I do."

He snorted and slapped his hands on his thighs. "I guess it's settled then."

But he didn't want it to be settled. He took his time as he moved about the room, locating his cravat, waistcoat, and jacket—just in case she had an epiphany and realized she couldn't live without him.

But she sat silently in the four-poster bed—beautiful, proud, and principled.

He heard the faint sounds of members of Lady Rufflebum's maids as they began to move about, performing their morning chores. If he stalled much longer, someone was going to discover him there, and Hazel would be forced to marry him regardless of her wishes.

But even *he* couldn't stoop that low. He wanted to be with her in the worst way, but he wanted her to marry him of her own volition. Not because she'd been compromised.

He hurried to the bed and brushed a kiss across her lips. "I'll be by the school later to visit with Kitty. Perhaps I'll see you before I drive back to London?"

She stared at her clasped hands in her lap. "Perhaps," she said, but her voice was so hollow it sent a skitter down his spine.

Hazel's armor was back in place, and this time it seemed as though she'd traded in her chain mail for full metal plates.

With leaden feet, he walked to the door, then faced her. "We're the same, you and I," he said softly. "You *say* you want love and a family. But you won't let me in."

"Why would I risk that?" Her voice cracked on the last word.

"Exactly." He resisted the urge to run back and haul her into his arms. "Like I said, we're the same."

Hazel found that the busier she was, the less time she had to dwell on Blade's parting words—and the ache in her chest.

So for the next few days, she threw herself into her lessons. First, she and the girls worked on translating portions of the *Aeneid*. Their Latin skills were decidedly lacking, but fortunately Beatrice's fascination with the Trojan War helped carry them through several verses.

The following afternoon, Dr. Gladwell gave an interesting lecture in which he demonstrated how to make a splint, fashion a tourniquet, and bandage a wound. By the end of class, the girls looked like *they'd* fought in the Trojan War. But Winnie, who seemed to have a knack for medicinal herbs and remedies, was delighted when the doctor praised her nursing skills.

Today they were rehearsing a few scenes from *Romeo and Juliet* that they planned to perform for Mrs. Paxton's boardinghouse guests. Kitty had sketched a backdrop of Verona's cobbled streets, Clara had fashioned makeshift costumes, and all the girls were thoroughly embracing their roles.

Indeed, Hazel could barely hear herself think over the click-clack of wooden swords wielded by half a dozen Montagues and Capulets—all of whom wore braids and dresses. Lucy, who had meticulously choreographed the entire fight scene, leapt off a desk, dove into a forward roll, and sprang to her feet, brandishing her driftwood sword like a Viking warrior.

Goodness. Hazel clapped her hands and waited for the shouts and moans of her budding thespians to subside.

"Well done, girls," she said approvingly. "Although Bea and Lucy, perhaps you could make your sword fight a bit less brutal. We don't want Mrs. Paxton's guests running for their smelling salts before they have a chance to enjoy the garden scene." To everyone, she said, "Please put away your costumes and props, and we'll resume rehearsal tomorrow."

As the girls bustled out of the classroom, Jane fanned herself with a clipboard and murmured, "*I* might need the smelling salts before we're done."

Hazel patted her shoulder. "I'll finish tidying up here. Why don't you rest before dinner?"

Jane shot her a grateful smile. "If you're certain."

"Absolutely," Hazel said, shooing her toward the door. But as Jane removed her apron, Hazel blurted, "May I ask you something?"

"Of course." Jane adjusted her spectacles and folded her

hands. "Would you like me to prepare a few lessons for next week?"

"No," Hazel said, frowning. "Nothing like that. I have a personal sort of question. I was wondering if you think I'm . . . hard."

Jane's brow knitted. "Hard?"

"Difficult to know," Hazel clarified, "or distant." The question had plagued her since the morning Blade had left her bed.

"I think that you are a private person," Jane said slowly, as if she was taking great care in choosing her words. "And there's certainly nothing wrong with that."

"True, but I'd like your honest opinion. Do I have a habit of . . . pushing people away?"

Jane leaned on the edge of a desk, her expression thoughtful. "You're kind, generous, and brave. You're fiercely devoted to your school and your students."

"But?" Hazel curled her fingers into her palms.

"But when it comes to personal matters," Jane ventured, "you tend to be guarded." She paused and tilted her head. "I hope I haven't offended you."

Hazel blew out a long, slow breath. "You haven't. You simply confirmed something I already suspected. Thank you for speaking frankly."

"What's this about?" Jane asked. "Has something happened?"

Hazel opened her mouth to answer in the negative but stopped herself. "Something *has* happened," she mused aloud. "I'm not certain what to do about it, but I do know this. I can't keep shutting out the people I care about. People like you."

"Thank you, Miss Lively."

"You should call me Hazel," she replied with a chuckle.

Jane beamed. "What a lovely name. It suits you."

Hazel smiled as she righted an overturned chair. "I didn't intend to keep you. Please, go and rest," she urged. "I'll see you at dinner."

As Jane walked past, she reached out and squeezed Hazel's arm. "If you need someone to talk to, you know where to find me."

"You've made me feel a little better already," she said sincerely. "Thank you."

Once she was alone, Hazel placed her hands on her hips and assessed the sorry state of her classroom.

Thankfully, restoring order was simple. One merely arranged the desks in neat rows, swept the floor, and erased the chalkboard.

Restoring order to one's life was a different matter entirely.

But she was determined to do just that. Her relationship with Blade was like the comet she'd hoped to see when she'd snuck onto the roof, years ago. Bright. Wondrous. Fleeting.

A once-in-a-lifetime, unforgettable experience.

Eventually, the awful hole in her heart would heal. The tears that constantly threatened would dry up. The loneliness and longing would fade.

Surely they would.

When everything in the classroom had been set to rights, she drew the curtains, closed the door, and headed to her office so she could pen a quick reply to a letter from Miss Haywinkle. But as she passed Jane's desk in the quiet antechamber, Hazel drew up short. Her office door was opened a crack, and through the narrow opening, a blur of movement caught her eye, sending a shiver down her spine.

Chances were that the intruder was Harold. Mrs. Paxton's cat had a habit of barging into Hazel's office, hopping onto the desk, and sitting on top of her journal. If he was feeling particularly ornery, he sometimes batted an inkwell to the floor for good measure.

Still, her heart hammered as she tiptoed through the antechamber. She held her breath, placed a palm against the door, and swung it open—revealing not a cat, but a student.

"Kitty?"

The girl stood behind Hazel's desk, her back to the door, but whirled around at the sound of her name. A deep pink stain crept up her neck. "Miss Lively," she croaked.

"What are you doing in here?"

"Hmm? I was just, er, looking for you. And then I noticed this frame on your shelf. I wanted a closer look." Kitty gestured toward the embroidered handkerchief that Hazel had framed years ago.

It was one of the few mementos from her childhood—a gift from her mother. In the week leading up to Hazel's seventh birthday, Mama had surreptitiously worked on it after dinner every night. On the morning of her birthday, Hazel found the handkerchief beside her breakfast plate. She unfolded the square of crisp white cotton to find a beautiful sprig of green leaves and a trio of rich brown hazelnuts above the initials HL. Mama had kissed her cheek and said that every proper young lady needed a monogrammed handkerchief.

"You mustn't trespass in private spaces," Hazel said firmly. "When you realized I wasn't here, you should have left."

"I know." Kitty had the good grace to look embarrassed but quickly recovered. "Are those your initials?"

Hazel ignored the question. "What did you wish to see me about?"

Kitty scurried from behind the desk, holding her wadded cape and wooden sword under one arm. "I had a question, but perhaps it's not the best time to ask."

"Are you certain?" Hazel swept her gaze over her desktop, relieved that nothing appeared to have been disturbed.

"Yes," Kitty said vaguely. "It's not important." She fidgeted and inched toward the door as if she couldn't wait to escape the office.

"How are your swimming lessons going?" Hazel asked.

"Poppy says I'm slightly less hopeless than I was at the start." Kitty shrugged. "She's been showing me how to fish, too. I like her."

"I thought you might." Hazel walked to her desk and settled into her chair. "I saw Mr. Sandford at the tea shop yesterday. He said you're assisting him with a project?"

"The new stables on South Street. Not as exciting as a castle or palace, but I suppose we all must start somewhere."

"I'm proud of you," Hazel said, refusing to let her make light of her accomplishment. "Mr. Sandford must be pleased with your progress if he's allowing you to contribute to the design."

"Yes." Kitty heaved a sigh. "But I'm forced to work with his grandson too, and he's terribly vexing."

Hazel arched a brow. "Is he?" Mr. Sandford's grandson was a strapping young lad and a few years older than Kitty.

Kitty stared at the toe of her slipper. "He mocked my idea to add scrollwork to the horse troughs. He said that they're meant to hold hay and slop, not flowers and champagne."

"Who says troughs can't be functional *and* beautiful?" Hazel said.

Kitty growled. "Drat. I wish I'd thought to say that."

Hazel shot her a sympathetic smile. "You can use it the next time someone dares to question your talent. Now, why don't you go upstairs and put your things away?"

Kitty nodded and headed toward door, then hesitated and turned around. "Miss Lively?"

Hazel looked up from her desk, expectant.

"I want to apologize for the way I acted that day in the cave."

Ah, yes. Hazel had done her best to forget Kitty's diatribe

during the paleontology lesson. "Thank you, Kitty. I accept your apology."

"You know," she mused, "I've lasted longer here than I have at any other school."

"Perhaps that's because Bellehaven Academy isn't like other schools."

Kitty rolled her vivid blue eyes as though she'd endured quite enough sentimentality for one day. "Truer words were never spoken," she quipped. She paused at the door and cast a genuine smile in Hazel's direction. "But I'm glad it's not."

Chapter 18

"You're lucky the Bluffs' Brew had a room for you," said Dunmire. The viscount sat at a table in the taproom across from Blade, idly swirling the ale in his glass.

"Luck had nothing to do with it," Blade grumbled. "I paid three times the usual rate."

Indeed, it seemed half of England had descended upon the small town for the sole purpose of witnessing the regatta tomorrow afternoon. But he had his own reasons for coming back to Bellehaven—just a week after his last visit.

"So who are you racing with?" Dunmire inquired.

Blade threw back his last swallow of ale. "I'm not racing," he said, firmly setting his pint glass on the worn tabletop.

The viscount narrowed his eyes and wagged a finger. "Playing your cards close to your chest, I see. Cunning, Bladenton. Very cunning."

"I'm not—never mind." There was no point in arguing with the viscount, who was as dim-witted as he was pompous. "Who's your partner?"

Dunmire grinned smugly. "Nathan Gutridge. Between my brains and his brawn, the other lads don't stand a chance."

"Right." Blade stood and slapped a few coins on the table.

"Best of luck. If you'll excuse me, I'm going to call it an evening."

"Already?" The viscount rubbed his chin, suspicious. "You know, all the sleep in the world won't help you defeat Gutridge and me."

Blade rolled his eyes. "The more you go on about the blasted race, the more I'm tempted to enter."

He was about to make his way out of the taproom when someone slapped him on the back.

"Bladenton. Welcome back."

Blade turned to find Gladwell standing beside him. "Doc," he said, inclining his head. "Nice to see you."

"Did I hear you're looking to enter the regatta? Turns out I need a partner."

Dunmire raised a brow. "What happened to Sutton?"

Gladwell shook his head. "Fell off a ladder today and dislocated his shoulder. I popped it back into place, but he'll be too stiff to row tomorrow." He poked an elbow in Blade's side. "What do you say?"

"I'm sure you can find someone else."

"I probably could," Gladwell said, nonchalant. "But we'd make a good team."

Blade raked a hand through his hair. "I'll think about it and let you know in the morning."

He'd come to Bellehaven for two reasons. First, because Kitty had written to tell him about a play she was performing at the boardinghouse tomorrow afternoon. In typical Kitty fashion, she'd complained about the endless rehearsals and amateur acting, but between the lines of her letter, he'd detected genuine enthusiasm. In any event, if the show was important enough for her to mention, it seemed as though he should be there to support her.

Second, he needed to talk to Hazel. He'd wanted to see

her tonight. The problem was that headmistresses didn't generally receive male visitors at nine o'clock in the evening. Or anytime, for that matter.

But damned if that would stop him from trying.

"Good night, gentlemen." He tipped his hat to Gladwell and Dunmire, then strode through the crowded bar and outside, into the balmy night.

Hazel opened her nightstand drawer and, for the third time that evening, searched the back corners. Her manual—the one with the rather scandalous engravings—was definitely not in that drawer. Nor was it in the chest at the foot of her bed or in the bottom of her armoire or anywhere else she'd looked in her little bedroom.

Oh God. She must have left it in her office. And although she was already in her nightgown, there was no way she'd be able to sleep until she assured herself that the book was in a safe location. She grabbed the dressing gown draped over her chair, stepped into her slippers, and—

Tap.

She froze and cocked an ear toward the window.

Tap, tap.

Odd, that. Perhaps a bird had perched on the sill, but there was a far more likely explanation. Namely, that the girls were up to something.

She tossed aside her dressing gown, turned down the lamp, and swept aside the curtains. As she peered through the windowpanes into the empty garden, a barrage of pebbles hit the glass.

Tap, tap, tap.

She quickly threw up the sash and leaned out. "Who's there?

"It's me." The voice, which ostensibly came from a bush,

sounded remarkably like Blade's. He stood up from behind the boxwood and gave a little wave. "Can you come down?" he asked in a stage whisper.

She craned her neck around to make sure no one was within earshot. "No," she said softly. "You shouldn't be here. How did you even know this was my room?"

"You said it was beneath the dormitory," he said proudly. "I took a chance."

"You took a risk," she corrected. "You weren't even supposed to be in Bellehaven this weekend."

"I wanted to talk to you." She couldn't see his face properly, but he sounded so vulnerable, so sincere, that her chest squeezed. How on earth was she supposed to move past her heartache when he kept saying daft, sweet things and making silly, romantic overtures? When he kept making her wish for things that could never be?

"It's late," she said. "And I have a very busy day tomorrow."

"I know about the regatta," he grumbled.

"And the girls are performing a play afterward."

"I heard. It was actually the inspiration for this visit. I was going to recite a few lines beneath your window, even though we both know I'm no Romeo."

She shook her head. "It doesn't matter. Nothing has changed. You and I are at an impasse."

"That may be true," he said. "But I can't help it if I want to be with you."

Her eyes burned with unshed tears, and she was grateful that the cloak of darkness kept Blade from seeing how torn she was. How close she was to running downstairs, taking his hand, and running off to a secluded cove where they could make love all night.

"I'm going to bed now," she said firmly.

"Hazel, wait." He stepped out from behind the bush, and

a beam of moonlight hit his face. Tiny leaves clung to his hair and rested on his shoulders. "Please," he whispered hoarsely, melting her insides like ice cream in July.

"We'll be at the docks for the regatta," she relented. "I'm sure Kitty would love for you to attend the play afterward."

"And you? Would you like it, too?" he asked, hopeful.

She choked back a sob. "Good night, Blade."

The crowd at the docks the next afternoon was even larger than Hazel had anticipated. Groups of spectators spanned the shore, contestants climbed into their boats, and the air buzzed with anticipation.

"I'd say this qualifies as a mad crush," Lucy said excitedly.

"Not as exciting as a ball," Kitty said drolly, "but beggars can't be choosers."

Hazel had walked to the inlet with her boarding students while Jane, who confessed she had no interest in the race, stayed behind to prepare for the performance later.

"If we should become separated," Hazel told the girls, "be sure to return home directly after the race. You'll need time to change into your costumes before the play."

"Oh, wait," Clara said. "I made something for each of you." She reached into her reticule and produced four scarves stitched together from colorful scraps of silk and satin.

"What are they for?" Lucy asked.

Clara passed the scarves around. "You wave them in the air and cheer as the boats race by."

Hazel ran hers over her palm, admiring the fine stiches and creative patchwork. "These are beautiful. Thank you, Clara."

"Let's test them out on the beach," Lucy cried. She grabbed Clara's hand and looked to Kitty. "Are you coming?"

"I'll catch up with you shortly."

As the girls raced toward the shore, Kitty's gaze flicked

across the faces in the crowd. Maybe she knew Blade was in town and was looking for him.

Hazel was doing her best *not* to look for him, and yet each time she saw a pair of broad shoulders, her belly did an odd little flip.

"Now that we have these"—Hazel flicked her scarf, letting it flutter in the breeze—"I suppose we should decide who we want to cheer for. Who would you like see win, Kitty?"

She twirled a long blond curl around her index finger, thoughtful. "Hmm. Perhaps Dr. Gladwell."

"Miss Lively!"

Hazel spun toward the harried female voice. "Poppy! How lovely to see you."

"Hullo." Poppy's freckled forehead creased as she rushed toward Hazel and Kitty. "Have you seen Dane?"

"Your brother?" Hazel shook her head. "No. But we only arrived a short time ago."

Poppy crossed her arms. "He didn't come home last night."

Hazel grimaced. Dane's reputation for mischief and mayhem was well established in Bellehaven. "Perhaps he stayed in town," she said. "I'm certain he'll turn up before long."

"You don't understand." She tapped her foot impatiently. "He was supposed to meet me here half an hour ago. So we could race."

Kitty gasped. "You're in the regatta?"

"We paid the entry fee—using most of my savings." Two spots of color stained Poppy's fair cheeks. "But I can't race by myself."

"We'll help you find him," Hazel said.

"He's probably passed out beneath a tree in someone's garden," Poppy muttered under her breath. "And of absolutely no use to me."

"Then we'll find you someone else to race with," Kitty said, matter-of-fact. She held a hand level to her brow and craned her neck. "There must be someone here who could row with you."

"No one will partner with me," Poppy said softly.

"Of course they will," Kitty said. "I've seen how you maneuver that fishing boat of yours. I'll bet you can row circles around anyone in the race."

Hazel didn't doubt it was true. Unfortunately, Poppy's skill was irrelevant to most of the people in the crowd—for two reasons.

First, because she was female.

Second, and perhaps more significant, because she was a fisherman's daughter.

A large-bellied, mustached man on the dock held a bullhorn to his mouth and announced, "All contestants must report to the dock immediately. The race begins in exactly ten minutes!"

"I was counting on that prize money to pay off my brother's debts." Poppy swiped at her eyes with the back of her hand. "I should have known better than to trust Dane."

Hazel swallowed. Knew what she had to do. "I'll race with you."

"You?" Poppy and Kitty cried in unison.

She shrugged. "I'm not the strongest rower, but I'm better than nobody."

"You'd do that for me?" Poppy asked softly.

"I'd be honored to be your partner." Hazel gave her arm an affectionate squeeze. "It's you who might question the wisdom of accepting my offer after you see how deplorable my rowing is."

Poppy chuckled then pressed a finger to her lips, contemplative. "Now that I think on it, there's someone else I know who handles the oars rather well."

"Who?" Hazel asked.

Poppy flicked her gaze to Kitty.

"Me?" Kitty asked, incredulous.

Poppy faced Hazel. "She helped me with the fishing nets a few mornings before her swimming lessons." To Kitty, she confessed, "I didn't want to give you a big head, but the truth is that you're a decent first mate. Er, first mistress."

Kitty spun toward Hazel, her blue eyes pleading. "May I do it, Miss Lively? Please?"

"Racers take your positions!" called the man with the bullhorn. "We begin in five minutes!"

Hazel nibbled her lip. A few short weeks ago, Kitty had been stranded in a boat; now she was begging to hop back in one. If Blade were here, the decision would be up to him. But Poppy and Kitty needed an answer now.

"Are you certain you want to do this? Your pretty gown could be well and ruined by the time you're done."

Kitty raised her chin. "I don't care about that. And you know I'm in good hands with Poppy."

"That's true." No harm would come to Kitty with Poppy and all the other contestants nearby. Her participation would, no doubt, raise some eyebrows, but Hazel refused to bow down to outdated notions regarding suitable activities for young women.

Kitty glanced back toward the docks. "So you'll let me?"

Hazel reached for the girl's hands and pressed them between her own. "Yes. But you must be careful. Promise me you'll listen to Poppy and stay seated so that we don't have to spend the rest of the afternoon fishing you out of the bay."

Kitty nodded solemnly. "I promise."

"One more thing." Hazel blew out a long breath.

"Yes?"

She looked earnestly at the pair of young women. "Win or lose, I couldn't be prouder of you both."

Poppy grinned and hooked an arm through Kitty's. "Come

on, then. Let's show the men of Bellehaven we can keep up with the best of them."

As they hurried toward the dock, Hazel called out, "The girls and I will be cheering for you!"

She wove her way through the throng just in time to watch as Poppy jumped into a boat and extended a hand to Kitty. Several onlookers gasped and snickered, but the pair of them held their heads high. They settled themselves on the benches, situated their oars in the rowlocks, and moved their boat into position alongside a dozen others.

An unnatural silence settled over the crowd as everyone waited for the race to begin, and Hazel held her breath.

"Kitty?" The voice, deep and eminently masculine, carried from the water to the shore, making Hazel's skin prickle with awareness. "Is that you?"

Good heavens. Blade was racing, too. He appeared to be partnered with Dr. Gladwell, just two boats away from Kitty and Poppy. And unless Hazel was mistaken, Lord Dunmire was in the boat between them, partnered with Nathan the barkeep.

"Uncle Beck?" Kitty called out, incredulous. "What are you doing in Bellehaven?"

Blade leaned forward to better see her and started to respond—

Just as the starting pistol fired.

The crack of gunfire echoed through the air.

Spectators erupted in raucous cheers.

The glass-like surface of the water turned frothy with the churning of forty-eight oars—and the annual Bellehaven Regatta was officially under way.

Chapter 19

For the love of—

Blade craned his neck to the left and blinked in disbelief.

Kitty, who normally turned up her nose at anything resembling physical activity, was sitting in a boat wrestling with a pair of heavy oars, while the fiery-haired woman on the bench behind her shouted directions.

What in the bloody hell was his niece up to? He and Hazel had already rescued her once, for crying out loud. Now she was going to risk her neck again *and* possibly make a spectacle of herself in front of the entire town.

"Come on, Bladenton," Gladwell called over his shoulder. "What's going on back there? We're already falling behind."

Sure enough, a few boats had pulled away from the pack. The blacksmith and stablemaster. Dunmire and Nathan. And, to the shock of everyone, Kitty and her partner.

Blade plunged his oars into the water and pulled them through, determined to make up for the slow start—and to keep an eye on Kitty in case anything went awry.

If and when her boat capsized, someone had to be ready to dive in and protect her from the small fleet coming up behind them. She could be struck in the head with an oar or the hull of a boat or—

· "You do realize this is a race?" the doctor shouted dryly. "At this rate, Dunmire and Nathan will row clear across the English Channel before we reach the finish line."

"Dunmire can bugger off for all I care," Blade grumbled.

Gladwell shot him a death glare. "Fine. But if it's all the same to you, I'd rather not lose to pair of young women."

Blade hazarded a glance in Kitty's direction and felt his chest swell. Her face was the picture of determination and concentration. She and her partner moved in perfect harmony, leaning into each stroke and pulling through with impressive grace. She was holding her own, and her boat was just a few lengths behind Dunmire's. "Watch it, Doc. You're talking about my niece."

But Blade wasn't keen on losing, either—especially not to the pretentious viscount. So he put his back into the next several strokes, and, before long, he and Gladwell were neck and neck with Kitty's boat. He looked over and gave her an encouraging nod, but she stared straight ahead, as though she feared the slightest break in her concentration might send her boat sailing directly into the reeds along the shore.

"Keep it up," the doctor shouted at Blade. "We're gaining on Dunmire."

Beads of sweat broke out on Blade's brow, and his forearms burned. Gladwell grunted with each stroke and cursed under his breath. But their efforts were paying off. They were creeping up on the viscount's stern. Nathan's shirt was soaked with sweat, and Dunmire's face was red as a radish.

"We'll pass them on the right," Blade said. There was more than enough room between the shore and Dunmire's boat, and the maneuver would place them in excellent position for the last stretch of the race. Kitty and her partner were a few lengths behind them now, away from the rest of the boats but keeping up their steady pace. With a little luck they'd finish in third place—an impressive feat.

Blade was vaguely aware of the crowd cheering, banners flying, and children running along the shore. But his sole focus was on winning, if only to prevent Dunmire from lording the silver cup over everyone at Lady Rufflebum's next dinner party.

He and the doc were only half a length behind now, poised to take the lead—until the bow of Dunmire's boat drifted right. Directly into their path.

"Look out," Gladwell warned. "We're coming up."

"No, you're not." The viscount's boat lurched farther to the right.

Nathan threw down his oars in disgust. "What the devil are you doing, Dunmire?"

Before the viscount could answer, the boats collided. The oars clashed. The hulls ran aground.

"Damn it!" Their boat was wedged between Dunmire's on one side and the mucky shore on the other. Blade swatted the long reeds away from his face. "Push us backward, Doc."

Gladwell knelt over the bow and tried to shove off the bank, but the boat wouldn't budge.

"Unfortunate," the viscount taunted. "There's no telling how long you'll be stuck in the silt."

To Blade's left, Kitty and her partner rowed furiously, slipping into first place. Despite his predicament, his heart squeezed in his chest. Kitty needed someone to believe in her, and that someone should be him. By God, it *was* him.

Dunmire frowned as the girls glided by. He jammed his oar between the hulls, clearly intending to push off, dislodge his boat, and retake the lead. "Excuse us, gentlemen. We have a race to win."

Blade scoffed. "You'll never catch them."

"You never know. We might inadvertently clip the side of their boat, too."

"The hell you will." Blade wrested the oar from Dunmire's hand, yanked it out of the rowlock, and—to the shock of the spectators above them on the shore—pitched the oar into a bunch of cattails.

"You bastard," Dunmire spat.

On the bank, the ladies gasped beneath their parasols.

"Better a bastard than a cheat," Blade quipped.

Doc held out a palm. "Easy, now."

Dunmire stood up in his boat, puffed out his chest, and glared.

Nathan tugged on the viscount's arm. "You two can discuss this later tonight over a pint at the Mermaid. Now sit down and cool off."

The barkeep was right. Blade's head told him the regatta was no place for a fight, but Dunmire could only push him so far.

"You should not have impugned my honor," the viscount said haughtily.

Blade snorted. "*You* should not have behaved like an arse."

Dunmire lunged at him, Blade grabbed him by the lapels, and they both tumbled overboard, thrashing in the knee-deep water.

They rolled in the muck, punching, wrestling, and cursing until Doc and Nathan hopped into the water and pried them apart.

Gladwell hooked Blade's arms behind his back and hoisted him to his feet. He stood there, dripping and panting, wondering how in hell a damned regatta had ended in a mud fight.

In the distance, the crowd erupted in cheers.

Kitty. She'd done it.

Blade broke free, splashed his way through the reeds, and climbed onto the shore. He ran toward the tents and large dais that had been set up near the finish line.

He wasn't certain what drove him or why he was so determined to see Kitty lift the silver cup. He only knew he needed to be there, and nothing—not his drenched clothes nor burgeoning black eye—was going to keep him away.

Hazel, Lucy, and Clara stood near the dais, shouting and waving their colorful scarves.

"I can't believe it!" Lucy jumped up and down. "They won!"

Clara beamed. "I'm not surprised."

Hazel could barely contain her happiness as Poppy and Kitty climbed out of their boat and onto the pier, waving triumphantly to the scores of spectators lining the path to the dais. As soon as Kitty saw Hazel, Lucy, and Clara, she ran over and threw her arms around them.

"My whole body is shaking," Kitty confessed. "I didn't think I could keep going, but I couldn't disappoint Poppy. I can't believe we won."

"We all believed in you," Clara said confidently.

Kitty arched a brow. "Even Miss Lively?"

Hazel opened her mouth to respond, but a deep voice beat her to it.

"No one cheered louder than Miss Lively."

"Uncle Beck!" Kitty's face lit up, and she clung to him, heedless of his sopping shirt and waistcoat.

Hazel blinked. Apparently, Blade had been dragged through mud and dusted with sand. A small cut above his brow was smeared with blood. He was utterly disheveled and disreputable.

But he'd never looked better to Hazel.

The tender, slightly awkward way he patted Kitty's back melted Hazel's insides. Somehow, he'd guessed that his niece needed her family there. He'd known that this wonderful, victorious moment in her young life would make her miss her parents in the worst way. That her joy would be tinged with sadness—because the people she loved most weren't there to share it.

Poppy rushed over, and Hazel hugged her. "Congratulations! I'm so delighted for you."

"I couldn't have done it without Kitty." Poppy wiped her brow with her sleeve. "She saved my skin—and my brother's. Because if I lost the race due to Dane's carelessness, I would have murdered him."

"Thank goodness it didn't come to that," Hazel teased. "Look, it's time for the award ceremony. You and Kitty must go."

Lucy and Clara followed the winners to the edge of the dais. Hazel stayed back, and Blade remained at her side while Mr. Martin, Bellehaven's mayor, formally presented the cup to Poppy and Kitty. Hazel *was* listening to all the kind things the mayor said, truly she was.

But she was understandably distracted by Blade's closeness. In her defense, his shirt was plastered to his arms and chest. His trousers were painted on his buttocks and thighs.

Heat rolled off his body, enveloping her in flames.

He shifted, moved nearer, and let his fingers surreptitiously caress the inside of her wrist.

Doing her level best to appear unaffected, she whispered, "I must assume that at some point during the regatta, you were attacked by pirates and forced to walk the plank. I can think of no other plausible explanation for your current state of disarray."

"You like me this way," he drawled, his breath tickling her ear.

"Like you've emerged from a swamp?"

"No. A bit dirty." His finger slid up her forearm, and her heart tripped in her chest. "But never fear. I'll make myself presentable before the play, and after . . ."

"After?"

"Perhaps we can spend some time together," he whispered. "Alone."

She swayed on her feet, barely resisting the urge to lean into him. "Perhaps."

Maybe she'd been too hasty in refusing Blade's proposal. True, he'd still not said anything of love, but his actions told her plenty. He'd come to Bellehaven of his own accord. He'd stood beneath her window last night. He'd been here for Kitty. Those things felt an awful lot like love, and a seedling of hope sprouted in her chest.

Meanwhile, on the stage, Polly and Kitty each held a handle on a silver cup and raised it between them, triumphant. The crowd broke out in applause; Blade and Hazel joined in. For once, everything was going her way. Indeed, it seemed everything was right with the world.

"Bladenton. I've been looking all over for you." The woman's voice was cultured, smooth, and sultry.

Blade stiffened. "Penelope. What are you doing in Bellehaven?"

An icy chill dripped down Hazel's spine.

"I should think it would be obvious," the stunning woman replied. All that Kitty had said about Lady Penelope was true, from her angel-like features to her fashionable gown to her unmistakable air of sophistication.

"When I heard you'd made the trip to Bellehaven," Penelope continued, "I decided I simply must come and witness the renowned regatta for myself. I must say, it did not disappoint."

"I wish you had told me," Blade said.

"And ruin the surprise? Never." Penelope smiled a bit too widely. "Aren't you going to introduce me to your companion?"

Blade rolled his shoulders as if doing so might help him

recover his manners. "Lady Penelope, this is Miss Lively, headmistress of the Bellehaven Academy of Deportment."

Hazel winced. He could have introduced her as a friend or even an acquaintance, but he'd gone with headmistress. Telling, that.

The woman's eyes widened. "You're Kitty's teacher. A pleasure to meet you, Miss Lively."

Hazel inclined her head. "The pleasure is mine."

"Bladenton tells me you've done wonders for our Kitty."

Blade shot Penelope a pointed, slightly skeptical glance.

"Forgive me. I confess I have already begun to think of her as my daughter." Penelope shot Hazel a conspiratorial glance. "After all, it will be official in a few months' time— once we're married."

Hazel waited for Blade to deny it, but he didn't.

As the silence stretched between them, her legs went numb below the knees.

Kitty hopped off the dais and scampered toward Blade. "Uncle Beck! Did you—" Upon spotting Penelope, she drew up short. "I hadn't realized you were coming to Belle-haven."

Penelope clucked her tongue and smoothed an errant lock of Kitty's hair into place. "The important thing is that I'm here—and I was fortunate enough to witness your historic victory. Well done, my dear."

Blade rubbed the back of his neck. "Penelope, I realize you've come a long way, but I cannot entertain you this after-noon. I'm attending a play at Kitty's school."

Penelope arched an elegant brow and narrowed her eyes at Kitty. "How intriguing. You must tell me more."

"We're performing scenes from *Romeo and Juliet*," Kitty said, but some of her earlier jubilation had faded. "We've been rehearsing all week with Miss Lively."

"*Romeo and Juliet*," Penelope mused. "Your headmistress

must have a romantic streak." She turned, unleashing the full force of her gaze on Hazel.

"It's not so much a romance as a tragedy," she said absently. She was still wondering how Blade could move on so quickly after their night together. Still grappling with the realization that she was speaking to the woman who would soon be his . . . wife.

"Clearly, I am in need of a refresher on Shakespearean plays." Penelope stared at Hazel, her face expectant.

Blast. She was fishing for an invitation, and Hazel had little choice but to extend one. "Of course, you are welcome to join us for the performance."

Blade frowned. "I don't think—"

"How kind of you, Miss Lively," Lady Penelope interjected. "I should be delighted to attend."

Chapter 20

"Ladies and gentlemen," Prudence announced, "welcome to Bellehaven Academy's first annual theater production."

The audience—which included Blade, Lady Penelope, a few parents, five ladies staying at the boardinghouse, and Mrs. Paxton—applauded enthusiastically. Only Harold appeared bored at the outset. He purred and yawned on Mrs. Paxton's lap, looking very dapper in the waistcoat that Clara had sewn for him.

With the girls' help, Hazel and Jane had transformed the schoolroom into a proper theater. They'd stacked the desks in the rear of the room, covered them with sheets, and arranged the chairs in a neat semicircle in front of a makeshift stage. Kitty's fanciful backdrop transported them to a medieval Italian village, and Clara's clever costumes allowed each of the girls to switch between multiple roles.

Any nervousness that the young actresses felt seemed to quickly dissipate. Lucy executed a perfect cartwheel before being mortally wounded and shouting, "A plague on both your houses." The audience clearly approved of the girls' dramatic interpretation, and by all accounts, the play was proving to be a smashing success.

Hazel watched from backstage, but, in truth, *she* was the

consummate actress. Pretending to be strong and confident. Happy and content.

In truth, she was a trembling mess.

Blade and Penelope sat next to each other in the first row. All of the guests assumed they were courting—and why wouldn't they? Lady Penelope had been born to play the part of a countess. With a simple swish of her skirts, she could command the attention of a room. With a mere toss of her head, she could attract every bachelor within miles.

Evidently, the bachelor she'd set her sights on was Blade.

"Bravo! Bravo!" Lady Penelope cried as the girls took their bows. Blade clapped and smiled broadly. Some of women dabbed at their eyes with handkerchiefs.

When the applause subsided, Prue stepped to the front of the makeshift stage. "Thank you all for attending our debut performance. Now we'd be delighted if you'd join us for tea in the dining room."

The parents and guests chatted animatedly as they filed out of the classroom; Jane and the girls followed suit. Only Blade and Lady Penelope lingered behind with Hazel, and she wondered if the afternoon could possibly become more awkward.

Penelope snaked her arm around Blade's and looked up at him, adoring. "Shall we make an appearance at the tea?"

"You go on," he said. "I was hoping to have a word with Miss Lively."

Penelope sniffed. "Then perhaps I shall return to the mayor's house and rest for a bit. I trust I'll see you at his dinner party tonight?"

Blade flicked his gaze to Hazel, then back to Penelope. "I'll see you there."

Her lips curled into a small but triumphant smile as she faced Hazel. "We are so grateful for all you've done for Kitty, but I think it's safe to say that she'll be returning to London after the summer. So in case we don't meet again, I wish you all the best with your school." With that, she glided out of the room, as graceful and icy as a skater at the frost fair.

Blade waited till they were alone and cursed under his breath. "I'm sorry about that. I didn't know Penelope was coming to Bellehaven. I'm shocked she did."

Hazel steeled her spine. "I only want to know if it's true."

"I have no intention of un-enrolling Kitty," he said firmly.

She shook her head. "Not that. The part where she said that you'd be married in a few months."

"Nothing has been set in stone," he said, frowning. "Yes, we discussed the possibility of marriage, but things changed when I met you."

"You're saying you don't have an understanding with Penelope?"

He dragged a hand through his hair. "Look, I asked you to marry me. Practically begged. You said no. As it turns out, she's my next best option, unless . . . you've reconsidered."

Hazel sank into one of the front-row chairs, and he sat beside her, so close that she could see the golden flecks in his eyes and the light stubble on his chin. "When we were on the beach today, celebrating Kitty's win, I realized two things," she said.

He reached for her hand and laced his fingers with hers, encouraging her to go on.

"First, that her victory was sweeter because you were there to see it."

"That's good, right?"

"Yes, but then Penelope arrived. When she said you were to be married, I thought my chest would crack open. That's when I realized the second thing—that I would never be content with less than your whole heart. Call me stubborn if you like, but there are certain things I refuse to compromise on—and one of them is love."

At the mention of the word, he flinched as though he'd stepped on a hot coal. "Love is what broke me. What almost killed me. We're both better off without it."

"I disagree. I think love could heal you—if you'd let it."

"You make it sound as though I have a choice in the matter."

"Don't you?"

"Not really." He rubbed his chest as if it ached. "It's a wasteland in here, Hazel. Trust me when I tell you I'm damaged."

"So you've said." She knew he was thinking about the mysterious Eliza. The girl who had once possessed his heart. The girl who'd thrown it away.

"You don't believe me?" His eyes searched hers, imploring.

"I think you feel more than you acknowledge."

"Maybe I do." He lifted her hand and pressed a kiss to the back, sending a frisson of pleasure through her body.

Every nerve ending in her body tingled with longing, with the desire to lean in and press her lips to his. "I must go. The parents, the girls . . . they're expecting me."

"Meet me later?"

She arched a brow. "I believe you have a dinner party to attend."

"I'll send my regrets. I want to see you," he said, his eyes imploring.

"I cannot meet you." She stood and smoothed her skirts, grateful that she'd located one last shred of common sense. "We've each made our choice. Now we must move on."

"Move on," he repeated flatly.

"Yes," she said, resolute.

He let out a long sigh. "I have some business in London, so I need to depart first thing in the morning. Will you tell Kitty I said goodbye and that I'll visit her again next week?"

"Of course."

"And perhaps you and I can talk as well?"

"I don't think we should." Her eyes brimmed with regret. "It's over, Blade."

He stared at her, clearly skeptical. "If you should need me, for anything, all you must do is say the word and I'll be on your doorstep. However, I won't press you further. No more hiding beneath your bed, no more throwing pebbles at your window."

"Thank you," she said, even as an unexpected wave of sadness swept over her. Life before Blade had been so predictable and proper—and now it would be again.

"This is it, then?"

Not trusting herself to speak, she nodded.

He backed away slowly, till their outstretched fingertips parted.

"I hope you find everything you seek. Happiness, family, love . . . you deserve all of it." He walked to the door and took one last look back. His expression was tormented, his voice suspiciously raspy. "Goodbye, Hazel," he said—and then he was gone.

She swallowed the goose egg in her throat and pinched the bridge of her nose so she wouldn't cry. Not now. Later, there'd be time for tears—after she'd thanked the parents and other audience members, after she'd sorted out her classroom and stored the sets and costumes.

Fortunately, she was something of an expert at bottling up pain and anguish. She could pour it all in, stick a cork in the top, and no one would know she'd just sent away the only person in the world who'd had a true glimpse of who she genuinely was.

The trick was tucking those feelings away. Not giving them too much time or space.

If she let a sniffle turn into a sob, she'd be done for, so

she went about her business, folding costumes and picking up props. She walked to the open window, breathed in a few gulps of ocean air, and smoothed a stray tendril behind her ear.

There. She was ready to face Jane, the girls, and their parents.

When she reached Mrs. Paxton's dining room, Hazel found her students engaged in a lively discussion about Lady Rufflebum's upcoming summer ball.

"It's the biggest event of the season," Prue explained to the other girls. "Ball gowns, dancing, champagne . . . The countess invites all the townspeople, and Mama says I'm old enough to go this year."

Mrs. Covington clucked her tongue. "You're old enough to attend, but you're *not* old enough for champagne."

Prue frowned and crossed her arms with a playful pout.

"I'd give anything to be in a room full of ball gowns," Clara said dreamily.

Upon seeing Hazel, Lucy piped up. "Miss Lively, will Kitty, Clara, and I be permitted to attend Lady Rufflebum's ball?"

Hazel pasted on a smile. "The countess was kind enough to extend an invitation to us, so . . . yes."

The girls erupted in cheers, causing Mrs. Paxton to jostle her teacup. "Young ladies," she scolded. "Please. A little decorum."

Oh dear. Hazel shot the girls a subtle but clear warning look. "You're quite right, Mrs. Paxton. Girls, perhaps one of you could check on Harold and offer him a treat."

Somewhat mollified, Mrs. Paxton redirected her attention to a scone. Relieved to have averted a potential crisis, Hazel sat down and poured herself a cup of tea. As she added a splash of cream, Mrs. Covington leaned across the table and addressed her in a stage whisper. "Miss Lively, I wondered if I might have a word?"

Alarms sounded in Hazel's head, but she attempted a serene smile. "Of course. What did you wish to discuss?"

"Perhaps we should remove ourselves to your office."

Hazel's teacup froze halfway to her mouth. "Certainly."

She returned the teacup to the saucer, led the way down the corridor, and schooled her expression into one of polite interest rather than panicked dread.

"I do hope you enjoyed the performance," Hazel said conversationally as they walked through the antechamber. "Prue showed tremendous poise and versatility playing the roles of Friar Laurence and Lady Capulet."

"The play was well done." Mrs. Covington followed Hazel into the office and sat in a chair opposite her. "But it's not the play I wish to discuss."

"No, I didn't think so," Hazel admitted. "What is on your mind?"

"The regatta this morning." Her nose wrinkled as though she'd caught a whiff of a dead fish on the beach. "Kitty may be the niece of a viscount, but I found her participation in the event most unbecoming. Abominably un-lady-like. It reflected quite poorly on her—and it didn't do your school any favors."

"With all due respect, Mrs. Covington, I disagree. Kitty showed athleticism, courage, and grace. Those are admirable qualities in a lady or gentleman."

"It was a gauche display." Mrs. Covington pursed her lips. "No rich, titled man is interested in pursuing a young woman who can best him in a rowing competition. Surely, you can understand that."

"I'll admit there may be some gentlemen who feel threatened by a woman who is independent and confident. However, those sorts of men deserve neither our time nor attention. If and when my students choose to marry, I expect they'll do very well for themselves."

"If and when . . . ?" Mrs. Covington shook her head as if she couldn't quite believe her ears. "Prue *will* marry, and I will insist on a good match. Whether we like it or not, Miss Lively, a woman's entire future hinges on her selection of a husband: her wealth, social standing, and security. I won't apologize for wanting those things for my daughter."

"I would never ask you to," Hazel said. "And I don't think that Prue's education here at Bellehaven Academy is at odds with those goals."

"I'm afraid I disagree." Mrs. Covington's eyes were one part exasperation, one part regret. "I must protect Prudence's reputation, and that means making sure that she only associates with young ladies who are . . . on a path similar to hers."

Hazel blinked. "I don't understand."

Mrs. Covington squirmed in her seat. "Lucy and Clara are darling girls, but they have no family to speak of. They will be lucky to marry decent, working-class men who can provide for their basic needs."

Hazel's blood went from a simmer to a boil in two seconds flat. She gripped the arms of her chair. "Lucy and Clara are wonderful students and dear friends to Prue, but they have nothing to do with her prospects."

Mrs. Covington sighed. "I should not be surprised that you are uninformed about the workings of the marriage mart. You are a sp—er, unmarried, after all."

"That is true," Hazel ground out. "I've never had a season in London or received a voucher to Almack's. But I *do* know something of survival and strength of character. Life sometimes takes us in unexpected directions, and we must be equipped to deal with those twists and turns."

"I will not allow my daughter to be subjected to the whims of fate, Miss Lively. Indeed, from the moment she took her first breath, I have dedicated myself to securing an outstanding match for her. Every decision I've made has been guided by this purpose, and since it appears that Bellehaven Academy's mission isn't aligned with my own, well . . ." Mrs. Covington stood and swallowed. "I'm withdrawing Prudence immediately. I must insist that she cut all ties to your other students—and Kitty in particular—as I believe a clean break will be easier for her."

Oh no. Panic numbed Hazel's fingertips. "Please, don't do this. It would break Prue's heart if she couldn't remain friends with the other girls."

"I know what's best for my daughter," Mrs. Covington said sharply. "Sadly, it is neither your fledgling establishment nor the unruly young women in your unconventional classroom. Good day to you." With that, she swept out of Hazel's office, leaving a trail of cloyingly sweet perfume in her wake.

Dear Jesus, what was happening? Prue had just begun to emerge from her shell, to find her confidence and courage. And now she was leaving Bellehaven Academy, forbidden from consorting with Hazel's other students.

It would be devastating for Prue.

And equally devastating for the school.

It was only a matter of time before Beatrice's and Winnie's parents started to question whether Bellehaven Academy was a suitable fit for their daughters. If they were to leave, Hazel would have no way of keeping the school afloat. More importantly, she'd have no means of supporting Lucy and Clara.

She'd be forced to close Bellehaven Academy's doors, take Lucy and Clara to London, and seek employment there. Perhaps she'd find a governess position—one that would allow her to bring the girls with her.

But the odds were not in her favor, dash it all.

She pushed herself out of her chair and rubbed the back of her neck as she paced the length of her office. She simply *had* to make Mrs. Covington reconsider. But changing her mind was going to take more than smooth words and vague promises. What Hazel needed was the backing of someone who was part of society's elite. A London insider who would vouch for her and assure Mrs. Covington that Bellehaven Academy would adequately prepare Prue to take her place among the ton. But it wasn't as though she was very well connected. Lady Rufflebum was a bit too fickle for Hazel to rely on, and she didn't know any fashionable titled women, apart from—

Gads. She froze mid-step and shivered. There *was* one person who could save her school and her girls. Hazel would have to swallow her pride, but it was her only chance at appeasing Mrs. Covington. The only way to ensure Lucy and Clara stayed out of the foundling home.

Hazel needed Lady Penelope to intervene. To offer to introduce Prue to a few esteemed members of her inner circle over the course of her first season. To ensure she made a favorable impression among the elite. Surely, the enticement of Lady Penelope's sponsorship of Prue would be impossible for Mrs. Covington to resist, regardless of her misgivings about Bellehaven Academy.

But Hazel didn't know her nearly well enough to prevail upon her for such a grand favor. No, the only chance of securing her assistance would be through Blade.

Which meant that Hazel would need to ask him to intercede, just when she was trying to move forward. Worse, it meant she would be indebted to Blade's future wife.

Hazel fought back a wave of nausea. But the truth was that Lady Penelope was Bellehaven Academy's best chance for survival, and if Hazel wanted Prue back in her classroom she had to act quickly.

She had to seek out Blade—tonight.

Chapter 21

Blade stepped out of the mayor's town house and jogged down the steps, gulping in the humid night air. The dinner party hadn't been as onerous as he'd anticipated. A dozen or so of Bellehaven's esteemed residents and assorted visitors from London had enjoyed several courses of expertly prepared food and multiple bottles of perfectly aged wine.

The mood had been festive, the conversation uncomplicated. He'd endured a bit of small talk about the state of the roads to and from London, the size of the mackerel this season, and, of course, plans to attend Lady Rufflebum's ball. Time slipped by, and long before the pineapple ice cream was served, Penelope had succeeded in charming everyone seated around the table, impressing them with her beauty and wit. Indeed, if there were such a thing as auditions for countesses, she would have been awarded the part on the spot.

He supposed it was a glimpse of what his future would be like. Elegant. Comfortable. Blissfully boring.

Life with Hazel would have been exactly the opposite. So why did he still long for it—and her? Saying goodbye to her had felt like extracting his heart from his chest and leaving it beating in her hands.

Maybe it was the after-dinner brandy that made him think about going to her, promises be damned. But he'd seen the torment in her eyes that afternoon. Known he was responsible for it. And he didn't want to hurt her more than he already had.

So he strolled down the quiet lane, forcing his feet to move in the direction of the Bluffs' Brew Inn. It was only a few blocks away, and, if he was lucky, the walk would clear his thoughts, which were currently muddled by haunting brown eyes, delectable lips, and a single rebellious curl.

He muttered a curse to himself, and, behind him, a shrub rustled, causing the skin on the back of his neck to prickle. He paused in front of a dark garden. Glanced up and down the deserted road.

Bellehaven wasn't exactly known for having pickpockets or hoodlums roaming its streets, but Blade's instincts told him he wasn't alone. Maybe Dunmire was looking to pick a fight after the regatta.

"Stop skulking behind the bushes and show yourself," Blade challenged.

There was a bit more rustling from the garden—then a figure, clad entirely in charcoal gray, stepped out from behind the hedge and slowly pushed back the hood of a cloak. "It's me."

"Hazel?" His entire body thrummed.

She raised a finger to her lips and quickly surveyed their surroundings. "We shouldn't be seen together out here. It would be difficult to explain."

"Agreed," he said, lowering his voice. "And yet, here we are. It can't be coincidence that you were hiding in a garden near the mayor's house."

"No. I needed to speak with you." There was an urgency, an edge to her voice that made his spine tingle.

"Are you all right? Has something happened?"

She would not meet his gaze. "Let's move away from the street before someone walks by."

"I didn't bring my coach," he said, scratching the back of his head.

"Follow me." She slipped on her hood, walked a bit farther down the lane, then led him onto a deserted footpath in the direction of the beach.

The moonlight illuminated the path, which twisted through chest-high grass. "Be careful you don't trip over a piece of driftwood."

"You needn't worry," she assured him. "We're almost to the beach."

As they walked, the rumble of the waves grew louder, the breeze off the ocean blew stronger, and Blade's sense of unease increased. Hazel wouldn't have risked meeting him like this unless she was in some sort of trouble—and that knowledge awoke an odd, fiercely protective streak inside him.

"Here we are," she said. They left the dunes and stepped onto a wide stretch of sand where it seemed as though they were the last two souls on earth. She faced him, shrugged off her hood, and swallowed. "Forgive me for sneaking up on you earlier. I didn't know how else to reach you."

"I'm glad you found me," he assured her. "Tell me what's wrong."

"Everything." Several strands of hair flew free from their pins and whipped at her cheeks. "But I might know a way to fix it."

He pointed at a pair of large boulders several yards away. "Let's sit over there, where you'll be sheltered from the wind—and we can talk properly." He slipped an arm around her shoulders, guided her to the far side of the rocks, and smoothed a spot of sand for her to sit.

She shot him a grateful smile. "This is better."

He reached for her hand and gave it a squeeze. Resisted the urge to haul her against him and kiss her senseless. "I'm listening."

She heaved a long sigh. "I require a favor. I hate to even ask you, but I am at loose ends."

He placed his palms on either side of her face and looked deep into her eyes. "Whatever is troubling you, we will face it together. Tell me what I can do."

"I appreciate your willingness to help. But this involves Lady Penelope, too."

Bloody hell. "How so?"

"I was hoping she could speak to Mrs. Covington. She withdrew Prue from Bellehaven Academy this afternoon."

"Why the devil would she do that? Prue seems perfectly happy. Kitty claims she's the cleverest girl of the bunch."

"Mrs. Covington fears that friendships with my girls will hamper Prue's chances of reaching the upper echelons of society—and though I hate to admit it, she may have a point."

Blade scoffed. "She threatened to pull Prudence out once before and changed her mind. Perhaps she will again."

"No," Hazel said, firm. "She was adamant that Prue have nothing more to do with Bellehaven Academy or any of my students."

"That seems cruel." He scratched the stubble on his jaw. "I assume Mrs. Covington didn't approve of Kitty's participation in the regatta today."

"She did not," Hazel confirmed. "And she thinks that flouting expectations about what it means to be a gently bred young lady reflects poorly on my school."

"Then she is even more of a closed-minded twit than I suspected," Blade said. "She will rue the day she walked away from Bellehaven Academy."

"I don't think you understand. It would take but a few

disparaging remarks from Mrs. Covington to completely un-
dermine my school's reputation. Once other prominent families learn of her dissatisfaction, they will want nothing to
do with Bellehaven Academy—or me. It is only a matter of
time before Beatrice's and Winnie's families pull them from
my classroom as well."

"How does Penelope figure into all of this?" he asked
warily.

"She is everything that Mrs. Covington wishes Prue to
be. If Lady Penelope vouched for my school and perhaps offered to introduce Prue into polite society—I feel certain
Mrs. Covington would reverse course."

He mumbled a curse. Involving Penelope was a bad idea
for at least two reasons. First, she viewed Hazel as a threat.
Second, she would expect something in return. "I could speak
to some acquaintances in London. Encourage them to enroll
their younger sisters and daughters."

Hazel shook her head. "It's too close to the end of the summer. Families don't move to Bellehaven at this time of year,
and by springtime it will be too late. I doubt my school will
survive the winter months."

"I could invest in Bellehaven Academy," he offered. "And
be a partner of sorts."

"That's incredibly kind of you," Hazel said. "But I don't
want to be financially dependent on anyone."

Her refusal was a subtle stab in his heart. "I'm not *anyone*. I'm your friend."

Hazel gazed at him, her expression apologetic. "Our past
would make any partnership between us terribly complicated. I am trying to move forward. You intend to marry
Lady Penelope."

Her words hung in the air, and though he longed to swat
them away, he couldn't—at least not in good conscience.

So for several heartbeats they sat in silence. Pale moonlight illuminated her beautiful face, and he tried to etch the image in his head, even as he knew his memory could never do it justice.

"There is another solution," he said soberly. "I could take Kitty back to London with me. If she were gone, maybe you could convince Mrs. Covington to re-enroll Prue."

"Absolutely not," Hazel said, adamant. "This is Kitty's home. She needs Bellehaven Academy, and honestly, we need her. I refuse to sacrifice one student for the sake of the whole. Families don't work that way. Besides, even if I succeeded in saving my business, I'd be losing the heart of what makes it special."

"I know what your school means to you, and I know you're not fond of compromising. But there's more than your future at stake. You have Clara and Lucy to consider as well."

"Yes, I—" She blinked. "You know their names?"

"How could I not?" Blade shrugged. "Kitty's constantly talking about them. She wants Clara to design a ball gown for her and swears Lucy could scale any cliff in Bellehaven using only her hands and feet."

"I do hope she's not planning to try," Hazel mumbled to herself before shaking her head. "I shall find a way to take care of her and Clara, no matter what happens," she vowed.

"I know you will." He dragged a hand through his hair and blew out a long breath. "If you are certain you want me to ask for Penelope's assistance, I'll speak to her before I return to London in the morning."

"I honestly believe Penelope is my only chance."

"A rather sobering thought."

"Do you think you can persuade her to agree?"

"I'll find a way," he assured her. In return, Penelope might demand that he procure a special license or whisk her away to Gretna Green. But Hazel's school meant everything to her. Oddly enough, that made it of the utmost importance to him—and he wouldn't fail her.

"Thank you." Hazel felt as though an enormous weight had been lifted off her chest. "I truly believe that once I make it past this little bump in the road, Bellehaven Academy will be a roaring success."

"I don't doubt it."

His faith in her made her happy and sad at the same time. It was odd—tragic, really—that he could believe in her so completely and still not believe in *them*.

"Thank you for understanding and interceding on my behalf." She shot him a half smile. "I promise you needn't worry about me popping out of every shrub you pass on the street."

Blade said nothing but stared at her with such a hot, raw intensity that her belly flipped and her knees went weak.

"You, Hazel Lively, are welcome to sneak up on me anytime you wish."

Oh God. A telltale pulsing started between her legs, and she was suddenly unbearably hot. She tugged the drawstring of her cloak free and shrugged it off.

He frowned and placed a large hand at her nape, sending delicious tingles through her limbs. "Are you feeling well?"

"Yes," she said, fully aware that her chest was heaving like she'd swum from one side of the bay to the other. "The problem is . . . that when you look at me in that particular *hungry* sort of way . . ."

His eyelids lowered and his nostrils flared. "You feel . . . aroused."

She pressed her knees together in a futile attempt to stop the pulsing. "Yes."

Somehow, his gaze grew even hotter. "There's a way to ease the ache, you know."

"I do know. I'm afraid I recall it all too well." Indeed, every time she closed her eyes, her head filled with visions of Blade hauling his shirt over his head, covering her body with his, and moving inside her till she shattered from the pure pleasure of it all. "But I, er, we, should not—cannot—do it again."

"While I would very much like to make love to you," he said gruffly, "I'm not talking about that." His hand drifted down her back, and his wicked fingers rubbed a small circle at the base of her spine.

"What, then?" She nibbled her lip, perplexed. "Kissing?"

His gaze dropped to her mouth. "No, although I'm inordinately fond of that, too."

"I don't understand." All she knew was that she wanted to straddle him—and that she shouldn't.

He leaned closer and brushed his lips across her cheek. "You can give yourself pleasure."

Oh.

"Would you like to try?"

"Yes," she breathed. "I believe I would."

Chapter 22

Blade spread Hazel's cloak on the sand, crawled to the center of it, and beckoned her with a smile. "Come, sit with me."

She sank onto the blanket, facing him expectantly.

"Take off your slippers." The rich, deep timbre of his voice made her nerve endings buzz with anticipation.

"You're doing it again," she said a little breathlessly, tossing her slippers aside. "You're looking at me as though you can see right through my clothes. That expression on your face—I don't know how or why, but it makes my corset feel two sizes too tight."

"We can certainly fix that." He turned her around, deliberately untied the back of her gown, and slowly loosened the laces of her corset. "Better?" he whispered.

"Much." His fingertips skimmed across her shoulders, tugging her sleeves down her arms; his lips lingered in the crook of her neck, lightly sucking her sensitive skin.

"Lean back against my chest," he said.

She moved closer, till her bottom pressed against his hard length and her hips were nestled between his muscular, outstretched legs. He pulled the neckline of her gown lower and lower, till her breasts were exposed to the cool night air.

"Blade," she breathed. "I didn't intend for this to happen to-night. I haven't changed my mind about us."

"I know." His fingertips trailed the length of her arms. "But perhaps, one night, while you're lying in your bed, you'll think of me . . . and do this."

She looked over her shoulder at his face, which was impossibly handsome in spite of his black eye. "Do what, precisely?"

"Whatever feels good." He growled and nipped at her lobe.

Tentatively, she swept a palm up her belly, between her breasts. Her skin tingled like she'd splashed it with cool water. "Like this?"

"A very good start." He licked the shell of her ear. "But I think you can do better."

"I shall try." She raked her nails lightly over the swells of her breasts and teased the undersides till the peaks grew painfully taut.

"That's it," he rasped. "Are you ready for more?"

"Mmm." She arched her back, surrendering to the lovely sensations she'd stirred in herself. "What did you have in mind?"

Blade growled and pressed a soothing kiss to her temple. "Lift the hem of your gown."

If someone had told her that morning that she'd even consider such a thing, she'd have assumed they'd just staggered out of the Salty Mermaid. But there she was, feeling wonderfully wicked as she leaned forward, lifted her skirts over her bent knees, and let the smooth fabric glide down her thighs.

He trailed molten kisses down her neck and across her shoulder, setting her blood on fire. "Now part your knees."

She hesitated, and he brushed the loose tendrils away from her face. "You needn't do anything you don't want to. But you can ease the ache if you wish. There's nothing wicked about it."

"I daresay it's a *little* improper," she breathed. "But maybe proper behavior does need the occasional holiday."

"My sentiments exactly." He chuckled as he slid his palms around her waist and hauled her against his chest.

She closed her eyes, parted her knees, and sighed as the breeze kissed her bare skin. It was lovely, but she still longed to lie with him as she had before. She craved the closeness, the connection, the intimacy.

"Blade," she begged.

"I'm here," he soothed. "But you are in control of your pleasure. You only have to do what pleases you."

"Right." Shyly, she reached between her legs and stroked herself, lightly at first, then a bit faster. A bit harder. Her body wound tight, and a low roar filled her head, mingling with the pounding of the ocean.

All the while, Blade was with her, spearing his fingers through her hair, caressing her breasts, whispering in her ear.

"I . . . I . . ." Her breath came in gasps, her core pulsed with need. But release was tantalizingly, excruciatingly, just beyond her reach.

As if he knew, Blade laid her flat on the cloak and leaned over her, stroking her face with a tenderness that melted her. "Imagine I am touching you. Tasting you. Making you mine," he murmured. "And know that I would if I could. You are everything, Hazel."

His words floated over her skin and caressed her with feather-light strokes. The air between them crackled with an energy that made the hairs on her arms stand on end.

Pleasure shot through her like a firecracker, lighting up her senses with a hundred sizzling sparks. Flooding her veins with a thousand glowing embers.

She rocked against him, moaning softly, and he wrapped her in his arms as she spiraled slowly back to the earth.

"You are perfect," he whispered. "And this . . . this was a night I'll never forget."

She laughed and buried her head in the crook of his arm. "Perhaps you should. I am rather mortified by my behavior."

He tipped her face to his and kissed her forehead. "You have nothing to be embarrassed about."

"I do feel better," she admitted. "But you . . ." She let her gaze drop to the front of his trousers.

"Do not worry about me," he said, adjusting himself. "I'm glad that we were able to spend one more evening together. I'm going to miss you."

"I shall miss you, too." She pulled her sleeves up her arms and presented her back to him.

He scowled at the laces of her corset, then reluctantly laced her up.

"Thank you."

He helped her to her feet, shook out her cloak, and draped it over her shoulders. "I'll walk you home."

"You don't need to—"

He held up a hand. "I insist. We'll stay on the side streets, and you'll keep your hood on. No one will suspect it's you."

She shot him a grateful smile as she emptied the sand out of her slippers. "Fine. I won't argue."

He laced his fingers through hers and led her down the beach. They walked along the water for a while, then followed a trail over the dunes to a street that was one block away from the school.

"We should part here," she said. "I'll be fine the rest of the way."

Blade held tightly to her hand. "I will speak to Penelope first thing in the morning and ask her to call on Mrs. Covington," he said. "If you don't hear from me, you may assume all has gone according to plan."

"Thank you again. Perhaps everything has worked out for the best." She tried to muster a bit of enthusiasm for the sentiment, but it fell miserably flat.

"I don't know if it's occurred to you," he said soberly, "but our relationship has been a series of goodbyes."

"That's true of most relationships." She thought of the tragic loss of her dear parents and Miss Haywinkle's unexpected retirement. She thought of former students who'd graduated and close friends who'd moved away. "They always end one way or another. But that doesn't mean they're not worth having."

He pressed a kiss to the back of her hand before releasing it. "I regret a great many things in my life. But I could never regret you."

Hazel took a measure of consolation from his words. She supposed she should be flattered that he'd never regret her. The problem was that he could never love her, either.

Still, she was determined to end the evening on a lighter note—if only so Blade wouldn't realize she was perilously close to tears. "I am glad I shan't fall into the same category as black eyes, ghastly hangovers, and reckless wagers."

"Rest assured that you, Hazel Lively, are and forevermore shall be, in a category entirely unto yourself."

The next morning, Blade sat across from Penelope in Bellehaven's tea shop, which was far more crowded than usual thanks to the vexing influx of tourists that the regatta had attracted. He supposed he *was* one of those tourists, strictly speaking, but he liked to think his status was slightly closer to that of a local. Lady Rufflebum was conspiring to have him join the Bellehaven cricket team, after all. Surely that counted for something.

"I beg your pardon." Penelope fluttered her eyelashes in a manner that suggested she was not begging his pardon at all, but rather demanding that he beg hers. "I have not even properly met this woman. Mrs. Covington, is it? Why would I deign to introduce her chit to the ton's elite?"

Blade took a fortifying gulp of coffee. Wished it were laced with something stronger. "Mrs. Covington is Prue's mother. She was at the play."

"Oh, well, then," Penelope said dryly, "I suppose that makes us bosom friends."

"I realize it's a bit of an imposition, but Kitty is very fond of Prue, and you are in a unique position to ease her way into polite society. If anyone can ensure a successful debut season for Prudence, you can." He was not above employing a bit of flattery, but in this case, it happened to be true.

"In a year or two, when Kitty is ready to make her debut, I shall be delighted to bring her out. But you cannot ask me to vouch for complete strangers, Bladenton." She pasted on a smile for the sake of the other patrons in the shop and continued speaking through her teeth. "I don't know anything about the Covingtons and certainly cannot attest to the character of their daughter."

"No one's asking you to take a blood oath or sing her praises to the queen," he said with a shrug. "Simply pay Mrs. Covington and Prue a call. Offer to secure them an invitation or two during Prue's first season. You may enjoy playing the role of mentor—and it will be excellent practice for Kitty's first season."

Penelope narrowed her eyes. "I do not require *practice*. And you still have not provided me a valid explanation as to why I should lend my expertise to this particular young woman."

"If Prue has a successful season, it will enhance the reputation of Kitty's school," he reasoned. "And that would certainly be a good thing."

Penelope laced her fingers beneath her chin. "Why is that?"

Some primitive instinct told Blade the question was much more dangerous than it seemed, but he hazarded an answer. "Because Bellehaven Academy has been good for Kitty. She's happy there."

"I had not realized your niece's happiness was so important to you," she said, clearly skeptical.

"If you and I are to be"—the next word momentarily jammed in his throat—"married, we must become accustomed to assisting each other. I'm asking you to do this as a favor to me."

"A favor to you," she repeated, arching a brow, "or to Miss Lively?"

Shit. He drummed his fingers on the small table between them and kept his face impassive. "You would be doing a kindness to many people—the Covingtons, Kitty, me, and, yes, Miss Lively."

"Am I correct in assuming that it was her suggestion to prevail upon me?"

Blade considered dodging the question, but the one and only redeeming quality of his relationship with Penelope was their ability to be honest with each other. "Miss Lively did suggest it. It seems Mrs. Covington was dismayed by Kitty's participation in the regatta and decided to withdraw her daughter from Bellehaven Academy. Your assistance would likely change Mrs. Covington's mind . . . and allow Prue to stay on as a student."

"Finally, we have arrived at the heart of the matter." For an interminable minute, she glared at Blade over the rim of her teacup. "I will do this favor for you," she said evenly. "But in return, you will do something for me."

"What do you want?" he said, mentally deducting a steep sum from his ledgers. "Jewelry? A generous allowance?"

She chuckled as though amused by his naïveté. "I want two things."

He winced and doubled the deduction. "Go on."

"First, you must promise that you'll never speak to Miss Lively again."

His stomach dropped like a rock. "Don't be ridiculous, Penelope. Miss Lively is Kitty's headmistress. I will, on occasion, have business to conduct and reason to converse with her."

"As your future wife, I am more than happy to attend to all matters related to Kitty's education. From here on out, there is no need for you bother with Bellehaven Academy."

He frowned. "It's not a bother. Besides, I cannot neglect Kitty. I refuse to stay away from her."

"I would never to ask you to forgo outings with your darling niece," Penelope said with suspect sweetness. "I shall simply accompany you whenever you find it necessary to visit this"—she eyed the provincial décor of the tea shop somewhat dubiously—"charming town."

"That hardly seems necessary," Blade balked. "Especially when it's obvious you much prefer London."

"Oh, I think it is necessary." She glanced at the neighboring tables and leaned closer. "I am not blind to your silly infatuation with the headmistress. I have no doubt that your feelings will fade. In the meantime, however, I refuse to look the part of a fool."

Blade released the handle of his cup so he wouldn't accidentally snap it off. "My relationship with Miss Lively is none of your concern," he ground out.

She shot him a serene smile. "Then neither is Prudence Covington."

Damn it. Hazel was counting on him, and deep in his gut, he knew what she'd want him to do. He dragged a hand down his face and tossed his napkin onto the table. "Fine. What is your second demand?"

She gave a breezy wave of her hand. "Nothing too onerous."

"I'll be the judge of that." His head was already pounding like he had the grandfather of all hangovers.

"The only other thing I would ask is that we publicly announce our engagement . . ."

He flinched. "I've already agreed to that."

". . . next week, at Lady Rufflebum's ball."

Good God. "I don't see the need to make a spectacle here in Bellehaven. Wouldn't you rather host an event yourself and make the announcement in Town?"

"Oddly enough, no." She folded her hands primly in her lap. "The countess's ball shall be the perfect opportunity to share the happy news—and I can start grooming Prue for her London season on the same evening. I should imagine everyone involved will be quite pleased."

Pleased? It was the stuff of nightmares. But the truth was that he'd already chosen this path. It was better to be consistently miserable than to risk another soul-crushing heartache. Better to keep his expectations low than to long for a life with Hazel—especially since he couldn't give her the love she deserved.

"Very well, Penelope." He rubbed his chest as if that might ease the unexpected tightness there. "I will give you what you want. Just promise me that you'll do right by Prudence Covington and that you won't malign Miss Lively in the process. Because if you hurt them or Bellehaven Academy, I will never, ever forgive you."

Chapter 23

After sleeping later than usual, Hazel quickly dressed, headed directly to her office, and locked the door behind her. She planned to cloister herself there for a few hours—for two reasons.

First, because after the events of the previous day, she felt as though she deserved an afternoon to lick her wounds. She may have managed to save her school, but there was nothing she could do to save Blade. He desired her, even cared for her. But he wouldn't love her—no matter how much she wanted him to. Each time she'd tried to knock on the door of his heart, he'd slammed it shut in her face. He'd alluded to horrendous heartache and unimaginable pain, and yet he'd never truly opened up to her. Never trusted her enough to expose the scars and allow her to heal him from the inside out.

But there was another reason she'd locked herself away in her office: She had yet to find her manual—her exceedingly explicit, extremely scandalous book.

She'd been so busy for the last twenty-four hours that she hadn't had a moment to properly search for it, but she'd concluded that is simply *had* to be in her office.

Indeed, she could clearly recall the last time she'd flipped through it. She'd been sitting on the windowsill, gazing at the gorgeous, provocative drawings, when Blade had unexpect-edly walked in. She'd quickly slipped one of her cards be-tween the pages as a bookmark and tucked it into her desk drawer at the first opportunity.

Or had she?

She pressed a hand to her chest where she felt the panicked drum of her heart through the folds of her fichu. Perhaps she'd been so flustered by Blade's arrival that she'd stuffed it onto a shelf or stowed it away in a cupboard.

Inhaling deeply, she forced herself to calmly walk to her desk, sit in her chair, and write a list of spots to look: draw-ers, closets, cupboards, shelves. She would methodically search each one, checking it off as she went, and eventually, she *would* locate the manual.

Before there was any possibility of it falling into the wrong hands.

Two hours later, she'd practically ransacked her office and checked off every item on her list. But she'd still failed to lo-cate the book.

She couldn't help wondering if someone had taken it, and the thought was absolutely mortifying. Particularly since her card—which was imprinted with her name and that of her school—was most certainly inside it.

Oh God. This was awful. Her temples throbbed and her palms turned clammy. She paced the perimeter of her office, formulating a new plan of action. Perhaps she should search her room again and completely empty out her trunk and portmanteau.

But first, she needed some fresh air—and a chance to clear her head. So she grabbed her bonnet and found herself walking in the direction of the tea shop, thinking perhaps she'd surprise Jane and the girls with pastries.

The prospect of an errand and a dose of ocean air did make

her feel marginally better—until she rounded the corner and spotted Blade and Penelope walking out of the shop.

Their backs were to her, and they strolled in the opposite direction, Penelope's hand in the crook of his arm, the pair of them resembling models in a dratted Bellehaven Bay advertisement.

A host of ugly emotions twisted in her belly: anger, envy, bitterness, hurt.

She supposed she *should* feel a sense of relief. Blade was only doing what she'd asked him to. He'd probably spoken to Penelope about helping Prue already. If all went well, Prue could soon be back in the classroom.

But Hazel's legs felt wooden and her insides hollow. She forced herself to walk through the shop's door, ringing a vexingly cheerful bell in the process. Somehow, she managed to order four rhubarb pastries, pay the clerk, and nod politely to another patron on her way out.

As she made her way home, she stared at the blue sky and listened to the seabirds squawking overhead. And she tried to convince herself that the image of Blade and Penelope promenading together wouldn't haunt her for the rest of her days.

Clutching the sack containing the treats in one hand, she marched through the door of the boardinghouse and climbed the stairs to the dormitory, where she found Lucy, Clara, and Kitty huddled around Kitty's bed.

"Good afternoon, girls," she said, holding the sack aloft. "Guess what I've brought you."

"Biscuits?" cried Clara.

"Cakes?" called Lucy.

Kitty merely slammed her sketchbook shut and shoved it under her mattress.

Hazel strode across the room and placed the sack on

Kitty's bed. "Rhubarb tarts," she said with a smile. "Enjoy them, and please be sure to save one for Miss Jane."

"Thank you!" they said, tearing into the sack with glee.

"You're quite welcome. I shall see all of you at—" Hazel froze and focused on a small oval object near Kitty's feet. "I believe you dropped something."

Kitty kicked it under the bedspread. "It's nothing."

Hazel hesitated. "It looks like a frame," she said slowly, hoping her suspicion was wrong.

"What on earth would I be doing with a frame?" Kitty asked nervously.

Lucy and Clara exchanged guilty glances.

"I don't know," Hazel said. "I could be mistaken, but it looked quite similar to *my* frame. The one displaying the handkerchief my mother embroidered for me."

Kitty blinked innocently. "You probably just saw the new case of pastels that Uncle Beck bought me."

"If that were true, you would simply show it to me." Hazel crossed her arms and stared impassively until Kitty's face crumpled.

"Very well." She reached beneath the bed, withdrew Hazel's framed handkerchief, and unceremoniously handed it to her.

Hazel ran her fingers over the glass front, ensuring it hadn't cracked. She examined the handkerchief inside, checking that her mother's careful, even stitches were intact. Only when she was satisfied that no harm had come to the frame did she lift her eyes to Kitty. "Why did you take this?"

Kitty sighed, only slightly remorseful. "I wanted to show it to Clara and Lucy."

"So you snuck into my office and brazenly took it without even bothering to ask?"

"I'm sorry." Kitty tossed a torrent of blond curls over one shoulder. "I didn't think you'd mind."

"We're sorry, too," Lucy and Clara chorused.

Hazel shook her head, disbelieving, and clutched the beloved frame to her chest. If Kitty had the audacity to take her most prized possession, there was no telling what else she might have absconded with.

Dear Jesus.

"Kitty, please come with me."

"Can't you simply punish me and be done with it?" she whined.

"Now," Hazel intoned.

A minute later, they were in Hazel's office again. She carefully placed the frame on the shelf where it belonged and sat behind her desk. Kitty slumped into the chair across from her, looking much as she had on the day Blade first brought her there.

Hazel had naively believed that the last several weeks had changed Kitty. That Bellehaven Academy had managed to accomplish what Kitty's other, more elite, boarding schools had not. To make her feel as though she belonged.

But despite all the promising signs, Kitty had reverted to her old ways. For the second time that day, Hazel's heart was breaking.

"You know how precious that handkerchief is to me," Hazel said, keeping her tone measured. "And yet you still took it. I don't understand."

Kitty stared at the floor. "I am sorry. I just wanted to show it to the other girls. I'd intended to return it before you realized it was missing, but you were in here, working."

Hazel frowned, recalling the time she'd caught Kitty snooping in her office. Apparently, she'd spent more time there than Hazel realized. "I'm going to ask you something, and I want you to answer me honestly."

"Very well."

"Where is the book?"

"What book?"

Hazel gripped the arms of her chair. "The book that you took from my office."

"I didn't take a book," Kitty said blithely. "It's as though you scarcely know me. If I were going to take anything, a book would be my very last choice."

"I'm afraid I don't believe you."

She had the audacity to look affronted. "I'm telling you the truth."

"You lied to me in the dormitory five minutes ago."

"That was different!" Kitty protested.

"Only because you were caught." Hazel stood and walked to the window. She was so angry, so disappointed, that she could hardly bear to look at Kitty. "You are confined to the dormitory for the next five days," she said flatly. "You may attend classes and take your meals in the dining room, but that is all."

Kitty gaped. "I'm supposed to visit Mr. Sandford tomorrow. We were going to review the final plans for the new stables."

"You'll have to send your regrets," Hazel said calmly.

"That's not fair." Kitty's voice shook. "You're punishing me for something I didn't do."

"I'm punishing you for taking my handkerchief and lying about it."

Kitty crossed her arms and scowled.

"However, if you do not return the book before dinner today," Hazel continued, "your punishment will be extended for an additional week."

"I don't have a bloody book!" She leapt out of her chair, huffing with indignation. "I don't even know what you're talking about. You must believe me."

"I wish that I could," Hazel said flatly.

"You can't lock me up in the dormitory for two weeks. I'd miss . . ." She pressed a hand to her forehead, aghast. "I'd miss Lady Rufflebum's ball."

"All the more reason for you to return the book, post-haste."

"You're being unreasonable and spiteful," Kitty sputtered. "And positively . . . *mean*!"

"That is all, Kitty. You may go."

She snorted. "I thought you were different from my other headmistresses. But you're as false as the rest of them, pretending to have our best interests at heart. Pretending to care when the truth is . . ." Tears filled her eyes and her voice cracked. "The truth is: You don't give a damn."

Kitty stormed out, slamming the door so hard that the walls shook.

Hazel waited till her footsteps faded, then laid her head on her desk—and cried.

"This just arrived for you, my lord."

Blade looked up from the ledger on his desk, rubbed his eyes, and blinked at his butler, who balanced a silver salver on his outstretched arm.

"Thank you, Wiggins." He took the letter from the platter, glanced at the envelope, and muttered a curse. It was from Penelope.

"Your dinner is still waiting in the dining room, sir. Would you like me to bring a tray here?"

"No need." Wiggins had announced dinner was served over an hour ago. "I'll head to the dining room momentarily."

"Very good, my lord." He gave a curt bow and left the study.

Blade closed the book on his desk, slid a finger under the letter's seal, and unfolded it.

Dearest Bladenton,

I have taken the first steps in fulfilling my part of our bargain. Earlier today, I called upon Mrs. Covington and offered my assistance during her daughter's debut season. I even managed, during the course of our conversation, to speak favorably of Bellehaven Academy. Mrs. Covington remained somewhat skeptical of the school's merits but indicated that she would consider re-enrolling Prudence after Lady Rufflebum's ball.

Speaking of the ball, I look forward to announcing our impending nuptials there and have already begun seeing to the necessary details. We shall be officially engaged within the week, and I feel certain that we both shall find the arrangement quite satisfactory.

Most sincerely yours,
Penelope

Blade dropped the letter like a hot iron, strode to the sideboard, and poured himself a brandy. From the moment he'd left the tea shop that morning, he'd had the unshakable feeling he was making a horrible mistake—not only in agreeing to marry Penelope, but in trusting her to save Hazel's school.

During the entire ride back to London, he'd debated what to do about it.

He wanted nothing more than to call off his plans with Penelope, but there was no telling how she'd react if he did. He didn't mind suffering the consequences, but he had a sickly suspicion that Hazel would be the one to end up in the crossfire. He had to protect her and make good on his promise to help her save her school.

Even if it meant resigning himself to an existence that was as barren and broken as his heart.

Chapter 24

Hazel walked into the dining room the next morning determined to make a fresh start. She was still smarting from the events of the weekend and would have preferred to stay in bed with the covers pulled over her head. But she couldn't afford to wallow in her troubles—not when her girls were counting on her. As always, duty called.

She bid good morning to Mrs. Paxton, who had just placed a fresh plate of toast on the buffet, and prepared a plate for herself before joining Lucy and Clara at the foot of the table.

"Hullo, girls," she said to the oddly somber pair. "Did you sleep well? You both look a bit peaked."

They exchanged a glance, and Lucy swallowed. "Is Kitty ever coming back?"

The hair on Hazel's arms stood on end. "I beg your pardon?"

"We know she shouldn't have taken your frame," said Clara. "But she was going to return it. Truly."

Hazel shook her head, hoping against hope that her suspicion was wrong. "Kitty isn't in the dormitory?"

Lucy shook her head sadly. "We haven't seen her since yesterday, when you asked her to go with you."

Hazel's fork slipped from her fingers and clattered onto her plate. "Oh dear."

"Lucy is worried that you sent her away for good, but I told her you wouldn't do that." Clara paused then bravely added, "Would you?"

"No. Of course not. I only spoke to her for a few moments. I assumed she returned directly to your room."

"All her things are still there," Clara said. "Even her sketchbook. It's not like Kitty to go anywhere without it."

"Do not fret." Hazel attempted a reassuring smile as she placed her napkin on the table and stood. "She cannot have gone far. I will find her. When Miss Jane arrives for breakfast, will you tell her that I'm making a few inquiries? If I am late for today's lesson, you may review the steps of the quadrille until I arrive."

"Yes, Miss Lively," the girls said in unison.

Hazel kept her composure until she left the dining room, but the moment she reached the corridor she sagged against the wall and pressed her fingertips to her forehead. Where could Kitty have gone?

She'd been in such a state when she stormed out of the office. She might have done something foolish such as hiring a coach to take her to London. Or spending the night in a cove where the high tide could be terribly dangerous. Sweet Jesus.

Right. There was no time for hysterics. Every second that Kitty was missing was a chance that harm might come to her. And if it did, Hazel would never forgive herself.

Her first stop was the Bluffs' Brew. The innkeeper said he hadn't seen Kitty, and the mail coach wasn't due until later in the day.

Hazel breathed a small sigh of relief. It was still possible that Kitty had found another means of leaving Bellehaven, but unlikely since she had no money with her. Chances were,

Kitty was still in town, and there were only so many places she could go.

While Hazel was near Main Street, she checked in at the tea shop, the Salty Mermaid, and Mr. Sandford's office. It seemed as though no one had seen or heard from Kitty since the regatta.

As Hazel made her inquiries, she endeavored to appear calm and collected, as though she weren't positively frantic over the fact that she'd apparently managed to lose one of her own students. Poor Kitty could be scared and shivering in a dark cave right now, or God forbid, floating out to sea in a rowboat.

Hazel's heart hammered in her chest as she hurried to the beach. Blade had entrusted his niece to her, and she'd let him down. Indeed, if Hazel couldn't locate Kitty very soon, she was going to have to send word to London, and Blade would, no doubt, be absolutely sick with worry.

She paused on the beach to catch her breath and clear her head. If she were Kitty, where would she go?

A couple of fishermen at the edge of the surf waved to her and shouted a greeting, and as she waved back, she thought of Poppy.

Kitty had to be with Poppy.

Hazel sent up a silent prayer that she was right and began the walk across town. An hour later, she stood on the doorstep of the humble cottage where Poppy lived with her father and brother. She took a deep breath and raised her fist, but the weathered wooden door swung open before she could knock.

"Ah, here you are," Poppy said with an impish grin. "I wondered how long it would take you to find her."

Hazel nearly cried with relief. "Thank heaven. Is she all right?"

"Well enough, I should think." Poppy wiped her hands on

her apron and glanced backward over her shoulder. "I'd invite you in, but the place is a bit of a mess."

"Perhaps you could persuade Kitty to come out and speak with me?"

"She's not inside," Poppy said, matter-of-fact, "but I can take you to her. I should probably explain a couple of things as well."

"Thank you," Hazel replied, confused, but grateful all the same.

Poppy hung her apron on a hook by the door and called over her shoulder, "I'll be back in a bit, Papa. Stay away from the stew until dinnertime." As she closed the door behind her, she muttered, "Last time he wandered near the stove to sneak a taste he nearly burned the house down."

"I'm sorry that you became wrapped up in this," Hazel said. "You already have more than enough on your plate."

Poppy shrugged and led Hazel down a grassy path that ran parallel to the shoreline. "The truth is, I was already wrapped up in it. First, you should know that I wanted to come and tell you that Kitty was with me, but she made me swear on my mother's grave that I wouldn't."

"Goodness."

"If I didn't agree, she threatened to hop on the first coach to London. I thought that she'd be safer with me."

"Most definitely," Hazel said. "You did the right thing."

Poppy crinkled her nose, and her freckles seemed to dance in the sunlight. "Before I take you to Kitty, there's something else I need to tell you."

Hazel's belly twisted. "What is it? Please say she's not hurt."

"No," Poppy assured her. She pointed to a large boulder overlooking the sea. "Let's sit for a moment."

All Hazel wanted was to lay eyes on Kitty and be certain

she was sound. But Poppy was not one for idle chat, and if she wanted to talk, it had to be important.

They climbed a step fashioned from a split log and sat on the surface of the rock, which was broad and flat, except for a deep crevice splitting it in half.

"It's beautiful up here," Hazel said.

"When I was a wee lass, I used to imagine that the glimmers of sun on the water were mermaids' tails," Poppy said with a chuckle. "Now I come here to remind myself there's a whole world beyond our tiny cottage and tattered fishing nets."

"Of course there is," Hazel said earnestly. "I've no doubt you shall see it one day."

Poppy arched a skeptical brow. "Perhaps. But for now, I rely on books." She reached into the crevice, carefully withdrew a small bundle covered in oilcloth, and handed it to Hazel.

"What's this?"

"One of the books you gave me last week."

Oh God. Hazel unwrapped the oilcloth and stared at the familiar cover. Her cheeks flamed. "Poppy, forgive me. It must have gotten mixed up in the batch I set aside for you. I . . . I'm positively mortified."

She smiled and brushed an auburn strand away from her face. "Don't be. I learned a great deal. It answered some questions I had . . . and raised others."

"Oh?" Hazel blinked.

"But that is a discussion for another time." Poppy hugged her knees to her chest. "Kitty mentioned that you were upset about a missing book. I suspected it might be this one."

"I accused her of stealing it from my office." Hazel felt ill. "I am a horrid person and an abominable headmistress."

"Poppycock. You made a mistake, Miss Lively."

"Hazel. Please, you must call me Hazel."

Poppy's blue eyes twinkled as though she were touched. "Kitty knows nothing about the book, so you can breathe easy on that account. She may have a need for it one day . . . but perhaps it's best if we wait a few years."

Hazel swallowed the lump in her throat. "Thank you. Can you take me to her now? I must apologize." She quickly wrapped the book and tucked it under her arm.

"Follow me." Poppy hopped off the boulder and made her way to a steep trail that seemed to lead toward the beach. "Watch your step—I'm afraid this ground isn't meant for delicate slippers."

Hazel tread carefully over the pebbly sand as they wound their way through tall grasses dotted with colorful wild-flowers. Eventually, they arrived at a small clearing with a view of the ocean. And in the center of the clearing, between two trees, was a charming lean-to built of wooden boards tied together with rope. Half covered in moss and trailing vines with purple blooms, it looked like something out of a fairy tale. Indeed, Hazel should not have been surprised to see seven dwarfs march out from behind the faded blue blanket that served as a front door.

Poppy waved an arm at the darling hut. "My private sanctuary," she said wryly. "At least it was, until now. It's where I go to read—and it's where Kitty slept last night."

As if on cue, Kitty swept aside the blanket and stepped outside, squinting in the afternoon sun. Her dress was wrinkled and her eyes puffy, as though she'd been crying. "Miss Lively," she said tentatively.

Hazel dropped the book, ran to Kitty, and wrapped her in a fierce hug. Tears of relief streamed down her cheeks. "Thank God," she murmured in Kitty's matted hair. "I'm so sorry. I know you didn't take the book. Everything will be all right."

"I'm sorry, too," Kitty sobbed against Hazel's chest. "I shouldn't have taken your handkerchief. I shouldn't have lied."

Hazel patted her back soothingly. This was the first time she'd ever embraced a student. She supposed she'd avoided displays of affection for fear of appearing weak or un-headmistress-like. But this one hug with Kitty had blasted through the walls between them like a keg of gunpowder.

Kitty may have appeared to be a sharp-tongued, self-assured, supremely talented young woman—and she *was* all those things. But she was also a frightened fifteen-year-old girl who wanted to be understood. Loved.

"We both made mistakes," Hazel said. "But as Poppy recently reminded me, if we're not making a few mistakes now and again, then we're not really living."

"Does this mean that my punishment has been lifted?" she asked hopefully.

"Not entirely." Hazel held her at arm's length to better see her face, then coaxed a smile out of her. "You will spend the rest of the week in the dormitory, but you may attend Lady Rufflebum's ball."

"I suppose that's fair," Kitty said with a sniffle. "I understand why you were so cross with me. Your handkerchief connects you to your mother . . . the way my locket connects me to mine." With that, she reached beneath the collar of her dress and pulled out a locket suspended from a delicate chain around her neck.

"That's beautiful," said Poppy. "I've never seen you wear it before."

"I always wear it," Kitty said, her expression solemn. "But beneath my clothes. Close to my heart."

"May we see it?" Hazel asked.

Kitty nodded and reverently lifted the gold locket away from her chest. Both Hazel and Poppy inched closer as she opened it, revealing two miniature portraits. "This is my father," she said, pointing to a man who looked very much like a younger, blonder, more carefree version of Blade.

"He is quite handsome," Poppy remarked.

"And this is my mother."

Hazel felt like she was staring at a goddess. "She's beautiful."

"The portrait doesn't do her justice," Kitty said, her eyes welling. "She was like the ocean—always moving, never still." She clicked the locket shut and turned it over, absently running a finger over the cursive engraving on the back.

"What does it say?" Poppy asked.

"Eliza," Kitty said reverently. "My mother's name was Eliza."

The hairs on the backs of Hazel's arms stood on end. That name . . . it couldn't be a coincidence.

Eliza was the first and only woman Blade loved—and she had married his younger brother.

Hazel began rotating puzzle pieces in her head, fitting them all together.

Blade's estrangement from Kitty's parents, his inability to love again, his unwillingness to belong to a true family—all of it made sense now.

The two people he cared about most had betrayed him, in his mind, at least. And they'd tragically died before he could make peace with them—leaving him to raise their only child, the niece he'd never met.

"Are you all right, Hazel?" Poppy asked.

Kitty's eyebrows shot up. "Hazel?"

"Still Miss Lively to you," she said firmly. To Poppy she replied, "I'm fine. Or, at least, I think I will be." Once she had a chance to talk to Blade—and tell him she understood.

But this moment, with Kitty and Poppy, felt just as significant. Just as revealing.

Not too long ago, Hazel would have meticulously swept all the unruly, inconvenient emotions they were feeling under a rug. And perhaps moved a heavy piece of furniture on top.

But she didn't want to do that anymore.

"I was just thinking," she began tentatively, "that all three of us lost our mothers far too early. And maybe that left a hole in each of our hearts."

Poppy swallowed and rubbed her chest. "Do you ever wonder how different your life might have been if they were still here with us?" she asked softly.

"I certainly wouldn't be at a boarding school in Belle-haven," Kitty said. "And I wouldn't feel lonely all the time, like a part of me is missing."

Poppy nodded, emphatic. "I wouldn't be making my living catching fish. And I wouldn't feel as though I was constantly swimming against the tide."

Hazel was silent for a moment, thinking about what Kitty and Poppy had said. Letting their pain become hers. "If my mother were still here, maybe I'd allow myself to feel more. To not be so . . . so hard." She blinked back tears.

Poppy reached out, impulsively clasping one of Hazel's hands. Kitty squeezed the other. They formed a small circle and gazed at one another with sad, earnest smiles.

"Perhaps there's a reason fate brought us together," Hazel said.

Poppy toed the ground with her half boot. "Maybe we're supposed to help each other plug the holes in our hearts."

"Maybe we don't have to feel so alone," Kitty said.

Hazel cleared her throat. "I'd like to make a proposal," she said, "that we form a special group of our own."

"Like a secret society?" Kitty asked excitedly.

"Er, if you'd like." Hazel shrugged.

Poppy arched an amused brow. "Does this group have rules?"

"Of course," Hazel improvised. "Nothing too onerous. First, we listen to each other."

Kitty and Poppy nodded their assent.

"Second, we support each other," Hazel continued.

They bobbed their heads again.

"Most important," Hazel said, "We promise to chase our dreams."

"I like that," Poppy said.

Kitty frowned. "Will our society have a name? I think it must, or it isn't a proper society at all."

Hazel suppressed a smile. "Agreed. A name is absolutely essential. What did you have in mind?"

"Hmm," Kitty mused. "Something that sounds sophisticated."

Poppy gave an impish grin. "I suppose that rules out my idea—the Mackerel Mavens."

Hazel gazed over her shoulder at the horizon where the indigo ocean met a blushing lilac sky. "This place is what drew us together. And it might just be the thing that heals us."

"How about the Belles of Bellehaven Bay?" Kitty said.

The trio glanced at each other, nodding approval.

"The Belles it is," Poppy agreed. "As long as I'm not expected to wear a ball gown and kid gloves." She flashed a saucy grin.

"You're not expected to be anyone other than who you are," Hazel said soberly. "None of us is."

Kitty exhaled deeply. "I feel marginally better."

"So do I," Hazel said. "But I know that Lucy and Clara were worried sick about you, and I'm certain Miss Jane is beside herself, too. Shall we return to school and let them know that all is well?"

Kitty nodded, and the three of them dropped hands. To Poppy, she said, "Thank you for letting me stay with you. I'm sorry I made you swear on your mother's grave not to tell."

"It's all right." Poppy said. "Belles stick together."

Hazel scooped up her book—still wrapped in oilcloth—and handed it to Poppy. "I don't think I'm going to need this anymore. Maybe you'd like to keep it?"

Poppy's blue eyes twinkled. "I shall take good care of it."

Kitty perked up. "Is that the infamous missing book? What's it about?"

"Biology," Hazel said simply. "And one day, you shall have the chance to study it as well."

Kitty rolled her eyes. "Lucky me," she said dryly.

Poppy laughed. "You may discover that science is more fascinating than you suspected."

"Or I may discover that I have about as much use for science as I do for advanced maths," Kitty retorted.

"Clearly, I have more work to do," Hazel said with a smile. She slipped an arm around Kitty's narrow shoulders. "Let's go home."

That night, as Hazel lay in her bed, she thought about Blade—and all she'd learned about him that day. Now she understood his reluctance to entrust his heart to another. She understood why family was inextricably tangled with pain and betrayal in his mind.

But she realized something else, too.

Blade had already begun to heal—and the proof was all around.

He'd come to visit Kitty last weekend. Not because he had to, but because he'd *wanted* to.

He'd agreed to help Hazel save her school. Not because he cared about the school, but because he cared about *her.*

There were countless other little signs. Pebbles on her window, his jacket around her shoulders, his fingers laced with hers.

Perhaps he wasn't quite ready to write love sonnets or

sing romantic ballads, but Blade wasn't the same cynical man who'd walked into her office at the beginning of the summer—and she had to tell him that, for two reasons.

First, because even if Blade didn't love her, he deserved to know that he could love *somebody*.

Second, because there was still a chance—a small one, to be sure—but a chance, nonetheless, that he *could* love her.

That was her dream.

And Belles *always* chased their dreams.

Chapter 25

Blade blinked twice at the note in his hands. Read it a third time to be certain he wasn't hallucinating.

Hazel was in London.

And she wanted to meet him at the park.

"Wiggins!" he bellowed.

The butler appeared in the study doorway. "My lord?"

"I'm going to the park for a bit."

"Very good, sir."

Blade rubbed the back of his neck. "Actually, it's not."

"I beg your pardon?"

"I'm meeting a young lady there, but I can't be seen with her. Or she can't be seen with me." He paced behind his desk. "Lady Penelope would be more than a little displeased."

Wiggins's usually pasty pallor turned pink. "I, er, believe I understand your dilemma, my lord."

"It's complicated," Blade said. "The woman is Kitty's headmistress, and she needs to speak with me and requested that I meet her."

"Surely Lady Penelope would understand."

Blade snorted. "No, she would not, and, unfortunately, she has more gossip-loving informants than France has spies.

If I were seen strolling in the park with another woman, she'd know about it before I could walk home and hang my hat."

"May I make a suggestion, my lord?"

"I wish you would, Wiggins."

The butler straightened his waistcoat, arched a bushy eyebrow, and proceeded to tell Blade the plan.

Hazel had not anticipated rain in St. James Park, which only proved how distracted she was.

This *was* London, after all.

"Miss Lively?"

Hazel spun around to find a cherub-faced older woman wearing a white cap and holding an umbrella. She was standing just off the pebbled path beneath a large chestnut tree.

"How do you know my name?"

The fair-haired woman glanced both ways down the path and lowered her voice before answering. "I work for Lord Bladenton," she said, handing Hazel his card. "He asked me to fetch you."

Blade hadn't bothered to come himself. Hazel tamped down a stab of disappointment, turned the card over, and read the brief inscription on the back. *Please come. I'll explain.—B*

"My name is Mrs. Wiggins," the woman said warmly. "Lord Bladenton's housekeeper. Forgive all the subterfuge. I've known the earl since he was a wee lad, and I must say this is the most curious request he's ever made, but I'm pleased to make your acquaintance."

"I'm pleased to meet you as well."

"Come along then." Mrs. Wiggins beckoned, holding the umbrella between them. Hazel gratefully ducked under and quickly discovered that while Mrs. Wiggins had the soft-spoken, kindly demeanor of a grandmother, she walked with the brisk, purposeful stride of a soldier. "It's only a few blocks to Bladenton House where we can give you a proper welcome."

Before long, the housekeeper was whisking Hazel through a grand garden and onto a stately terrace that made Lady Rufflebum's beautiful house in Bellehaven seem positively rustic by comparison.

"Here we are." Mrs. Wiggins opened a French door and waved Hazel through—into the most gorgeous ballroom Hazel had ever seen. Pale light from the immense windows illuminated oak floors inlaid with intricate mahogany medallions, towering walls covered in exquisite artwork, and a vast ceiling painted with fanciful pastoral scenes.

"Oh my," Hazel breathed.

"I should have liked to bring you through the front door, but the earl insisted that discretion was necessary," Mrs. Wiggins explained, somewhat embarrassed.

"Thank you for escorting me here," Hazel said. But she began to wonder if she'd made a mistake. This was Blade's world—and it couldn't have been more different from the modest boardinghouse she called home.

As if she could read Hazel's thoughts, Mrs. Wiggins clucked her tongue. "The earl seemed most eager to see you. He's waiting in the drawing room, and he was pacing like a caged animal when I left him there."

Hazel felt as though she owed the woman an explanation. "I'm headmistress of the school that his niece attends," she said. "Kitty is fine, but I had a few matters that I needed to discuss with him—in person."

Mrs. Wiggins nodded as if this made perfect sense. Never mind the fact that headmistresses did not pay visits to the homes of earls.

As they wound their way through a maze of corridors, rooms, and staircases, the housekeeper pointed out interesting tidbits. "This bust is a likeness of Lord Bladenton's grand-father . . . I remember when the earl used to slide through this hallway in his stockinged feet . . . He and his brother once rode down this staircase on a wooden sled."

Hazel soaked in the knowledge, savoring the rare glimpses into Blade's past. She filed away the clues from his childhood, hoping they'd shed light on the man he'd become.

"The drawing room is just through there." Mrs. Wiggins paused and gestured toward a door several yards away. "Would you like me to accompany you, Miss Lively?"

"Pardon?"

"I can serve as a chaperone if you'd like."

"Oh." Hazel blushed. "I should have thought of that. You must think me quite bereft of manners."

"Not at all. Mr. Wiggins and I are the only souls who know you're here, and you needn't worry about either of us talking out of turn. But if you're concerned about the appearance of impropriety, I can tuck myself in a corner of the drawing room while you speak to the earl."

Hazel smiled, touched. "That won't be necessary, thank you. I trust the earl—and you as well."

"Very good." The apples of her cheeks glowed with approval. "There's a hot pot of tea inside and a plate of scones. Just ring if you require anything at all."

Hazel thanked the housekeeper and glided into the drawing room. Blade stood near the fireplace, glaring at his pocket watch. His hair stood on end as though he'd raked it with his fingers a dozen or more times. His cravat was dreadfully askew.

And still, he made her belly flutter.

"Blade."

He turned to her, swallowed up the ground between them in three long strides, and drew up short—as if he'd just remembered he shouldn't sweep her into his arms. His chest was a scant few inches from hers. "Hazel," he breathed.

The air around them was charged with energy. It would only take one tremulous touch, one heated glance to spark a fire.

"Are you all right?" There was an edge to his voice. A hint of desperation. "Please say you're all right."

"I am," she assured him. "Are you . . . going to invite me in?"

He muttered a curse. "Of course," he said, extending an arm toward the center of the room. "Please make yourself comfortable—and forgive me. I was shocked to learn that you were in London."

"I hope it wasn't an unpleasant surprise," she teased. She crossed the plush, pale-green carpet and sank onto a velvet bench seat in an alcove full of silk pillows. Raindrops pattered on the mullioned window behind her. With a stack of books and the occasional cup of tea, she'd be content to spend the rest of her life right there.

"I'm always glad to see you, Hazel."

He sat beside her, and the nook suddenly seemed less conducive to reading and more conducive to . . . other things.

"How did you travel here?" He pinched the bridge of his nose. "Please tell me you didn't take the mail coach."

Hazel shook her head. "I came in Lady Rufflebum's coach, with her companion. When I learned that Miss Whitford was visiting her sister in town for the day, I asked if I could come along and visit a friend."

He arched a dark brow. "A friend?"

"The countess and her companion may be operating under the erroneous assumption that the friend is a woman I went to school with," she admitted. "I wouldn't have fibbed if it wasn't important."

"Whatever the reason, I'm glad you're here." The raw sincerity in his voice warmed her insides. "I didn't want to meet in the park where someone might see us."

Hazel's belly sank. "Because of Penelope?"

Blade started to reach for Hazel's hand, then crossed his arms and nodded. "She's not above spreading gossip—and it can be vicious. I don't give a damn what she says about me, but I won't permit her to speak ill of you or Bellehaven Academy."

Hazel shrugged off a prickle of apprehension and mustered a smile. "This setting is far better than the park, and Mrs. Wiggins is a delight."

"She is," he agreed. "But you did not come here to meet my former nanny."

"That's true." Hazel wriggled off her slippers and tucked her legs beneath her skirt so she could face Blade. "I have something to say, and you might not like it. That is, it might sting for a bit."

He frowned. "What do you mean?"

She took a deep breath, like she was about to tear off a bandage. "I know about Eliza. I know that she was Kitty's mother, and your first love. I know that she married your brother, and that you were estranged from them both."

Blade turned ghostly pale. He looked away, as though he needed a moment to compose himself before meeting her gaze. "You didn't need to come all the way from Bellehaven to tell me that," he said dryly. "It's not as though I'd forgotten."

"I know. I came here to tell you that I understand. That I'm sorry you lost them both. Twice."

"Jesus, Hazel." He propped his elbows on his knees and dropped his head into his hands. "You *don't* understand. If you did, you wouldn't be bringing it up right now. You'd know that I do my damnedest to get through every day not thinking about Simon and Eliza. Not thinking about—" His voice cracked. "Fuck."

"Tell me." Hazel reached for one of his hands, peeled his clenched fingers open, and pressed a kiss to his palm. "Tell me everything. The very worst parts. Let the demons out . . . let me fight them alongside you."

He hesitated, then tugged his hand away. "It's . . . it's not the sort of thing you should have to hear."

"Are you afraid my ears are too delicate? Because I assure you, they're not. Nothing you can say will scare me away, Blade. Nothing can change the way I feel about you."

"I don't believe that," he said flatly.

She raised her chin. "Then try me."

"Bloody hell." He leaned forward again and drew in a deep, ragged breath. "Fine. The second worst day of my life was the day I turned twenty-two. Eliza and I were engaged. I'd traveled to London to buy her a ring and couldn't wait to show it to her. Couldn't wait to begin our life together.

"I returned home a day earlier than expected. A maid tried to stop me from going directly to my room." Blade barked a hollow laugh. "But I wanted to change my clothes before I visited Eliza. So I walked in."

"Oh no." She pressed a hand to her heart. Felt it thump with dread.

"Simon was lying in *my* bloody bed. And Eliza—the woman who'd sworn she loved me—was on top of him." He squeezed his eyes shut, as if he was trying to unsee it.

"Oh my God." Hazel's throat constricted. "I'm sorry."

"I staggered into the hallway. Retched on the carpet. Then I walked back into my room. Eliza was wrapped in a sheet, crying. Simon had one leg in his trousers and was tripping over himself, trying to explain.

"I couldn't stand the sight of them. I told them to leave, to never come back." Blade's jaw twitched. "They never did."

Hazel brushed an errant lock from his forehead and let her fingers drift though his hair. "You must have been devastated."

"I would have given my life for either of them," he said, softer. "I thought we'd all grow old together. Eliza and I would have a large, happy brood. Simon would marry and have a nursery-full of his own. But that single moment—when I discovered how they'd betrayed me—obliterated everything I thought I knew about marriage and family and love."

"And yet," Hazel said slowly, "it was only the second worst day?"

"Right." Blade gripped the edge of the bench seat, turning his knuckles white. "The worst day of my life was fifteen years later, when a frantic footman arrived on my doorstep. There had been a carriage accident. Simon and Eliza were both gravely injured but hanging on. My brother was begging to see me.

"And I knew I'd made a mistake." His voice cracked on the last syllable. "In refusing to speak to him all those years. In shutting him out. He'd written me scores of times—at least once a month. And I never opened his letters. Every time I stuffed one in a drawer, I told myself I was avoiding further pain. But there was a twisted side of me that savored the thought of punishing him."

Hazel caressed the back of his neck. "You're not to blame, you know."

He scoffed at that. "I saddled my horse and rode to Somerset like the hounds of hell were at my heels. I needed to see Simon and tell him that in spite of everything, he was still my brother. But when I got there . . . it was too late. He was gone. Eliza, too."

"I'm sorry," Hazel breathed.

He grabbed fistfuls of his hair. "A maid ushered me to their room. They were lying beside each other in a four-poster bed, broken and bruised. Through her sobs, the maid said their dying wish was for me to act as guardian to Kitty. Until that very second, I didn't even know I *had* a niece," he sputtered. "Why would they entrust her to me? What the devil do I know about raising a girl?"

"More than you think," Hazel murmured. She rubbed his back in light, soothing strokes.

"So now you know," he said soberly. "I lost the people I loved most. Twice. I can't risk a third time, Hazel. I don't think I'd survive it."

Chapter 26

In recounting the darkest days of his life, Blade had cast up all the poison that had been churning in his gut for the last fifteen years. The truth was messy and foul, but he'd expelled it. Put it right out there for Hazel to see.

And she was still there. Holding his hand, rubbing his shoulders, telling him everything would be all right.

"What you've endured . . . it's awful. I won't pretend it's not. But you're not alone anymore," she whispered. Her empathy radiated through him, smoothing the jagged edges of his pain. "Even when I'm not physically with you, I will *always* be on your side."

His chest ached. "I don't deserve that sort of loyalty."

"Of course you do." She squeezed his hand as though she could convince him through sheer force of will. "The anger, the grief, the guilt—they will fade. After all you've been through, you deserve some happiness, Blade."

The hell he did. "I'd settle for not being miserable."

"You should aim higher." Her voice was playful, her eyes dead serious.

His throat constricted. "Don't you see, Hazel? On the day that Simon and Eliza died, I lost a part of my soul. The part that believed in love and family. It's not that I'm still pining over Eliza—I stopped loving her years ago. But what's left of my heart is scorched earth. *Nothing* is going to grow there."

"What if I told you it already has?" Hazel said earnestly.

He shook his head. "What?"

"At the beginning of the summer you were Kitty's reluctant guardian. Now you're a doting uncle."

He scoffed. "I bought her a few trinkets. That hardly qualifies as doting."

"I'm not talking about gifts," Hazel countered. "You listened to her. You cheered when she won the regatta. You came to watch her act in the play."

He rubbed the back of his neck. "I'm not one to shirk my duties."

"Kitty is more than a duty to you. I think you did those things because you *care* about her."

"Of course I care about her." Blade blinked, caught off guard by his own admission. He cared about Kitty. Wanted her to be happy. Would do anything to protect her.

"That's not all. You care about me, too."

"Hazel." Jesus. The last thing he wanted to do was hurt her. "I won't deny I care for you. But I still can't love you the way you want to be loved."

"Let me tell you how I want to be loved," she said slowly. "I want a man who will carry me out of the surf and wrap me in his coat. A man who will take me to dinner under the stars and lie with me, listening to the ocean. A man who tells me his secrets and listens to mine." She paused and laced her fingers through his. "I want a man who derives pleasure from giving me pleasure. *That* is how I want to be loved."

Her words rained down on him like a balm to his soul. After everything he'd told her, Hazel *still* saw something good in him. And for the first time in fifteen long years, he felt a glimmer of hopefulness.

The irony was it had come a few days too late.

Hazel sat beside him, impossibly beautiful, completely vulnerable. The rebellious curl at her temple had sprung free, transporting him to the day he'd first walked into her office. He'd once thought that curl was an aberration—completely at odds with who she was. Now he knew better.

"I want to be with you, Hazel," he said. "More than anything. But I made a promise."

"To Penelope," she said.

"Yes. Ours will not be a true marriage. I will never love her."

"It's not the stuff of dreams, is it?" Hazel said.

Blade shrugged. "It's what Penelope wants. The fancy house, the ball invitations, the generous allowance . . . I suppose they're enough for her."

For several heartbeats, they sat in silence.

Then Hazel said, "I meant what I said earlier. I shall always be on your side. I will always want what's best for you . . . even if it's not what's best for me."

He cupped her cheeks in his palms. "You deserve every happiness in the world. I'm sorry I wasn't able to give it to you."

"But you *have* made me happy." She tipped her forehead to his. "You cracked open my shell. You made me realize that there's nothing wrong with being a little soft."

"I like the soft side of you, Hazel." God, but it was difficult to think clearly when she was touching him. "Almost as much as I like your prim fichus and bonnets."

"I came here because I needed you to know two things," she breathed. "First, you are not nearly as hopeless as you believe. Second . . . I love you."

Her words pierced his chest like an arrow. Made his heart burst with joy and ooze despair at the same time. Because he wanted to say the words back to her—but couldn't. It wouldn't be fair. Not when he knew that love was all she'd ever wanted. Not when he would announce his engagement in a few days' time. "Hazel . . ."

She brushed her lips across his, silencing him. "You don't have to say anything. It's enough for me that you know. I love you, Blade."

He captured her mouth in a kiss that was both primal and tender, hoping it said all the things he couldn't. That he wished things were different. That she'd dragged him out of the darkness. That he never wanted to let her go.

He ran his hands over her body, committing every curve to memory. He tangled his tongue with hers, savoring the sweet, slightly spicy taste of her.

She kissed him with an abandon that thrilled him. She nipped at his lip, raked her nails down the back of his jacket. "I don't have much time," she murmured against his mouth, even as she slipped her hand inside his trousers and wrapped her fingers around him.

"Christ." His cock twitched in her palm, and he had to hold his breath for five seconds so he wouldn't come instantly.

"I want you to lie back." She pressed a hand to his chest, easing his head onto a pillow. He bent one leg on the bench and braced the other on the floor, thinking she meant to lie on top of him.

Instead, she sat between his thighs and unbuttoned his trousers. Lowered her head. Slowly, took him in her mouth.

He gasped from the sheer bliss of it.

She was tentative at first, gently stroking with her tongue and molding her lips around him. But then she took him deeper, sucking him so sweetly he thought he'd die of pleasure.

Hazel loved him. She'd told him. Shown him. And he wanted to bask in the glow of it—stay in this moment—forever.

But the sight of her head between his legs and the warm, wet feel of her mouth on his cock was too perfect. Little moans in the back of her throat vibrated through him. Drove him to the edge of release.

"Hazel," he rasped. He cradled her head in one hand. "I can't . . . I'm about to . . ."

She gazed at him, brown eyes shining, and sucked harder. Took him deeper.

Fuck. His climax hit him like a hurricane—raw, elemental, powerful. And for that one moment in time, he surrendered to it. Everything he'd lost. Everything he longed for. And everything he felt for Hazel. He let the storm rip through him. Rode it out till the end.

When he opened his eyes, she was still there, her head resting on his chest, her fingers splayed over his pounding heart.

"I don't think you have any idea . . . how amazing you are." And he wasn't just talking about the pleasure she'd given him—though there *was* that. He was talking about her courage and selflessness. Her unique ability to grab him by the cravat and pull him, inch by inch, out of the darkness . . . and make him a better man.

"I'm glad I came to see you today," she said softly. "Even though it will hurt to leave. If I hadn't told you how I feel, I think I would always regret it."

Panic swirled in his gut. "Surely you don't have to leave already?"

She sat up and shot him a winsome smile. "Miss Whitford is going to retrieve me from Gunter's in less than an hour."

"You could send word that you're staying the night with your friend. I'll take you back to Bellehaven in the morning."

She shook her head, regretful. "I've already shirked my duties for one day. I have lessons to teach tomorrow and can't impose on Jane again."

"Fine," he said. "Then we'll return later tonight. I'll have you back in Bellehaven before your class begins."

"Tempting as that is, it would be difficult to explain why I was returning in your coach."

He knew she was right, but he couldn't bear to say good-bye to her again, not when his head was still grappling with everything she'd told him. Maybe, just maybe, he could convince Penelope that marriage to him was a bad idea. Maybe he *could* be the sort of man that Hazel needed and deserved.

He sat up, buttoned his trousers, and looked at Hazel earnestly. "There's something I must tell you before you go."

"Yes?" She blinked at him, expectant.

"It kills me to say this. But when Penelope agreed to help Prue, she demanded something in return."

Hazel swallowed. "What?"

"To announce our engagement . . . at Lady Rufflebum's ball."

The color drained from her cheeks. "I see."

"I will speak with her. Maybe I can convince her to change her mind. But I gave my word that I'd marry her. It seemed like the only way to save Bellehaven Academy. Your school—your girls—they're everything to you. I thought it was what you wanted."

"I thought so, too." She stood and pressed a palm to her forehead. "My girls *are* everything to me. But so are you. I wish that I didn't have to choose."

"You shouldn't have to. I'm sorry Hazel."

She shook her head. "You're not to blame. You were only doing what I asked."

"Believe me, if I could go back and start the summer over again, I'd do things differently," he said. "But unless Penelope agrees to release me from the deal we made, I will have to marry her . . . and I will have to announce our betrothal at the ball."

* * *

Hazel paced the length of Blade's drawing room, feeling as though she was moving underwater. She heard all that he had said, but it sounded strange and distorted, as if she were in the middle of a bad dream.

She'd known that Blade had promised to marry Penelope. She'd known that he'd done it partly for her. But she hadn't known it would hurt so keenly to hear him say it.

Still, she didn't regret baring her soul to him. She didn't regret anything they'd done. What she regretted were the things they couldn't share—a future, a family, a lifetime of loving each other.

"What about Kitty?" she said. "Will she be able to stay in Bellehaven?"

"Absolutely," Blade confirmed. "At least until she's ready to return to London. But she's happy with you and Lucy and Clara."

"And you'll still visit?"

"I will," he hesitated. "But it will be different. I won't be alone."

She nodded. That was probably for the best—at least until sufficient time had passed that she could look at him without wanting to run into his arms and bury her head in the crook of his neck. That day seemed very distant indeed.

"I should go." She looked out the window behind him, where rivulets of rain trickled down the glass.

"I will take you to Gunter's," he said firmly, and she didn't argue. "You should eat and drink something while I order the coach," he added, gesturing to the elaborate tea tray.

She nodded again as he strode from the room and forced herself to nibble on a scone.

But there was no delaying the inevitable. A few minutes later, she sat beside him on the plush velvet squabs of his coach, safe and cozy, as they rumbled through the puddle-filled London streets. They didn't speak, but he held her hand, brushing his thumb over her palm every few seconds, and she knew that this was precisely the feeling she would miss. The feeling of being connected to someone on a level that transcended mere words. The certainty that no matter how difficult life became, someone was there, making the burden lighter by simply caring.

When the coach rolled to a stop, just down the corner from the confectionery shop, her belly lurched, rebelling at the thought of leaving him.

"Miss Whitford will be here any moment now," she said. He held tight to her hand.

He leaned in and gave her a soft, slow kiss—the kind that made the world stand still. "Thank you for not giving up on me. Even when I'd given up on myself."

She didn't trust herself to speak but managed a smile as he opened the door of the coach and helped her step down onto the pavement.

"I'll see you at the ball," he said gruffly.

She forced her feet to move in the direction of the shop's front door, grateful that the rain provided cover for her tears. She felt Blade's gaze follow her as she walked away, but she had the prickling sensation that someone else watched her, too. When she entered the shop, she hazarded a glance through the large bay window, but no one seemed to have followed her.

The sad, painful truth was that she was alone. Again.

Poppy breezed into Hazel's office the next afternoon like a beam of sunlight breaking through gray skies. She called a cheerful greeting, placed her basket of books on a chair, and began stacking them in one arm. "Thank you for the wonderful selection this week," she began, then paused. "You look rather . . . tired." Her brow creased in concern. "Are you feeling well?"

Hazel started to say that she felt perfectly fine, but she was weary of pretending—and somehow she knew that Poppy, who was the closest thing she had a sister, would understand. "I went to London yesterday . . . to visit someone."

"Did you?" Poppy's blue eyes widened. "Was the some-one . . . a gentleman?"

"Yes." Hazel sank into her chair, propped an elbow on the desk, and rested her chin on the heel of her hand. "It was a risky and reckless thing to do, and yet I'm certain it was the right thing."

Poppy set the books on the edge of the desk and took a seat across from her. "Then you should not second-guess your decision." She searched Hazel's face. "You care for him?"

A knot lodged in Hazel's throat. "I do."

"And he cares for you?"

"Yes, but . . ."

"But," Poppy repeated, her expression grim. "I'm sorry there's a *but*."

"I am, too." It felt good to confide in someone—like loos-ening one's corset after a grueling day. "I suppose I'll be fine eventually. But right now . . . all I want to do is crawl into my bed, pull the covers over my head, and cry."

Poppy reached across the desk and squeezed her fingers. "Any man would be lucky to have you. Perhaps, in time, he will come around."

"Our time has run out, I'm afraid," Hazel said. "Even if it hadn't, I'm not sure we could have made it work. We are from completely different worlds, he and I."

Poppy pursed her pink lips, narrowed her eyes shrewdly, and tapped an index finger on the arm of her chair. "This man, would he happen to be an earl?"

Sweet Jesus. "How . . . how did you know?"

"I saw you together after the regatta. There was something

in the way you looked at each other—as though the rest of the crowd wasn't even there."

Hazel groaned. "Was it so obvious?"

"It was to me." Poppy tilted her head thoughtfully. "Are you certain that there's no chance for a future?"

"He will be announcing his engagement to Lady Penelope at the ball this weekend." She pressed a hand to her belly, willing her lunch to stay put.

"Bloody hell."

"Precisely," Hazel agreed. "I wish that I did not have to witness it, but I don't see how I can avoid it. The girls have been looking forward to the ball all summer, and they'd be devastated if I told them we weren't going."

"It was all Kitty could talk about during her last swimming lesson."

"You'll be there, won't you?"

"At Lady Rufflebum's?" Poppy shuddered. "Balls are not for me."

"Nonsense," Hazel said. "You'll know everyone there, and it would make me feel so much better to have a friend nearby. Please, say you'll go."

Poppy's blue eyes turned soft, and she exhaled in resignation. "Fine. I shall put in an appearance. I suppose I can wear the gown you gave me."

"You will be beautiful, as always," Hazel said. "Thank you for understanding."

"It's the least I can do for a fellow Belle," Poppy said with a grin. "As for the earl, if you'd like someone to fill his fancy coach with three-day old chum, I'm your girl."

Hazel chuckled. "Only you could make me laugh when I'm—"

A knock sounded at the door, and she quickly swiped at her eyes before calling, "Come in."

Kitty, Lucy, and Clara filed into the room, greeted Poppy,

and flanked Hazel in perfect formation. Kitty clutched a small satchel, Lucy held a pad of paper, and Clara had a measuring tape draped around her neck.

"Hullo, girls," Hazel said. "Is everything all right?"

"We've come to make some last-minute notes prior to the ball," Kitty said, matter-of-fact. "Would you mind if Clara took a few measurements?"

"Er, I suppose not."

Clara was already moving behind her, stretching the tape from the tip of one shoulder to the other. "Fifteen and three-quarters inches," she said to Lucy, who dutifully recorded the number in her pad. Clara slipped the tape around Hazel's rib cage and called out another number.

"Is all this fuss necessary?" Hazel clucked her tongue at Clara. "You said you were only making a few alterations to my old gown."

"Just a few," Clara repeated, blinking her dark eyes innocently. "I had to raise the waist, of course, and lower the neckline. We all agreed that the sleeves required a bit of gathering. And obviously, there are the necessary embellishments—it would hardly be a ball gown without a bit of whimsy."

The other girls murmured their agreement.

Oh dear. "A bit of whimsy is fine, but I shouldn't want anything too conspicuous."

Clara's small hands froze. "You trust me, don't you, Miss Lively?"

"Of course I do."

She exhaled and continued moving and measuring. "I shall not disappoint you."

Kitty set her satchel on the desk, withdrew two hair combs, and held them above Hazel's ear. To Poppy, she said, "Mother-of-pearl or silver filigree?"

"The silver," Poppy replied definitively.

Kitty nodded. "I shall pin the side just so," she said, modeling the hairstyle with her own golden locks, "and allow the rest to fall over her shoulder."

"That sounds rather elaborate," Hazel protested.

"It sounds rather lovely," Poppy countered.

Clara took a few steps back and squinted as though she were envisioning Hazel's gown and hair in her head. "The overall effect will be stunning," she said confidently. To her cohorts, she said, "I believe we have what we need."

They nodded, gathered up their supplies, and marched out of the office.

"I see what you mean about the girls," Poppy said. "They are rather obsessed with the ball."

"We've been practicing the quadrille all week long." Hazel smiled wryly. "And reviewing our etiquette."

Poppy scrunched her freckled nose. "I, for one, will be happy when the summer is ended, the tourists have gone, and Lady Rufflebum's ball is over."

"I suppose all summers must come to an end." Hazel heaved a sigh. "I shan't forget this one for a very long time."

Chapter 27

"Blade." Penelope looked over the gleaming pianoforte she'd been playing and stood with the sort of grace that suggested she'd been practicing since leaving the cradle. "What a pleasant surprise."

He entered her tastefully appointed drawing room with trepidation and greeted her hard-of-hearing aunt, who was engrossed in a book in the far corner.

"Please, sit," Penelope said. "I shall ring for tea."

"No need." He took a seat in an armchair while she perched on an adjacent sofa. "I won't stay long. I wanted to speak to you before you travel to Bellehaven."

"Then it's a good thing you called today. I'm leaving for the seaside tomorrow."

"So soon?"

"I plan to visit Mrs. Covington and spend a bit of time coaching Prudence in advance of the ball."

"That's kind of you," he said, knowing full well that kindness had nothing to do with it.

"Prudence is a rather plain girl, but I've no doubt she'll blossom under my tutelage. Her mother seems most grateful. I do believe she's planning to re-enroll Prue as soon as next week. And if her daughter makes a splash at Lady Rufflebum's ball, she intends to recommend Bellehaven Academy to all her wealthy friends."

"I realize that you are lending your assistance to the Covingtons because I asked you to," he said slowly, "and I do appreciate it."

"I was reluctant at first. I had no idea that being virtuous would feel so rewarding. I daresay it's done wonders for my complexion." She smoothed her fingertips across a porcelain cheek and flashed him a self-deprecating smile—the sort he might have once found charming.

"There's something else I must ask of you," he said soberly. "And it's no small matter."

One elegant eyebrow twitched. "Go on."

"I'd like you to release me from our agreement."

She cocked an ear as though she couldn't have possibly heard him correctly. "Which agreement might that be?"

"To marry. I don't think we should, Penelope."

"This is a most unexpected development," she said smoothly.

"I know. We had an understanding."

"Have," she corrected. "We *have* an understanding."

"Circumstances have changed. I thought I'd be happy to sire an heir and live a life apart from my wife. Now I know that I want more—as should you."

She pursed her lips, plucked a slightly faded white rose from the vase on the table beside her, and rolled the stem between her fingers. "This rose is from a duke," she said conversationally. "A duke who called on me last week. He seemed quite eager to further our acquaintance, but I discouraged his attentions . . . because of our agreement."

"I don't blame you for being angry." Blade raked a hand through his hair. "I'm not proud of my behavior. I have always honored my commitments, but in this case, I'm utterly convinced that following through would do greater harm than calling it off. If you insist that we go forward with a loveless marriage, I will have no choice but to acquiesce to your wishes. But I'm asking you—begging you, for both our sakes—to release me from this arrangement."

Penelope stood and slowly circled his chair as she tapped the ivory petals of the flower against her palm. "You act as though you know what is best for me, for my future."

Shit. "That was not my intention. However, I've no doubt you shall have many more suitors—gentlemen who would be far better matches than I."

"I disagree," she said with a calmness that chilled him to his core. "Do not forget that I have been married before. I know what sort of husband I want and, more important, what sort I *don't* want. Intense passion—which often passes for love—leads to nothing but myriad problems." She bit her lip as though she'd said too much, then continued. "I entered into an arrangement with you seeking status, security, and freedom. I intend to have those things, Bladenton. Which is why I will not release you from our agreement."

He swore under his breath. "Please, reconsider."

"I know what this is about," she said lightly. "The headmistress. You may not believe me now, but I am doing you both a favor. You would not be content with a wife who spends her days trying to teach ill-bred girls how to pass as proper ladies."

He gripped the arms of the chair. "Don't disparage Haz—, er, Miss Lively or her students," he warned.

"And Miss Lively," Penelope continued, "would not be content with a husband who is incapable of genuine affection."

All the doubt, pain, and guilt of the last fifteen years bubbled up in his throat, threatening to choke him. But then he remembered what Hazel had said—that he'd already changed. "My marriage to Miss Lively would be different."

Penelope stopped in front of him and clucked her tongue. "Perhaps it would be, for a few weeks. Maybe even a few months. But then you would revert to your old ways. You'd grow impatient with all the time she spends at her school. You'd become jealous of Bellehaven Academy."

"That's utterly ridiculous," he spat.

"Is it?" she crooned. "Think about it, Blade. She'll be holed up in her office planning lessons when she should be in your drawing room planning dinner parties. Miss Lively will never put you ahead of her beloved school—and she'll resent you for wanting her to." With that, Penelope dropped the wilted rose in his lap and glided back to the sofa.

Holy hell. He'd hoped that he'd be able to reason with her. That she'd appreciate his honesty. Instead, she was trying to crucify him with it. Clearly, there would be no changing her mind.

As he glimpsed a future without Hazel, a heavy, suffocating dread settled on his shoulders. The walls began to encroach; all the hope he'd briefly felt drained through his feet.

"I'm glad we had this talk," Penelope said smoothly. "But now I must go and begin packing for my trip. I've had an exquisite gown made for Lady Rufflebum's ball, naturally. All eyes will be on us as we announce our engagement—and I intend to look my best."

Blade murmured a farewell and headed for the door as fast as he could. As soon as he was outside, he leaned against an iron rail and gulped in a lungful of air.

No matter how much he longed to walk away from the promise he'd made to Penelope, he was bound by it. He had to live with the consequences.

What absolutely gutted him, though, was that Hazel would have to live with them, too.

* * *

Hazel sat in her bed, reading Blade's letter for the dozenth time that day.

> *Dearest Hazel,*
> *It is with a heavy heart that I must tell you that my attempt to extract myself from my prior commitment was unsuccessful. Honor requires me to keep my word, no matter how much I wish it weren't so. I have many regrets, but the greatest is hurting you.*
> *I hope you have a life full of all the things you desire— the sound of the ocean, the warmth of family, and the joy of love. For my part, I shall content myself with memories. Indeed, I shall never see another fichu without thinking—most ardently—of you.*
>
> *B.*

She sniffled, rolled over in her bed, and pounded a fist in her pillow. Oh, she'd known there was precious little chance of a future with Blade, and she supposed she should have taken some comfort from the fact that he'd tried to break things off with Penelope. In truth, he'd penned a lovely letter.

Only it hadn't mentioned love.

After everything they'd been through. After everything she'd risked. This brief letter was all that was left behind—a vague impression, like an ammonite fossil in the cliffs.

A loud knock sounded at her door, jolting her upright. Good heavens. She could not recall the last time someone had come to her bedroom.

"It's me, Miss Lively," Kitty called from the corridor. "I've come to style your hair."

Hazel blinked at the clock on her mantel. "Already?" she replied, stuffing the letter beneath her pillow. She checked her face in the mirror above the washstand, frowned at her

puffy eyes, and cinched the sash of her dressing gown before opening the door. Kitty stood in the hall, wearing a few
dozen curling papers in her hair, her expressive face beaming with anticipation.

"The day has finally arrived," she said with her usual dramatic flair. "Can you believe that we both shall attend our
first ball tonight?"

"A momentous occasion." Hazel smiled, wishing she felt
an inkling of Kitty's enthusiasm. "But we needn't leave for
another two hours."

"That soon? We haven't a moment to waste." Kitty swept
past her, set a box on Hazel's desk, and pulled out the chair.
"Please, sit so I may begin. I daresay it will take me a quarter of an hour just to remove all the pins you have in there."

Hazel chuckled. If someone had told her at the beginning of the summer that she'd allow one of her students to
style her hair, she'd have told them they'd sooner see a snow
squall in August. But Kitty and the girls had pleaded with
Hazel, reasoning that they were all representing Bellehaven
Academy, and that they should work together to ensure they
made a favorable impression at their first major social event.
It had been hard for Hazel to disagree, especially when they
presented such a united and impassioned front—rather like
a family.

So she sat and resigned herself to Kitty's ministrations.
"How are the other girls?"

"Clara's resting," Kitty said, pulling a brush through Hazel's hair. "She was up half the night, fussing with her needle and thread—as usual."

"Goodness. I hope she didn't overtax herself on my account."

Kitty shrugged. "You know how she adores a sewing project."

"And Lucy?"

"She's running a few errands with Miss Jane. I suspect they'll return at any moment." Kitty's forehead creased as she methodically twisted, pinned, and curled. "You have a great deal more hair than I realized," she said, as if this were a surprising but rather welcome development.

"How was your visit with Mr. Sandford yesterday? Are you pleased with the plans for the new stables?"

"Mmm." Kitty removed the pin she'd held between her lips. "Mr. Sandford incorporated some of my suggestions along with some of his grandson's. I am not sure how those diametrically opposed ideas will work together, but I shall be eager to see how the stables take shape when they begin construction next week."

Hazel arched a brow. "And will Mr. Sandford's grandson be attending the ball tonight?"

"I'm certain I don't know or care," Kitty said, a bit too vehemently. "But I suspect he's too busy swinging a hammer to bother with donning a proper evening jacket."

"In any event, you shan't have a shortage of dance partners."

"And neither shall you." Kitty took a step back, looking quite satisfied as she surveyed her work.

She flipped open the lid on the wooden box, withdrew a pair of pretty combs, and carefully tucked them into the twists at Hazel's crown. Then she applied a bit of light, citrus-scented pomade to the riot of curls that tumbled over Hazel's shoulder. "There," she said at last. "That will do quite nicely."

"Shall I have a look?" Hazel asked, eager for a glance in the mirror. She didn't doubt Kitty's expertise in this area, but she did worry that the style would be too elaborate for her liking.

"Not yet," Kitty said firmly. She went to the washstand, dipped a cloth in the water basin, and handed it to her. "Press this to your eyes."

"Why?"

"It will help with the swelling."

Hazel opened her mouth to object, then realized it was futile and pressed the cool cloth to her eyelids. Meanwhile, Kitty rummaged through the box.

"These teardrop earrings will add a lovely bit of sparkle." Hazel felt a pinch on each lobe. "They were a gift from my parents," Kitty said wistfully.

"Then you must keep them safe," Hazel said. "Or wear them yourself."

"No," Kitty insisted. "Clara, Lucy, and I all agreed that these would be perfect . . . and it makes me happy to see you wearing them."

Hazel's throat grew thick with emotion. "That's very sweet," she said, touched. "I promise to take good care of them."

"Now we must add a bit of color to your face."

Hazel removed the cloth from her eyes to find Kitty unscrewing the top on a pot of rouge. "Where on earth did you get that?"

She dipped a finger into the pot and dabbed the apple of Hazel's cheek. "I bought it from one of the older girls at my last boarding school. She bribed her mother's lady's maid to nick it for her."

Hazel wasn't sure if she should be horrified or impressed. "You realize that you're far too young and pretty to require rouge?"

"Yes," Kitty said, matter-of-fact. She used a tiny brush to apply a touch of the paint to Hazel's lips. "But it's helpful on occasion. We all have days when we must give nature some assistance."

"I suppose that's true, but—"

"Ah, here are Lucy and Clara." Kitty waved them into the room.

"Miss Lively!" Lucy exclaimed. "Your hair is so beautiful. Why must I be cursed with orange hair?"

"You're blessed," Hazel corrected, "with hair the color of ripe strawberries and spun gold."

Clara glided farther into the room wearing a secretive smile and holding Hazel's old dress behind her back. "Are you ready to see your new ball gown?" she asked.

Hazel chuckled at her characterization of the dress as a ball gown—especially since it was five years old and a rather drab shade of tan. But she knew better than to underestimate Clara's talent. "I am always eager to see your creations," she said truthfully.

Clara presented the dress with a flourish, holding it beneath her own chin for display.

And the sight of it took Hazel's breath away.

The shape had changed dramatically—long, straight sleeves had been replaced with delicate puffs. The waist had been raised and adorned with green satin ribbon; the neckline had been lowered and trimmed with delicate white lace. The fabric color, which had once seemed plain, now glowed like polished bronze beside the dress's striking accents.

But what drew Hazel's eyes the most was the exquisite embroidery along the gown's hem. "Is that . . . ?" She swallowed the lump in her throat and moved closer to examine Clara's expert needlework. Felt her heart lurch. "It's . . . the hazelnut design from my handkerchief."

"The very same one," Clara said proudly. "I made it a bit smaller and repeated it all the way around the hem at varying heights, for added interest. The rich browns and lush greens work brilliantly with this material. But more important, we all agreed that the hazelnuts helped to make this gown uniquely *you*."

Suddenly weak-kneed, Hazel gripped the back of her

chair. "That afternoon in the dormitory, when you took my framed handkerchief—this was why."

"We should have asked," Lucy said, apologetic. "But we didn't want to ruin the surprise."

"No." Hazel shook her head, adamant. "I should have realized you had a good reason, and I'm sorry." She went to the girls and hugged them each in turn, savoring the feel of their slender, surprisingly strong arms around her waist. Hazel was no expert, but it seemed to her that this must be what families did: making mistakes, forgiving each other, and growing closer as a result.

"I must be the luckiest headmistress in the entire world," she continued. "Not because the three of you conspired to make me the most beautiful gown in the British Empire, but because you conspired to do something so thoughtful and generous. Thank you."

Kitty swiped at her eyes suspiciously but quickly composed herself. "Before you get too carried away, perhaps we should see if the gown actually fits you."

Clara propped a fist on her hip, slightly offended. "Of course it will fit."

"I'm sure it shall," Hazel quickly agreed. "And I'm most eager to try it on."

Clara handed her the dress, which she took behind her dressing screen. She shrugged off her robe and carefully stepped into the wondrous creation, which seemed to skim every curve of her body without squeezing in the slightest. It exposed a bit more skin than Hazel was accustomed to showing, and yet she loved it.

When she stepped out from behind the screen, the girls squealed with delight. "Come, let me lace you up," said Kitty, moving behind her.

"Here are your slippers," Lucy set a pair of light-pink shoes on the floor at her feet.

"Where did those come from?" Hazel asked.

"They're Miss Jane's. She said you wore the same size, and we wanted something simple, so as not to detract from your gown."

"You've thought of everything," Hazel said warmly, stepping into the slippers.

Clara fussed with the dress's sleeves, making sure they were situated just so on Hazel's shoulders, while Kitty finished tying the laces at her back.

At last, the girls stepped away, admiring the fruits of their labor.

"Perfect," Lucy said happily.

"The first stare of fashion," Clara declared.

"Flawless," said Kitty. "And I suppose it's time you saw for yourself."

She grabbed Hazel's hand, led her to the mirror, and smiled at their reflections.

Hazel's jaw went slack. The woman who stared back was most definitely her—but another version of her. A version that would be perfectly at ease waltzing in a London ballroom or sitting in a private box at the opera.

Her thick brown curls were swept to one side; emerald earrings dangled from her lobes. All the accessories were beautiful—but Clara's gown was a bit of magic.

Granted, it wasn't as though a gorgeous dress could mend her broken heart. It certainly couldn't prevent Blade and Penelope from announcing their engagement in a few hours' time. But it *did* manage to make Hazel smile, and that in itself was something of a miracle.

"I don't know what to say, girls, except thank you. You gave me something I hadn't realized I'd been wishing for."

Lucy laced her fingers beneath her chin. "Tonight is going to be the best night ever."

Kitty nodded dreamily. "I can't wait for Uncle Beck to see Miss Lively."

Oh dear. "Kitty, you mustn't think that your uncle and I . . ." She felt her cheeks heat. "That is, we are merely friends."

"If you say so." Kitty patted the back of her own head, as though she'd just recalled she'd yet to remove her curling papers. She grabbed her box from Hazel's desk and began herding the girls from the room. "Come on, we must dress ourselves now. Lady Rufflebum's coach will be here to retrieve us in less than an hour."

They scurried toward the door, but Clara drew up short and spun around. She gazed at Hazel, her dark eyes wise and earnest. "I'm glad you like the gown, Miss Lively."

"I adore it," Hazel corrected. "And I shall treasure it, always, because you made it."

She nibbled her lip, pensive. "There is one, simple favor I should like to ask in return."

"Of course, Clara." Hazel placed a hand on her thin shoulder. "What is it?"

"Promise me," she said slowly, "that you will never—ever—attempt to cover that neckline with a fichu."

Hazel shot Clara a conspiratorial smile. "I wouldn't dream of it."

Chapter 28

"You're looking well," Blade said tightly. Penelope had attached herself to his arm shortly after he'd arrived at Lady Rufflebum's ball. Now they were taking a turn about the room—and he was making one more valiant attempt to minimize the damage he'd caused.

"Not the most effusive of compliments," Penelope said wryly, "but I shall take what I can get." She glanced around the large room, admiring the streams of ribbons in varying shades of white and blue that hung from every column, sconce, and window frame. The long satin strands billowed in the evening breeze, mimicking the undulations of the ocean. "I must say, the countess has gone to extraordinary lengths to decorate the ballroom."

"Indeed." But the truth was he didn't give a damn about the bloody ribbons or the vases stuffed with flowers. He wasn't impressed by the scores of glowing candles or the massive ceiling mural featuring Poseidon and his chariot drawn by fish-tailed horses. He only wanted to see Hazel—and to be certain she was all right.

His eyes flicked to the ballroom entrance, where a batch of newly arrived guests were being announced, but Hazel wasn't among them.

"I'm delighted we have such a beautiful setting in which to announce our engagement," Penelope said. "It shall be quite memorable."

Blade paused and faced her. "About that. I would rather not create a spectacle here."

"You promised," she said through her teeth. "I wasted two hours yesterday attempting to coach the Covington chit on how to engage her dance partners in witty repartee. I am fulfilling my side of the bargain, and you shall do the same."

He reached into the breast pocket of his jacket, withdrew the envelope he'd placed there, and handed it to Penelope.

She narrowed her eyes, suspicious. "What's this?"

"The announcement of our"—he swallowed, willing his tongue into submission—"engagement. It's addressed to the offices of *The London Hearsay*."

"I'm afraid I don't follow."

"You can give it to a footman right now and request that it be delivered immediately. In three days' time, it will appear in the paper, for all the ton to see. And I will not be able to take it back."

She pursed her lips and tapped the edge of the envelope with a gloved fingertip. "I suppose it does provide some form of insurance."

"Send it now," he urged. "Instead of making the public announcement tonight. We needn't cause a scene here. Doing so would only rub salt in the wound."

"In Miss Lively's wound, you mean," she said pointedly.

"I've hurt her enough already."

"You needn't worry," Penelope intoned. "The headmistress seems remarkably strong. Rather immune to emotion."

Blade swore under his breath. Decided to try a different tack. "This is not our engagement ball," he reminded her. "Lady Rufflebum takes great pride in this annual event, and it would be rude to usurp the attention from her—to use it for our own purposes."

Penelope tossed her head, and the tall, unnaturally pink feather in her headdress quivered in response. "Actually, the countess could not be more pleased. I have already informed her that you intend to make a special announcement just after midnight. She's arranged for a champagne toast."

Shit. "I was a fool to agree to this," he said, more to himself than to her. "Mad to think it would work."

"Perhaps." She flashed him a frosty smile as she folded the envelope and surreptitiously tucked it into her bosom. "However, it's all but done now. We *will* make the announcement this evening at midnight. And if you don't have the ballocks to do it, then I shall do it for you."

Lady Rufflebum had generously offered to send her coach to bring Hazel and the girls to the ball. For Lucy and Clara, the brief ride in a luxurious coach was nearly as exciting as the prospect of the ball.

"So this is what it feels like to be a queen," Lucy announced. She and Clara looked like a darling pair of dolls in their new dresses, sitting on a plush velvet seat opposite Hazel and Kitty. "I could become accustomed to this life."

"You'll still be going to sleep in the dormitory tonight, along with Clara and me," Kitty pointed out. "So enjoy the fairy tale while you may."

"I intend to," Lucy said firmly.

"But do not worry, Miss Lively," Clara added. "We shall be on our best behavior tonight."

Hazel's chest squeezed. "I know you shall. All I ask is that you look out for each other and be kind. Do that, and you'll make Bellehaven Academy—and me—proud."

They nodded like dutiful soldiers taking their marching orders.

Kitty smoothed the skirt of her pale-pink gown. "I intend to track down Prue, find out where she's been all week, and persuade her to return to the classroom. I miss her."

The younger girls bobbed their heads, murmuring their agreement.

"I miss her, too," Hazel said. "But the decision is Mrs. Covington's. She must do what she deems best for Prue."

"Is that why you're sad?" Clara asked.

Hazel swallowed. Clara had always been too perceptive by half. "Yes, partly."

"Why else?" Lucy asked.

Drat. Hazel couldn't very well admit to the girls that she dreaded seeing the man she loved announce his engagement to another woman, so she told them a modified version of the truth. "I suppose I'm feeling melancholy because tonight's ball marks the end of the season. That means summer—and all the lovely things that came with it—will soon be drawing to a close."

"I'm not fond of endings," Clara said softly.

Hazel reached across the coach and squeezed her hand. The last thing she'd wanted was to dampen the girls' excitement. "Then we'll think of tonight as a beginning—the beginning of a new and grand adventure."

"Precisely," Kitty said. "According to the latest issue of *The Debutante's Revenge*, 'One should never let a perfectly good ball go to waste.' I suggest that we all follow the sage advice of the authoress—and make the most out of the evening."

Kitty's words still echoed in Hazel's head half an hour later as she and the girls glided into Lady Rufflebum's breathtaking ballroom. Decorated in soothing hues of blue and white, the room looked like an underwater palace—or an ancient temple from the city of Atlantis. Hundreds of shimmering ribbons hung from the high ceilings, creating a fanciful maze for guests to navigate. The dance floor had been painted to resemble the ocean floor, complete with conch shells, seaweed, and the occasional crab.

"It's beautiful," Kitty breathed. "I want to sketch it right now."

"Everyone is staring at us," whispered Lucy.

"No," said Clara. "They're staring at Miss Lively."

Hazel's face heated. It did feel as though she was on display. Rather like she was a newly finished statue, and someone had just whipped off the sheet at a public unveiling. "They're not accustomed to seeing me in a gown as pretty as this. They're admiring your handiwork, Clara."

"The best gowns don't compete with beauty, they complement it," she replied quite seriously.

Hazel managed to smile and hold her head high despite the fact that several pairs of quizzing glasses were pointed in her direction.

"I think I see Prue," Lucy said, gesturing across the room. "In the white dress, walking through the ribbons by the terrace doors."

"Let's go." Kitty linked arms with the younger girls. "Are you coming, Miss Lively?"

Hazel hesitated, unsure how Mrs. Covington would react. She'd made it clear that Prue was to have nothing to do with Bellehaven Academy or its students. But even Mrs. Covington couldn't prevent the girls from seeing one another at the social event of the season. "You three go on and give Prue my best."

Her heart swelled with pride as she watched them weave their way through the crowd, a trio of guppies swimming against the current. She took a deep breath and let her gaze sweep over the room, hoping to locate Jane and Poppy.

In truth, she was also searching for a pair of broad shoulders and a ruggedly handsome face. She'd told herself that she wouldn't. That seeing Blade would only heighten the pain. But his pull over her far exceeded her willpower. It was like trying to turn down the lamp before reading the last chapter of a favorite book—it simply couldn't be done.

"Looking for someone in particular, Miss Lively?" The voice, feminine and cultured, triggered a riot of ugly emotions in her belly, but Hazel kept her face impassive as she turned around.

"Good evening, Lady Penelope," she said. "I was just trying to find my friends."

Penelope raised a skeptical eyebrow. "It's quite a crush. Lady Rufflebum has seen fit to invite all manner of—" She tilted her head and cast a critical eye over Hazel, starting at her crown and slowly working her way down to the toes of her slippers. "I hardly recognize you tonight without your usual hairpins, sensible apron, and sturdy boots." Her mouth curled into a smile that did not reach her eyes. "That is a compliment, by the way."

Hazel longed to fire back with a barb, but in spite of everything, she was still hopeful that Lady Penelope would rescue Bellehaven Academy. That a glowing endorsement from her would help keep the school afloat. "Thank you."

"You must give me the name of your modiste," Penelope said smoothly. "Her design has a distinct . . . flair."

Hazel smiled inwardly. "She hasn't established her own shop—yet. However, I shall let you know if she decides to take on additional clients."

Penelope nodded, seemingly mollified. "I wondered if you and I might have a word . . . in private?" she added, raising the gooseflesh on the backs of Hazel's arms.

"I should probably remain here, where I can keep watch over Kitty and the girls."

"This won't take long." Penelope closed her fingers around Hazel's wrist with a vise-like grip and glided toward the

French doors at the rear of the room, towing Hazel in her wake. A minute later they stood in the glow of the lanterns suspended above Lady Rufflebum's terrace. Quite alone.

Hazel wished she were anywhere but there—and with anyone but Penelope.

"What did you wish to discuss?" she said, doing her best to keep her tone professional. Mildly detached.

Penelope strolled across the flagstones, her golden gown floating around her legs. "I thought it was high time that you and I were frank with each other."

Warning bells sounded in Hazel's head. "I don't know what you mean."

Penelope stood at the edge of the terrace and gazed at the garden beyond like a princess surveying her kingdom. "Lord Bladenton and I intend to announce our engagement tonight—as you well know."

Hazel saw no point in denying it. "Yes."

"Nothing—and I do mean *nothing*—may interfere with that."

Her blood heated to a low boil. "I'm not certain what you're implying, Lady Penelope."

She spun on her heel and faced Hazel, blue eyes blazing. "I won't allow you to jeopardize my future with Bladenton."

Hazel curled her fingers into her palms and counted to three in her head. "I am not the master of anyone's destiny. Lord Bladenton shall determine his own future." Indeed, it seemed he'd already made his choice.

"And yet, for reasons I can't quite fathom, you appear to have some sway over the earl." She eyed the mildly daring neckline of Hazel's gown. "I can't risk him making a stupid, rash decision this evening—which is why I'm having this chat with you."

Lady Penelope's scorn was frightening in its intensity, but Hazel refused to cower. She raised her chin and glared back.

Hard on the outside. "Idle threats don't intimidate me," she said, keeping her voice low and even.

"Oh, there's nothing idle about this." Penelope bared her white, even teeth. "You see, I know what's been going on here in Bellehaven—and in London. It's rather shocking, even to me."

Fear prickled at the skin between Hazel's shoulder blades. "I don't know what you're talking about."

"It's the height of scandal, actually. A prim headmistress dallying with a rakish earl. The gossip pages will be in raptures over it . . . but I cannot imagine that the parents of your students will be similarly delighted."

Dear God. Hazel's mouth turned ash dry.

"I know all about your illicit affair . . . your sordid trysts."

"You don't know anything," Hazel ground out, but beneath the skirt of her gown, her knees trembled.

"Let me be clear." Penelope spoke slowly, as if she were addressing a child. "If Blade doesn't announce our engagement at midnight, I shall make an announcement of my own. Lady Rufflebum, her esteemed guests, and the whole of Bellehaven—including your own students—will learn the disgraceful truth. That you have been thoroughly compromised by the earl and are utterly unfit to run a school for deportment. You will be forced to close the doors of your precious Bellehaven Academy. Forever."

Panic flooded Hazel's veins. Such a scandal *would* be the end of Bellehaven Academy—and her livelihood. She'd have no way to support Lucy and Clara. She'd have to say goodbye to Kitty, Poppy, and Jane. She'd lose the wonderful family they'd begun to build.

She closed her eyes for two heartbeats, then met Penelope's icy gaze, searching for a shred of compassion. "If you were to do such a hateful, such a spiteful thing, you would ruin more lives than mine."

"Regrettably, yes." Penelope pursed her lips thoughtfully. "I take no pleasure in hurting you, but I *will* do what I must to ensure my next marriage is nothing like my first."

"I don't understand."

"It's neither here nor there." Penelope frowned as though she'd revealed more than she'd intended. "But trust me when I say it's in everyone's interests that the engagement is announced at midnight, as planned." She patted her head, adjusting the tilt of the pink plume at her crown as she made her way back to the house. "Indeed, the future of your school depends upon it."

Chapter 29

Blade had spotted Kitty chatting animatedly with her friends on the perimeter of the dance floor, so he knew Hazel must be at the ball . . . but he'd yet to see her.

Maybe she was avoiding him—and he couldn't say he blamed her.

"Good to see you, Bladenton." Dunmire slapped him on the back as if they were lifelong chums, which they most definitely were not. The viscount raised his brandy glass in a mock salute. "The countess certainly knows how to host an event, doesn't she? This would be a mad crush even by London's standards."

"True." Blade took a gulp of his own drink and let his gaze sweep across the ballroom.

"Plenty of beauties to choose from tonight," Dunmire quipped. "Almost an embarrassment of riches. Look at the pink dress over there." He thrust his chin in Poppy's direction. "It's the girl who won the regatta if I'm not mistaken. Certainly cleaned up nicely. I wouldn't mind luring her into Lady Rufflebum's silver closet."

Blade clenched his jaw and faced the viscount. "Stay away from her."

Dunmire raised a palm as if he couldn't quite believe he

was under attack. "Didn't realize you were interested in her, old chap. I assumed your tastes ran more toward Lady Penelope's type. Any man would be lucky to have her warming his bed."

Blade glared at him. "I'm not having this conversation with you."

"Suit yourself." Dunmire shrugged and backed away slowly. "I'll leave you to your brooding."

Bastard. Blade suspected Poppy was capable of taking care of herself but decided the least he could do was warn her. Only she seemed to have disappeared, too.

"There you are, Uncle Beck!" Kitty kissed him on the cheek then did a little twirl. "How do you like my gown?"

She made him chuckle in spite of his foul mood. "It's lovely."

"You're looking rather dashing yourself," she said.

He scrubbed the back of his neck. "There's something I need to tell you," he began.

She blinked at him, expectant. "Yes?"

"I'm going to be . . ."—damn it, but this was hard—"making some changes soon. You're bound to be affected, too, but I want you to know that I won't allow anything to come between you and me. You have my word."

For the space of several breaths, she stared at him, her expression impassive, and he wondered if she'd heard him over the din of the party. But then she reached out and squeezed his hand tightly. "I won't allow anything to come between us, either. You have *my* word."

"Good." He cleared the knot from his throat and managed a smile. "Now, shouldn't you be dancing? Or cavorting with your friends?"

"Do you truly think that I'm so one-dimensional, Uncle?" Kitty looked mildly wounded. "That I'm completely preoccupied with gowns and gossip?"

"What?" Blade felt as though he'd blundered into a fox trap. "Of course not."

She linked her arm through his and pulled him toward the French doors. "Come with me. I want to show you something."

She guided him across the deserted terrace and beyond, into the garden. "Where are we going?"

"To view my latest source of inspiration."

"Inspiration for what?" he asked warily.

"A new design project. After much debate, I've concluded that what Bladenton Manor requires is—" She paused for dramatic effect. "—a *greenhouse*." She gazed up at him, hopeful. "Wouldn't you agree?"

No, he would not. Bladenton Manor needed a greenhouse about as much as it needed a moat, but since the fox trap was still top of mind, he nodded. "Absolutely. I'm always curious to hear what you're planning."

"It's just down this path . . . there. Have a look at the roofline. The entire structure is simple and clean, very utilitarian. But I was thinking that we'd create something special for Bladenton Manor. Instead of a predictable rectangular structure, I should like to try an octagonal design. Imagine a brick foundation topped with beautiful mullioned arched windows and a roof so clear you could almost reach up and touch the stars."

"Mmm," he murmured.

"Are you listening, Uncle Beck?"

"Yes, of course."

She paused at the greenhouse's doorstep and pursed her lips, clearly skeptical. "Let's go in."

"It's too dark to properly see anything. Besides, I don't think we should be snooping around Lady Rufflebum's grounds."

"The countess told me I could explore the greenhouse any

time I liked," Kitty assured him. "There must be a lamp in-side."

"Fine," he grumbled. He pulled open the door, and the scents of earth, lime, and lilacs filled his head. "I'll see if I can find a lamp. Stay here so you don't bump into something and ruin your gown."

He wandered inside the structure, pausing to admire the view of the crescent moon through the glass ceiling before stepping farther into the foliage.

"I think I see a table to the right," Kitty called out from the doorway, just as Blade collided with it, bumping his thigh on the sharp corner.

"Found it," he replied dryly. He ran his hands over wooden surface and discovered what felt like a bucket of gardening tools and a half-full watering can.

"Any luck?" called Kitty.

"Not yet."

"Maybe the table just past that one."

He shuffled farther into the greenhouse, blindly swatting palm fronds away from his face.

Bam. The glass door to the greenhouse slammed shut, raising the hairs on the backs of his arms. He spun around. "Kitty?"

"I'm out here." Her muffled voice came from the other side of the glass, and he reached the door in five large strides. She frowned as she fiddled with the handle outside.

"What are you doing?"

"Trying to open the door." She rolled her eyes, as if the answer should have been obvious. "The breeze caught it, and now . . . well, it appears to be stuck."

"Back up," he instructed. "I'll push it open."

"Careful. The countess will have your head if you dam-age her door."

"I'm not going to break it. Just give it a firm shove." He

grabbed the handle, twisted it, and pushed. The door didn't budge.

"Oh dear."

"Don't worry," he scoffed. He jiggled the handle and pressed a foot against the bottom of the wooden frame till it creaked in protest. But the door still didn't move.

Kitty wrung her hands. "Maybe I should go fetch assistance."

"Assistance?" he repeated, incredulous. "No need. It's just a little stuck. I'm sure I can jar it loose."

He pounded on the casing till the glass rattled. Shook the door until his forehead broke out in a sweat. Tried using his shoulder as a battering ram. It was useless. In fact, the more he pushed, the more the door resisted.

"I'll enlist a member of the countess's staff to help," Kitty said through the panes. "Just don't . . . break anything. I'll return shortly."

"Wait—"

But she'd already left and was scurrying toward the house. He raked both hands through his hair and muttered a curse. Granted, it wasn't exactly a tragedy that he was missing the obligatory waltz, inane small talk, and weak lemonade, but it *was* frustrating to be trapped in a glorified shed. Especially since he knew Hazel wasn't far away.

All he wanted was to bask in her glow for one more night.

"Hazel?" Poppy's eyes rounded and she reached for Hazel's shoulders, holding her at arm's length. "You look stunning in that gown—like you could be the heroine in my favorite sort of novel."

"You don't know how relieved I am to see you." She pulled Poppy into a fierce embrace. They were near the rear of the ballroom, where the orchestra wasn't so loud and the crowd wasn't too thick.

Poppy's freckled brow knit in concern. "Has something happened?"

Hazel swallowed. "Let's just say that Lady Penelope doesn't care much for me or Bellehaven Academy."

She crinkled her nose. "I don't care much for *her*. Is there anything I can do?"

"No. I don't know why I mentioned it. You should be enjoying the evening. Half the young men in Bellehaven Bay were smitten with you already, and after seeing you in that dress tonight, I'd wager the other half are well on their way."

Poppy scoffed. "I'm not interested in anyone here. Lord Dunmire was ogling me earlier."

"He's arrogant and accustomed to getting what he wants. Be careful."

"Don't worry. If he tries anything, I'm prepared to defend myself." She flicked her gaze downward and surreptitiously lifted the hem of her gown, revealing a leather sheath strapped to her calf.

"Is that . . . ?"

"My fillet knife," Poppy confirmed. "It comes in handy for more than cod."

Hazel chuckled. "I don't think I want to know."

"Miss Lively, there you are!" Prue hurried over, looking rather grown-up with her hair coiled in a braid at her crown. She greeted Poppy with a warm smile, then turned to Hazel. "I've missed Bellehaven Academy—and you."

"I've missed you, too," Hazel said sincerely. "More than you know. You look very pretty and fashionable, by the way—just like a London debutante."

"Well, I'm not a debutante yet, thank goodness. I'm hoping Mama will let me wait another year or two before I must concern myself with a court dress and Almack's vouchers." Prue frowned, fiddled with the sash of her apricot gown, then sighed. "But I am determined to pursue my studies regardless," she said firmly. "And to that end, I have a favor to ask."

"You're welcome to borrow books from school anytime you like," Hazel offered. "As long as your mother has no objection."

"Actually, I was wondering if you could do something for me tonight. It shouldn't take long but will necessitate leaving the ballroom."

"I confess I'm intrigued," Hazel teased, certain that Prue merely wanted to inquire about a portrait in the countess's gallery or perhaps a map in the library. "Would you like to come along, Poppy?"

"You go on," she said breezily. "I'll remain here and ensure that Kitty and the rest of the girls are staying away from the champagne."

"Good thinking," Hazel murmured. "We shan't be long."

Prue linked an arm through hers and steered her out of the ballroom, down a corridor, and into a deserted drawing room. "Mama and I had tea with the countess a couple of days ago," she explained, "and Lady Rufflebum kindly gave us a tour of her gardens and greenhouse. There were a couple of plant varieties that she couldn't identify and I'm most eager to know what they are."

This was precisely what Hazel loved about Prue—her scientific curiosity, her relentless pursuit of knowledge, and her keen interest in nature. "I'm not certain I'll know the names of the plants, but we can certainly have a look, take some mental notes, and consult a book on flora tomorrow."

"I just knew you'd be able to help," Prue said enthusiastically. "The greenhouse is through these doors, a short way down the path."

Hazel hesitated near the French doors. Moonlight illuminated the walkway, but they'd need a better source of light to inspect the plants. "Shall we bring a lamp?"

Prue shook her head. "No need—I recall seeing one there."

They stepped outside onto the winding stone path and followed it through the lush garden. It seemed that the farther they moved from the house, the quieter the night grew.

"I'm sorry to steal you away from ball," Prue said.

"Don't be silly. I'm always glad to spend time with you." Prue's quiet, thoughtful personality was just what Hazel needed, truthfully. Any activity that took her mind off Blade was a welcome distraction.

"Here we are," Prue said breathlessly. Almost as if she were . . . nervous.

"Did you tell your mother where you were going?" Hazel asked. "I know she's not fond of Bellehaven Academy at the moment, but you mustn't keep secrets from her."

"You're right," Prue whispered, chastened. "But now that we're here, it doesn't make sense to turn back. We can look at the plants and return to the ballroom before she realizes I'm missing." Prue kicked something away from the base of the door, reached for the handle, and opened it.

Against her better judgment, Hazel walked in.

And heard the door slam behind her.

She turned toward the door just in time to see Prue and Kitty running away. When she tried to open the door, it wouldn't budge.

"Kitty?" The voice that called from inside the greenhouse was gruff, masculine, and oh so familiar. There was only one person who could make her heart pound like thunder. Who could make her belly flutter like a hummingbird's wings. Blade.

"She and Prue just ran toward the house," she replied. "I believe they've locked us in here."

He took a few steps closer and held the candle between them. "*Hazel?*" he said, incredulous.

"It's me," she confirmed, swallowing the awful lump in her throat. She'd known it would be difficult to see him, but she'd assumed they'd be in a ballroom, surrounded by scores of people. That she'd have the buffer of her friends and her girls.

He stood there, staring at her, still and silent as a statue.

Oh God. What if he'd come to the greenhouse for a tryst? What if Lady Penelope was hiding behind him, straightening her gown and fixing her hair?

"You look . . . gorgeous," he breathed.

"What are you doing here?"

He blinked and shook his head. "Kitty claimed she wanted to show me something. Next thing I knew, I was locked inside. You?"

Hazel exhaled, relieved that Penelope wasn't lurking behind the potting soil after all. "Prue brought me. I think she and Kitty must have wedged something beneath the door. I can't be certain, but I suspect Poppy was in on the plan, too."

He strode to the door, made a valiant but futile attempt to open it, then pounded his fist on the frame in frustration. "Why would they scheme to trap us in a greenhouse?" He turned and snapped his gaze to hers. "Unless they want us to be discovered together."

"Right." Hazel swallowed. "I'd be compromised." She didn't have to say what they were both thinking—that they'd have no choice but to marry. And despite her feelings for Blade, she didn't want to marry him if it meant settling for less than all of him.

"Bloody hell," he muttered, which, did not make her feel better in the slightest. He reached for her hand and pulled her past a long table lined with pots of herbs and cabbage. "Come with me."

Chapter 30

Hazel blinked at Blade as he paced the narrow aisle in the center of the greenhouse. His midnight-blue evening jacket hugged his broad shoulders; his buckskin trousers showcased his taut backside. The sight was almost enough to make her forget their terrible predicament—but not quite.

There was no doubt that Poppy, Kitty, and Prue had good intentions, but Hazel was still furious with them for orchestrating this devious little plot. Worse, she was heartsick over Blade's impending engagement. And she was more than a little terrified of Penelope. "There's something you should know."

He froze mid-step, his forehead creased with concern. "Go on."

"Penelope spoke to me earlier."

"I hope she didn't say anything to upset you."

"She knows about us, Blade. Or at least she claims to. She said that if your engagement isn't announced tonight, she'll expose us."

"Shit." His jaw clenched. "Hazel . . . I'm sorry. You don't deserve any of this. If Penelope had a grievance, she should have taken it up with me—not you."

"But I have more to lose. If I'm at the center of the scandal, Bellehaven Academy will be destroyed."

"I won't let that happen." His eyes gleamed with determination as he shrugged off his jacket. "I'm going to get us out of here before we're discovered."

"What?" Hazel leaned forward. "How?"

"I'm tempted to break the glass, but that would only attract attention—and lead to a host of other questions. So I'll climb through that window." He pointed to a small opening near the greenhouse roof, at least twenty feet off the ground.

"You cannot be serious."

He shoved a table beneath the window, toppling several pots in the process. "I'm dead serious."

"Even if you manage to climb up there, you'll break your neck on the way down."

He shrugged, unfazed, and placed an overturned crate on the table. "I'll try to land in a bush."

As he climbed onto the crate, the table rocked on wobbly legs, and she rushed over to steady it. "I'm not certain this will hold you." The wooden boards beneath the box bowed and creaked under his weight.

He frowned. "Stand back, Hazel. I don't want you to get hurt."

She stayed rooted to her spot. "Then come down from there."

He reached up, his body flush with the wall of windows, and gripped the ledge of the opening with his fingertips. "We don't have much time. If Penelope or one of the other guests finds us here, it's over. Your reputation, your school . . . you could lose everything."

"You don't have to do this, Blade."

"Of course I do." He grunted as he hoisted himself, slowly muscling his way upward till his elbows rested on the sill, his shoulders were wedged inside the window frame, and the rest of his body hung against the glass panes.

Her heart pounded at the thought of him hurling himself through the window. He'd be leaping headfirst, and from what she could see, there was nary a shrub in sight outside.

"Why?" she demanded, not caring that her voice echoed through the greenhouse. "Why must you be so stubborn? Why do you insist on risking life and limb?"

"Why?" he repeated, still breathless from his exertions. "*Why?* Because I love you, damn it."

Her body warmed, glowing from within. "You love me?"

He muttered a curse. "I've wanted to tell you for a while now . . . but I thought it would complicate matters."

"It certainly does," Hazel murmured. Blade loved her—and that changed everything. "Will you please come down and talk to me?" she pleaded.

He shook his head. "I love you, Hazel Lively. And I happen to know there's nothing in this world that's more important to you than your school and your girls. They're your family, and I'll be damned if anyone is going to take them away from you."

With that, he started wriggling his torso through the opening, grunting each time he inched forward.

"Blade, stop."

Either he didn't hear her, or he wasn't listening. The upper half of his body hung outside of the greenhouse, at least twenty feet above the ground. With one more thrust, he'd be falling. And she couldn't stand by while he did something so endearingly foolish.

She scrambled onto the table, climbed onto the crate, and grabbed hold of one of his boots.

"What the devil are you doing?" he shouted, incredulous.

"I should think it would be obvious." She wrapped her forearm around his trunk-like thigh and yanked hard, grateful that gravity was on her side.

"Let go, Hazel. A little fall won't hurt me. My head is harder than you know."

"I have some inkling how hard your head is." She pulled with all her might, pleased to see him slip backward a bit.

"Trust me," he cajoled. "I could be outside, opening the greenhouse door for you in less than a minute. We'll be back in the ballroom before anyone's the wiser."

"Or, in less than a minute, I could be calling for Dr. Gladwell to come and set your broken bones. That's if you're lucky."

He snorted and tried to wriggle out of her grasp. "Lucky?"

"If you're unlucky, I'll be calling for the coroner." She grabbed his shirttails with both fists and pulled with every ounce of strength she possessed. "Come. Back. Down."

A loud ripping sound rang through the air. Blade's chest and shoulders slid back, inside the opening, and he was falling.

The crate broke, the table collapsed. Hazel clung to him as they tumbled from the platform. He turned his body, cushioning her landing on the greenhouse floor. All the pots that had been on the table crashed to the floor, covering them in layers of soil, leaves, and petals.

"Oh my God, Hazel." Blade cupped her face in his hands, wiping the dirt from her eyes. "Are you all right?"

"I think so." She gingerly moved her limbs, and when she sat up, discovered she was straddling Blade. He was sprawled flat on his back, wearing a few scraps where his shirt should have been.

That was precisely how Lady Rufflebum found them when she scurried into the greenhouse. "Good heavens." She pressed a hand to her quivering chest; her expression alternating between shock and horror. "Miss Lively . . . Lord Bladenton . . . what on earth have you done to my orchids?"

Hazel froze. She knew she should say something. And probably cover her legs. And definitely dismount Blade.

But a loud buzzing filled her head, and her body refused to obey her brain. She simply sat astride him while others rushed into the greenhouse. The countess's companion. Lord Dunmire. Lady Penelope. Poppy, Kitty, and the girls. Even more guests gathered outside the greenhouse, their noses pressed to the glass as they gawked. Every curious gaze was fixed on her and Blade.

His lips were moving, but Hazel couldn't make out the words—not with the strange humming in her ears. His large, sure hands were on her waist, gently lifting her off his hips as he sat up. He lumbered to his feet, helped her stand, and briefly, surreptitiously, squeezed her hand.

The gentle pressure of his palm against hers broke the spell, and she remembered what he'd said just moments before. He loved her.

"Despite how it may have appeared," Blade said smoothly, "nothing untoward occurred here."

A couple of disbelieving titters erupted from the crowd. Hazel noticed more than a few women staring appreciatively at Blade's rippled torso.

He made a futile attempt to cover his chest with the shreds of his shirt, then shrugged. "Miss Lively and I were trapped, so I—rather stupidly in retrospect—tried to climb through the window."

"How heroic," Prue breathed dreamily.

"The point is," Blade continued, "this spectacle is entirely my fault. Miss Lively was trying to prevent me from breaking my neck, and I deeply regret any harm I caused her with my recklessness." He turned to her, his dark eyes earnest. "Please forgive me, Miss Lively."

"There's nothing to forgive," she choked out.

The crowd fell unnaturally quiet; indeed, the only sound was the swoosh of Lady Rufflebum's fan.

"I also want to vouch for Bellehaven Academy," Blade continued. "It's far from your typical finishing school, but any young woman would be fortunate to have Miss Lively in her life, nurturing her talents and helping her grow. This town *needs* Bellehaven Academy, and nothing that's happened here tonight should jeopardize Miss Lively's school. Because I happen to know it is everything to her."

"It's *not* everything," Hazel blurted. She swallowed, taking a moment to compose herself. "I used to think it was. But it's not more important than my girls. It's not more important than family. And it definitely not more important than love."

Blade shuffled his feet and leaned close to her ear. "What are you doing, Hazel? We can fix this."

"I don't want to," she whispered back.

As the words sank in, his eyes grew wide and he grinned, flashing the rakish dimple that never ceased to melt her insides. "Carry on, then."

"The truth is," she continued loudly, "that I fell in love. With Lord Bladenton."

A collective gasp filled the greenhouse, echoing off the glass ceiling. The countess's fan waved in double time.

Hazel turned to him, brushed a clump of plant roots from his shoulder, and reached for his hand. "I love you, Blade. And that means I choose you first. I choose *us* first. Now and always."

Lady Penelope emerged from the crowd, her piercing blue eyes shooting darts at Hazel. "This is all quite touching," she said with a nervous chuckle. "However, a one-sided infatuation does not a love story make. Bladenton," she said pointedly, "I know you had planned to make your speech at midnight, but perhaps now would be a better time."

"I couldn't agree more," Blade said, but his eyes never left Hazel's. "When I first came to Bellehaven, I couldn't wait to leave. I was running from my responsibilities, my past, and my feelings. Miss Hazel Lively, you were the reason I stopped running. You made me want to stay."

He swept an errant curl away from her face, and his fingers trailed down the side of her neck, making her knees go weak. "I would never ask you to choose between your school or me. I want you to follow your passions wherever they lead you . . . as long as they always bring you home to me."

The ground tilted a little. Perhaps she'd bumped her head in the fall, and this was all a bizarre, lovely dream.

But no. Poppy and Kitty were smiling at her. Jane was dabbing her eyes. Clara, Lucy, Prue, and the other girls had linked arms like a little battalion, ready to come to her aid if necessary.

All the while, Blade stood there, staring at her as if she were the only person in the greenhouse. "I love you, Hazel. In a modest fichu or a beautiful ball gown. With your hair tamed into a tidy twist or blowing wild on the beach. I love your fiery determination and your soft acceptance. Mostly, I love that you were a tough nut to crack—and that you opened to me."

Her eyes welled and her heart felt as though it would burst. "Blade."

"I want to listen to the ocean with you. Build a life and make a family with you, starting with Kitty and the rest of the girls. I want to wake to your smile every morning and lay my head next to yours every night—if you'll let me. Will you marry me, Hazel?"

The greenhouse fell silent again, and everyone—inside the glass walls and out—leaned in, eager to hear her response.

"Yes!" she shouted.

"Yes!" the girls repeated, jumping up and down. "She said *yes!*"

Blade swept her into his arms and twirled her around, oblivious to the dirt, dust, and leaf bits that swirled at their feet.

"There shall be a champagne toast in the ballroom!" Lady Rufflebum cried. "Let us away at once!"

"Wait," Lady Penelope interjected, bringing the celebration to a screeching halt. Everyone turned to her expectant, and Hazel's stomach dropped. "Before we raise our glasses to the happy couple, I have something to share. It's a letter," she said pointedly, "and I think you'll find it rather enlightening."

Penelope's pink feather shook indignantly as she placed one hand on a shapely hip and made a great show of reaching into her corset with the other.

"Bloody hell," Blade muttered.

"Something I should know about?" Hazel asked nervously.

"I'll explain. Just know it doesn't change anything."

Hazel held her breath, but after several awkward seconds of searching her bosom, Penelope was unable to produce anything—except a frustrated whimper.

"I may be able to shed some light on Lady Penelope's missing letter." Lord Dunmire marched forward like a trial lawyer preparing to introduce new evidence. "I believe it fell from her bodice earlier . . . while she was in the silver closet."

"The silver closet?" Lady Rufflebum repeated, incredulous.

"Precisely," Dunmire said. "I happened to see it and picked it up."

Seething, Penelope held out her palm. "I should like to have my letter back, my lord."

Dunmire tugged on the bottom of his waistcoat. "I am afraid that's impossible, my dear, as I disposed of it."

She arched a disbelieving brow. "I beg your pardon?"

"Disposed of it. Ripped it to shreds. Tossed it to the winds."

"Why . . . why would you do that?" she demanded.

Dunmire brushed a pink downy barb off the sleeve of his evening jacket, watching as it floated to the ground. "It seemed rather irrelevant after the silver closet," he said with a wink. "Besides, you have a better option. Namely, me."

Lady Penelope opened her mouth as if she'd object, then folded her arms and stared at the viscount, wary—and mildly intrigued. "Forgive me if I remain unconvinced."

Dunmire shrugged. "Your trepidation is understandable, but we needn't rush. I shall make it my mission to persuade you that we are compatible—and that you may trust me."

She whirled and swept out of the greenhouse with the viscount close on her heels, spurring another round of raucous cheers.

"To the ballroom!" the countess ordered. But while the guests streamed out, she toddled over to Hazel and Blade. "I'm quite pleased for you," she said sincerely. "But you," she said, jabbing a bejeweled finger at Blade's chest, "are going to owe me for those orchids."

"Of course," Blade assured her. "I apologize for the mess. You must send me a bill for the damages."

The countess barked a laugh. "I don't want your money, Bladenton. I want your sweat. At the cricket match next summer—and every summer after that."

"Done."

"Uncle Beck! Miss Lively!" Kitty rushed over and hugged them both. "Thank heaven you're all right. I would have felt awful if you'd been hurt in the fall."

Blade snorted and shrugged on his jacket, which somehow made his lack of a shirt even more noticeable. "And yet you have no remorse for locking us in the greenhouse?"

Kitty batted her eyes innocently. "I can't imagine what you're talking about."

The rest of the girls gathered around, giddy with excitement. "I hope you're not cross with me, Miss Lively," Prue said, "but we all voted. And we decided that, sometimes, proper behavior *does* take a holiday."

"Perhaps," Hazel conceded. "But only once in a blue moon." To Clara, she said, "I'm sorry that I spoiled your masterpiece. We will do our best to clean it—maybe it can be salvaged."

"Maybe." Clara smiled serenely. "But it doesn't really matter. The gown has already worked its magic."

Prue's mother hurried toward them, and Hazel made a futile attempt to shake the potting soil from her skirts. "Felicitations to you both," said Mrs. Covington. "Miss Lively, I wondered if I might have word?"

"Of course."

"I believe I was a bit hasty to pull Prudence out of Bellehaven Academy. She's been so unhappy the past week, and tonight . . . well, now that she's in the company of her friends, it feels as though I have my daughter back."

"Prue is more than welcome to return. We've all missed her."

"She'll be in class on Monday," Mrs. Covington said firmly. "Your methods are unconventional . . . but, after tonight, I'm thinking that unconventional might be just what Prue needs."

Hazel's chest warmed. "I'm glad you think so."

"Besides," Mrs. Covington said behind the cover of her fan, "any headmistress who can land a dashing earl must be doing something right." With that, she snapped her fan shut and headed toward the greenhouse door.

"How's everything over here?" Blade's arms slipped around Hazel's waist, and she felt the hard wall of his chest at her back. "Have I missed anything?"

"Prue's coming back." She smiled up at him. "And tonight . . . well, it's been the best night of my entire life. I couldn't ask for anything more."

"Then I guess you're not interested in the surprise I have for you."

"On the contrary." She leaned back, pressing her bottom against his thighs. "I'm very interested."

"Sweet Jesus," he rasped. "Can we leave the girls?"

Hazel looked around the almost empty greenhouse. Jane was already herding their charges toward the ballroom. Poppy met Hazel's gaze and made a shooing motion. "They're in good hands," she confirmed. "So, where are we going?"

He shot her a lopsided grin, the sort that must have melted millions of hearts. The difference was that now, Blade was all hers.

Taking her by the hand, he said, "Come with me."

Chapter 31

Blade took Hazel to the ocean. To the moonlit cove between the rocks where the water was calm and the sand was soft.

They peeled off their clothes as they ran into the surf. Her slippers, his boots. Her gown, his trousers. Hazel had never felt so free.

Only a few hours ago, she'd thought her time with Blade was over. But now they were floating on their backs, holding hands, and staring up at the star-soaked sky. She couldn't wipe the smile off her face. Because their story was only beginning.

He scooped her into his strong arms, held her against the statue-worthy contours of his chest, and gazed into her eyes. His dark hair gleamed in the pale light of the moon, and a constellation of droplets dotted his broad shoulders. She could scarcely believe he was hers—and that he was looking at her like she was the center of his world. His forever.

"If someone had told me a few short months ago," he mused, "that I'd be swimming naked in the ocean with the headmistress of Bellehaven Academy, I would have given them directions to Bedlam."

"And yet, here we are," she said with a happy sigh.

"Here we are." He spun her around till they were both

dizzy. Smiled like he'd found a pirate's treasure trove. Kissed her as though she was the answer to all his prayers.

She wrapped her arms around his neck as he carried her out of the water and across the sand to the large, soft quilt they'd spread at the foot of a cliff. When he placed her on the blanket and stretched out beside her, her pulse raced, and a frisson of awareness shot through her limbs.

He lifted a damp curl from her forehead, twirled it around his finger, and stared straight into her soul. "I love you, Hazel Lively."

God, it felt good to say the words. To know he could give Hazel the love she deserved. To know he could make her happy.

And damn, but he was determined to make her happy. Starting right now.

Droplets fell from his hair onto her shoulders, and he licked each one off her warm skin, sucking and nibbling his way across her collarbone and over her breasts. When she arched her back, he drew a nipple in his mouth and teased it till she whimpered softly.

He took his time as he kissed a trail down her belly, circled her navel, and drifted farther south, teasing and tasting. Giving her pleasure every way he knew how.

Her hips lifted off the quilt.

Her fingers tangled in his hair.

And when she came apart, shouting his name into the night, he thought his heart would burst.

She nestled her head in the crook of his arm and let her fingers glide down his back, over his thighs, everywhere. Like an intrepid explorer charting new territory, she roamed his body with her hands and mouth, driving him half mad with desire.

When at last he thrust inside her, it felt like coming home.

His heart hammered in his chest, his blood pounded in his ears, and the whole world stood still—for Hazel and him. His head was filled with her. Dark, silky tresses and honey-scented skin. Long, lithe limbs and sweetly enticing curves. A boundless thirst for knowledge and a hunger for amorous pursuits.

But at her center she was simply Hazel—the woman who'd banished the darkness from his soul. The woman who'd made him believe in love.

She met him thrust for thrust, spurring him on with soft moans and subtle squeezes, and before long they were both panting. Reaching. Reeling.

He leaned close to her ear and flicked his tongue over the shell. "You're beautiful, Hazel—and you're mine, always."

She whimpered, then cried out as she climaxed, drawing him deeper . . . until pleasure thundered through him, too. He buried his face in her neck and let release take him, imprinting her on his heart. Forever.

Two days later, Hazel was in her office, enrolling her third new student of the morning. Evidently, a heartfelt speech by a half-dressed earl with god-like pectoral muscles was a far more effective advertisement for her school than her engraved cards had ever been.

"We're delighted to welcome you to Bellehaven Academy." Hazel walked around her desk, shook her newest student's hand, and smiled. "I look forward to seeing you in class next week."

Hazel ushered the girl and her mother out, and, upon finding the antechamber blessedly free of visitors, called to Jane who was working diligently at her desk. "Could I speak to you for a moment?"

"Of course." Jane adjusted her spectacles and followed Hazel back into her office.

They settled into their seats, and Jane looked at Hazel, expectant.

"I want to say thank you," Hazel began.

"Whatever for?"

"For believing in this school from the start. For stepping in to teach lessons. For caring about our girls. And for being my friend."

Jane's cheeks pinkened. "There's no need to thank me. I adore working with you."

"I'm happy you feel that way." Hazel reached into a drawer and withdrew the package she'd picked up from the engraver's that morning. "This is for you."

"For me?" Jane slipped the velvet sleeve off the walnut block and beamed as she read the words etched on the brass plate. MISS JANE MORELAND, TEACHER, BELLEHAVEN ACADEMY. She blinked at Hazel, her eyes shining with emotion.

"I would have offered you the position sooner if I could have. Now that our enrollment is increasing, we can afford to make it official . . . if you'd like to. What do you say?"

"Yes!" Jane hugged the desk plate to her chest. "Thank you for trusting me. To be a part of this . . . it's an honor."

"Bellehaven Academy is lucky to have you, and so am I." Hazel felt her throat clog as she embraced her friend. "Now go. I want you to take the afternoon off and celebrate properly."

Jane balked. "But there could be more prospective students."

"I insist," Hazel said firmly.

"Very well." Jane sniffled as she proudly polished the nameplate with the cuff of her sleeve. "Perhaps I'll drop by the bakery and surprise my parents with the news."

"An excellent idea," Hazel said, gently pushing her in the direction of the door.

Jane had scarcely left the room before another knock sounded.

Gads. At this rate, Hazel would have to hire another teacher before luncheon. "Please, give me a moment to clear my desk," she said, "and I shall be right with you."

"No need to tidy your office for me." Blade strode in, his broad shoulders, narrow hips, and devilish grin all conspiring to make her belly flutter.

"Lord Bladenton." She kept her tone professional as she tucked a pencil behind her ear and crossed her arms. "This establishment is for girls only, I'm afraid."

He shut the door and arched a brow, dark eyes gleaming. "I was hoping you'd make an exception for me." He sat in one of the chairs opposite her and set an oddly shaped parcel on her blotter.

"What's this?"

"A pre-wedding present for my future countess. Open it."

She carefully removed the wrapping, revealing a huge conch shell with a pointed spire, cream-colored swirls, and a smooth peach interior. "Oh, Blade. It's lovely."

"It's so you can listen to the ocean," he explained earnestly. "Anytime you like."

Her eyes welled with happy tears. "Thank you."

"That's not the best part, though." He leaned forward and clasped her hands in his. "Would you like to know where I found it?"

"Where?"

"Near the cliff where we had our picnic."

She sniffled. "Now I love it even more."

"I happened to be there yesterday," he said, suspiciously nonchalant. "Looking at a nearby property . . . that's for sale."

"You were?" she choked out.

He nodded. "I thought that maybe after class this afternoon we could take a drive, visit it together. You could see if it would suit your needs. For your school . . . and for our family."

Her throat grew thick with emotion. The absolute best kind. "I don't know what to say, except I love you."

He stood, rounded the desk, and gathered her into his arms. "Your dreams are my dreams, Hazel. Your girls are our girls. We need a place that's home for all of us—Kitty, Clara, Lucy, and any other children we're blessed with."

She kissed him then, with all the joy, love, and passion in her soul. In one smooth motion, he lifted her, propped her bottom on the edge of the desk, and slid a hand beneath her skirt. His sure fingers traced circles on the insides of her thighs, teasing her with hints of the pleasure to come.

Perhaps that was why she didn't mind that her inkwell toppled off the desk. Barely noticed that her lesson plans floated to the floor. Laughed when her hair sprang free from its knot.

"All of this," she murmured. "It's more than I dared wish for. But here you are."

"Here *we* are." He cradled her head in his hands, kissing her with a tenderness that made time stand still.

Every brush of his lips was a taste of happiness.

A promise that he'd always be by her side.

A whisper that they belonged—and that, together, they'd found home.

Don't Miss the Next Book
in the *Rogues to Lovers* Series
by Anna Bennett

ONE DUKE DOWN

Available January 2023 from
St. Martin's Paperbacks